DENIAL

Abuse, Addiction, and a Life Derailed

By
Nanette Kirsch

This book is dedicated to the Wagner family: Mara, Caleb, Margaret, Audrey, Stephen, and Annie Wagner. David's love for each of you brought joy to his life and sustained him throughout his days.

WHAT OTHERS ARE SAYING ABOUT *DENIAL*

"No person of even modest goodwill would argue with the idea that the sexual abuse of children is among the worst horrors that exist in our culture, and that any meaningful concept of justice must deal with such conduct with the gravity it deserves. A great deal of good writing has gone into making those kinds of arguments and to raising consciousness about how much more prevalent these crimes are than anyone likes to acknowledge.

"*Denial* picks up where so much of that writing leaves off. It is the story of how sexual abuse plays out over the course of a life. For a victim of childhood sexual abuse, the criminal act is only the first episode in a long story in which trauma is often compounded with shame and silence, the harms of which can manifest themselves in myriad ways as the survivor tries to learn to cope on his or her own with something that no one is really prepared to face alone. *Denial* tells the story of how this happened in one life and does so honestly, without either soft-selling things that are dark and difficult or exploiting extremely emotional content for cheap sympathy.

"Chances are there is someone in your life who is a victim of sexual abuse who has never told you so (and may never have told anyone). My hope is that *Denial* helps crack the door of silence so that more victims get the support they need before the harm that was done to them compounds."

— JAY EXUM,
FORMER ASSISTANT UNITED STATES ATTORNEY,
UNITED STATES DEPARTMENT OF JUSTICE

"As someone who has dedicated his life to leading victims of sexual abuse and addiction to restoration and wholeness in Jesus Christ, I found *Denial* to be a powerful and transformational work, both for exemplifying the profound effects of sexual abuse on body, mind, and spirit, and for providing a unique, 360 perspective. This story radically challenged my own thinking about therapeutic intervention and convicted me that we are not doing nearly enough to support sexual abuse victims in their recovery."

— ROB JACKSON, MS, LPC,
CHRISTIAN FAMILY UNIVERSITY
(christianfamilyuniversity.com)

"*Denial* gives life and perspective to the discussion of abuse. Reading about the deep lifelong consequences victims encounter has helped shape the way I work with and counsel those living through their own shame and denial."

— JEFF OLIVE,
SENIOR PASTOR OF UNITED METHODIST CHURCH,
CONROE, TEXAS

ACKNOWLEDGMENTS

The journey to write this book has been a labor of love for more than three years. One of the greatest blessings has been the opportunity to meet and engage with so many people who care about David and Mara Wagner and their family and supported this book as an act of love. I am grateful for their time, and I hope they will find that this work honors the trust they extended.

Rob Jackson of Christian Family University volunteered his time to help analyze David's writings and to provide a clinical perspective on the complexities of his experiences specific to and resulting from childhood sexual abuse. Rob continually points to the Holy Spirit as counselor and comforter, a valuable contribution to this book and no doubt to the clients he serves. Thank you.

Numerous other experts have given generously of their time out of a commitment to helping people harmed by childhood sexual abuse, including Donald B. Little, Jay Exum, Bob Jones, Bethany Howard, and Karen Hiney. Thank you.

Another blessing of this project was the chance to reconnect with my high school English teacher, Georgia Johnson (Mrs. J), the woman who inspired my vocation, and from whom I am still learning some thirty years later. Her mastery and love of the English language, and her consistent encouragement, motivated me from beginning to end. I am always grateful for her love and friendship, and expert editing pen.

The most valuable friends are those you can trust to speak truth. Laura and Kevin Horner, Jeff Olive, Mary Forbes, Kathy Shieldes-Harry, Kelley Skoloda, and DeAnn Marshall all took time to provide candid feedback.

Kit Tosello, who edited this work, brought such excellence to her craft, and the entire team at Deep River Books has been a blessing in every step of the process. Thank you so much for your faith, encouragement, and expertise.

My husband, Craig, and my four children believed in me and supported me every step of the way. Thank you for sacrificing your own needs (like laundry) to help me create the space to do this. I love you all.

Finally, and most humbly, I thank Mara Wagner, who gave me the privilege of doing this work. I have strived to be worthy of the unconditional trust she extended to me throughout the process. It was gratifying to see Mara slowly relinquishing her pain to the pages of the book. Margaret and Audrey shared their memories that helped me capture David as their father. And Caleb took his role as the eldest son seriously, helping to discern how to share this work in a way that honored and protected his family.

David Wagner was my friend. Stepping along the intricate pathways of his life has been a rare, personal, and at times heart-wrenching journey. There is peace and sadness in the parting. I will miss him.

CONTENTS

PREFACE

The body is not meant for sexual immorality but for
the Lord, and the Lord for the body.

1 Corinthians 6:13

My husband and I first became friends with David Wagner in
college. We remained close to him personally and professionally,
as well as to his wife, Mara, and their five children, for more
than twenty-five years.

Mara first asked me to write this story in 2009. She sent
me boxes of documents, letters, depositions, and other artifacts,
which I kept unopened for nearly five years. That's when I confronted challenges in my own marriage stemming from the lingering effects of sexual abuse I had suffered in high school. As
God healed my wounds, he equipped me to tell David's story
with the empathy and compassion of a fellow survivor, one
restored to wholeness by Jesus Christ.

As I began to open those boxes, I read and reread David's
journal and was struck by his faith; even after years of suffering
he was still crying out to the Lord. This evoked the question
in me that inspired and guided this story: *Where was God in
David's suffering?*

David was an innocent, naïve boy of twelve when he became
the target of a sexual predator for the first time. Why didn't
God rescue him from the abuse or at least step in later as David
stumbled blindly through his pain?

Over a more than two-year quest, God revealed an answer that satisfied my soul: *God was with David.*

"What comfort is that," you may ask, "if he didn't do anything to help an innocent child caught in the grip of evil?" After all, if your best friend was "with you" as you were being robbed and beaten, and stood idly by, you might conclude he wasn't much of a friend at all.

Here is where I discovered the beauty woven through the fabric of David's life story. God was with David . . . every minute of every day. He suffered beside him as he was being abused. He was in his brother's love, reaching out, listening, seeking joy, and sitting quietly beside him in his unspoken pain. He was with him in his teacher's loving concern, offering a lifeline of trust and support. He was there reminding him of the abuse years later, calling him to end his denial, encouraging him to speak the truth that would shatter the lies holding him captive. He poured blessing upon blessing over David with a loving wife; five beautiful, healthy children; so many friends; and a level of success that validated his shaken sense of capability and worth.

As much as the Lord loved and pursued David—and pursues each of us—he would not do so at the cost of David's free will. In the end, the choices remained David's to make; even when he made the wrong ones, God was with him still.

> Can anything ever separate us from Christ's love? Does it mean he no longer loves us if we have trouble or calamity, or are persecuted, or hungry, or destitute, or in danger, or threatened with death? (As the Scriptures say, "For your sake we are killed every day; we are being slaughtered like sheep.") No, despite all these things, overwhelming victory is ours through Christ, who loved us. (Romans 8:31–39)

Why then couldn't David feel God's presence or experience his healing comfort? The answer, I believe, underscores why sexual abuse is such a powerful form of spiritual warfare. Children who are sexually violated by a trusted adult are devastated on every level: physical, emotional, and psychological, as well as spiritual. In the shadow of abuse, victims often react by casting intimacy as their enemy, the threat from which they seek to protect themselves.

Yet as human beings we were created for intimacy. It is in our human love relationships we learn the kind of love, selflessness, and intimacy that leads us closer to God. Jesus revealed God to be essentially relational, a triune being—Father, Son, and Holy Spirit, living and moving in perfect, loving harmony. "God is love" (1 John 4:8); he values relationship so deeply that, while we were his enemies (as sin is the enemy of love), he gave his own son to save us. Jesus also taught that God's Spirit of Truth "lives with you and will be in you" (John 14:17).

In human love relationships, the deepest expression of intimacy is through sexuality. While Christianity is often portrayed as holding a negative or restrictive view of human sexuality, within the covenant of marriage, the opposite is true.

"Christianity gave the world a revolutionary view of sex. . . . Don't you see that this is the highest view of sexuality possible?" Reverend Timothy Keller says in his teaching on Paul's letter to the Corinthian church (1 Cor. 6–7). "Paul is saying, the gospel says that human sexuality is a dim reflection of what it is going to be like to fall into the arms of the Lord on the final day."[1]

To a survivor of sexual abuse, these ideas sound downright terrifying, even to the point of being repulsive, especially if she believes that God, who was supposed to be her protector, turned his back in her hour of greatest need.

With this context in mind then, let's return to the question of why David struggled to feel God's presence. The very elements of his human nature that were designed to lead him toward God—the ability to love and trust, the willingness to make himself vulnerable to another—were desecrated by evil.

And that precious gift of sexuality, the physical expression of intimacy and God's invitation to experience the divine ecstasy of creation, was broken to pieces in the heart, soul, and body of this innocent child.

As if that were not enough, the perpetrator in David's case was a trusted spiritual leader, compounding these effects immeasurably. Perhaps situations like his are what prompted Matthew to write,

> But whoever causes one of these little ones who believe in me to sin, it would be better for him to have a great millstone fastened around his neck and to be drowned in the depth of the sea. (Matthew 18:6)

Further, abuse imprinted a lie deep in David's heart that he was unworthy. Like a rifle in the hands of a toddler, the nefarious, premature awakening of a child's sexuality is a dangerous thing. A victim's immature psyche is unable to distinguish the irresistible appeal of physical stimulation from its evil source. Deep shame follows survivors into adulthood, based on the misperception that they desired or even sought out the abuse, when in truth they were in an innocent, if misguided, pursuit of pleasure. As a result, victims incorrectly hold themselves accountable for the abuse, fostering lifelong denial and silence.

In a final, cruel twist of fate, David, like so many other victims, was left perilously blind to these crucial connections. The trauma of sexual abuse is so intense that children often *dissociate*—a psychological term for a mental defense mechanism people often describe as "floating above the scene" or "watching from a safe distance, as if a spectator."

Dissociation further reinforces denial by blurring the connection between childhood sexual abuse and the distorted thoughts and emotions, and compulsive behaviors, that plague many survivors in adulthood, manifesting in substance abuse, sexual addiction, verbal/emotional/physical abuse, homophobia, depression, suicide, and more.

Denial was written to help survivors break free of these devastating outcomes. It is a clarion call, through one man's heartbreaking story, to end the shame and secrecy surrounding sexual abuse in all its forms. It's also an invitation for survivors to step into the light of truth, and courageously speak out about the violence that robbed them of their childhoods and continues to threaten their lives.

Denial was written with these three guiding principles:

1. Its primary inspiration is the five Wagner children. I began this journey to give them context for what happened to their father as they reach adulthood, so they can find mercy for his suffering, grace for his failures, and confidence that through it all his love for each of them was one thing that never wavered.

2. David's very personal, and at times gut-wrenching, story is shared to offer hope to the millions of sexual abuse survivors, particularly those impacted by clergy sex abuse. In early 2014, the Vatican reported to a United Nations panel that it had dismissed 848 priests and disciplined 2,571 others for sexual abuse over the past decade.[2] Considering that a pedophile abuses an average of 260 children during a lifetime, this suggests potential for close to a million victims from these cases alone.[3]

It is important to note that one of the reasons the Catholic Church is under a spotlight is that it is the only religious denomination to release detailed data about its own.[4] Insurance companies that insure against sexual misconduct, and thus have financial incentive to accurately characterize the risk, put Catholic churches at no higher risk than other denominations.[5]

In fact, sexual abuse occurs primarily outside church walls. One in ten people will be sexually abused by age eighteen.[6] The not-for-profit organization Parents for Megan's Law estimates there are sixty million survivors of childhood sexual abuse in the United States,[7] a staggering number of wounded people in need of help.

I wrote this story based on my belief and personal experience that Jesus Christ is the true path to healing of body, mind, and spirit; that he delivers freedom from the shame, self-contempt, and anger sexual abuse engenders; and most importantly, that he holds the key to restoring the relational intimacy with others and with God we were created to enjoy. The end of this book and the website (denialbook.com) offer resources to help survivors and families seeking recovery.

3. Lastly, this book is intentional in seeking to do no harm. *Denial* is the story of a life irreparably harmed by evil; it is also the story of human failing, as the damage from the abuse rippled into David's adult life and hurt those close to him. Ultimately, however, it is the story of a *life*, one filled with goodness, love, and laughter, in addition to pain.

Names and locations were changed, and some characters and content have been fictionalized to tell a coherent story and protect the innocent. The documentation in the book (letters, journals, depositions, etc.) is included verbatim, even where identities have been changed. Within these ethical and legal boundaries, I have strived to create an honest, candid, and compassionate telling of David's story.

I expect some people may be tempted to view this book as an attack on the Catholic Church; it is not.

Childhood sexual abuse is a powerful form of spiritual warfare waged through fallen human beings. As followers of Jesus, all Christians, like all people of goodwill, are called to denounce acts of evil wherever they occur, advocate for justice, and embrace and support survivors. Perpetrators must be held accountable legally and morally for their actions, yet they too are deserving of our prayers for forgiveness and healing.

A Reading from the Book of Isaiah

In those days the prophet said, "Seek the Lord while He may be found, call him while he is near. Let the wicked change his ways and the unjust man his thoughts. He should return to the Lord and he will have mercy on him. For God is ready to forgive him.

"For my thoughts are not your thoughts, nor your ways my ways," says the Lord. "For as the heavens are above the earth so are my ways above your ways and my thoughts above your thoughts.

"And as the rain and snow come down from heaven and stay to soak the earth and make it spring and give seed to the sower and bread to the hungry, so shall my word be. It shall go forth from me not to return empty, but it shall do whatever I please and it shall prosper in the things for which I sent it."

This is the word of the Lord.

*Notation on handwritten Scripture
passage by his mother:*

*"David. Second time he read Epistle when
in the second grade. Feb. 1973"*

Based on a true story.

PART ONE

The Wounding

But Jesus said, "Let the little children come to me
and do not hinder them, for to such belongs the
kingdom of heaven."

Matthew 19:14

CHAPTER 1

Altar Boy

Beware of false prophets who come to you in sheep's
clothing but inwardly are ravenous wolves. You will
recognize them by their fruits.

Matthew 7:15

1977–1978
Erie, Pennsylvania

*"For all the ways I have harmed others I ask for forgiveness. For all
the ways I have been harmed by others I offer forgiveness."* David
recited his daily prayer as he tugged open the heavy wooden
doors of St. Florian Catholic Church.

His brothers had been altar boys before him, a tradition that
paused for ten years until David came of age. Finally David was
the one to represent the Wagner family at weekly Mass, extending the legacy that had made his family a more familiar fixture
on the altar than most of the priests.

David enjoyed the privileges that came with his status, such
as being the one to carry the crucifix in processions, ring the
bells during the consecration of the Eucharist, or add incense to
the thurible during funerals. His family sat in the third pew on

the right every Sunday, on holy days of obligation, and on Ash Wednesday, which was not technically a holy day.

David loved being an altar boy almost as much as he loved baseball, and his fervor reignited his mother's hope, the hope shared by so many Catholic mothers like her, that one of her sons would become a priest. Again today David was first to arrive. In the solitude of these cold, stone walls, he could most tangibly experience the presence of God. Like the Tabernacle of Moses, the edifice itself proclaimed God's absolute authority.

He looked around the empty sacristy. Even in this relatively insignificant anteroom, used to prepare for Mass, a high reverence for God was fully on display. Every detail evoked an august sensuality, from the imposing dark wood furnishings to the deep plush and scarlet hue of the carpeting.

Even the air was rarefied; laden with incense, chrism oil, and altar flowers from thousands of Masses. Lighting was scarce, which kept the space at a perpetual dusk that cast long shadows into the deepest corners of the room and amplified the silence.

A dark mahogany armoire held the priests' vestments. Carved, high-back wooden chairs with red velvet seats flanked a built-in cabinet with brass handles. Only priests were permitted to sit in those chairs, but David had sat in one on another early morning, and found it to be profoundly uncomfortable.

The cabinet itself stored the linens used in the celebration of the Mass. The top drawers held the altar cloths the priests used to wipe away their iniquities during the Liturgy of the Eucharist. The bottom drawers contained the altar linens, hand-stitched by some of the parish women. These ladies dedicated countless hours to ensure that every detail of the altar was seasonally appropriate and aesthetically pleasing.

On top of the cabinet sat a gold chalice, crystal wine goblet, and two small glass pitchers used for Holy Communion.

David retrieved a red cassock from the rack of altar-boy vestments hung in order by size. Last year David had used the ones at the end closest to the back door. But now, his lanky frame led him to the far right of the rack, to the ones reserved for the tallest altar boys, even though he was only in sixth grade.

Getting first choice of cassocks was another reason David liked to arrive first. He checked his appearance in the mirror on the inside of the armoire door. His cassock stopped just above the hem of his uniform slacks, an important detail to avoid a revival of last year's running joke that altar boys flew commando. He pulled the white surplice over his head and wished for the hundredth time that it didn't have lace on the bottom. He smoothed the folds of his vestment; then eyed his penny loafers, coins inserted with Abe's face up, and hoped his mother would be seated on the aisle to see him.

David turned his attention to the preparation of the gifts. This type of extra effort got you called up for funerals and weddings, events that meant two coveted perks to an altar boy: getting out of class, and big tips, especially if you didn't wear sneakers. He counted out the hosts from a baggie and placed them one by one in the chalice. Then he unscrewed the cap of the wine bottle, releasing its syrupy bouquet.

David wondered who would say Mass today. If it was Father John, he knew to fill the wine pitcher to the brim and the water pitcher only halfway; Father liked to save a big swig for cleanup after Holy Communion, and he didn't like it too watered down. Once consecrated, all the wine had to be consumed; the hosts were stored in a chalice kept locked in the tabernacle. David always wondered why it had to be locked. After all, who would steal hosts that had been transubstantiated into the living body of Christ? He couldn't think of a worse sin.

Maybe Father Tom would say Mass this morning. He preferred rich food to strong drink, but he was stern and rigid about
the particulars of the Mass, which forced David to focus more
on getting the details right than on the celebration itself. With
any luck it would be the new priest, whom David knew nothing
about. All anyone had seen of him so far was his red Mustang, a
source of curiosity among all the boys. David hoped to be first
to meet him and maybe even first to get a ride in that car.

As David turned to put the wine back in the cabinet, he was
startled by the presence of someone else in the sacristy. It was
the new priest. David was surprised by how young he looked.
Most of the priests were old, at least in their forties. The man
was dressed traditionally in an alb, a white, ankle-length tunic
with a green cincture tied at the waist. Underneath were the
trademark black clerical slacks and shirt with a white neckband
worn only by Roman Catholic priests.

The priest stood at the open armoire looking for a vestment.
He chose a green chasuble—green, because it was ordinary time
on the church calendar. He vanished briefly beneath the circular
garment before his head popped out of the hole at its center.
As he fixed his hair in the mirror, he caught David's eye in the
reflection.

"David Wagner, Father," he said quickly, reaching out his
hand to introduce himself. Father's loose, long brown hair made
him look a little like a lost member of The Partridge Family. He
was only about an inch taller than David, even in his Docksiders.

He just might be cool, David surmised, at least for a priest.

"James Jarzombek," he said, shaking David's hand. "You can
call me Father Jimmy."

"Good to meet you, Father."

Just then, Joe burst into the sacristy with only five minutes
until the start of Mass. Joe was one of David's best friends. He

had earned a reputation as the class brainiac, but only because he wasn't as funny as David, so people assumed he was smarter. David relished any opportunity to one-up his good friend, so it looked like today was off to a great start.

Joe grinned sheepishly at David as he hurried to get dressed. He introduced himself to Father, probably wondering if he was the type of guy who would make a big deal out of tardiness. When no reprimand came, Joe fell in line behind David, and the two boys led the way from the sacristy to the narthex at the back of the church with Father following. In his rush, Joe had failed to notice that his cassock was too short, ending at his knees, but David didn't.

The organ exhaled the opening chords of "Joyful, Joyful, We Adore Thee," signaling the start of Mass. As the faithful rose to their feet, David stepped to the front of the line and inhaled the fragrance of his faith, a rare fusion of incense that had baked into the walls; candle wax that had carried thousands of intentions heavenward for a dollar apiece; and the newer, cheaper scent of old-lady perfume.

His eyes surveyed the front of the church for his mother, as he recalled his sister's warning on his first day as an altar boy: "Remember, Davey, don't wave to people in church, because you aren't in the theater but the House of Our Lord."

He lifted the crucifix high on its pole and pushed his shoulders back. Father Jimmy, hands pressed solemnly at his chest, smiled benevolently to the congregation. David couldn't help grinning discreetly at his mother as he passed by.

Following Mass and a few minutes chatting up Father Jimmy, David and Joe strolled slowly back to school, delaying the inevitable return to class.

"Why'd you do it?" Joe asked, referring to the strike David had organized in science class the week before.

"Dissection, Joe. It's all about dissection. Class 6-2 got to dissect first, and we had to leapfrog them." David laughed at his own joke and at the recollection of fifteen sixth graders marching up and down the hallways behind him in mock protest.

The whole thing lasted only a few minutes before the principal, Sister Annalise, got wind of it and positioned herself cross-armed at the end of the hall, right in front of the statue of the Virgin Mary. In the lecture that followed, she attempted to expand the Fourth Commandment, "Honor your father and mother," to include teachers and administrators, but David found the link dubious at best, and completely unconvincing as far as his future with practical jokes.

His best friend, Nicole, was the only reason the consequences were no more severe. Her doe eyes and big smile made her the picture of innocence. She had a healthy respect for her parents' authority, and simply explained to Sister Annalise that the strike was actually a good thing because the students were expressing their interest in more hands-on learning. It seemed to assuage Sister's anger. David realized again why Nicole had been his best friend since preschool; they were a perfect team.

"You must admit I negotiated a good settlement," David said, glancing at Joe for acknowledgment. Joe had book smarts, but he lacked David's appetite for risk—something David's big brother, Matthew, had said was the mark of a true leader. David's willingness to take risks for laughs had paid off handsomely so far in his school career.

Before last week's strike, David's sixth-grade year had been most notable for the infamous pencil drop. He hatched the plan to try to add some spark to an otherwise boring day. He quietly directed everyone in Sister Susan's class to drop their pencils at precisely 1:38 p.m. At 1:37, kids began looking nervously at

David, who couldn't believe they were getting so worked up over a simple prank. He nodded that it was a go.

As the second hand swept toward the twelve, Ticonderoga #2s rained down from the desks to the linoleum, startling Sister and marring her otherwise perfect blackboard penmanship. She spun around in search of the culprit, so David quickly threw up the lid to his desk and ducked inside, pretending to search for a book. When he saw Sister's black shoes appear beside his desk out of the corner of his eye, he swallowed hard and lifted his head, his red cheeks giving him away. David returned her glare with a practiced, if unconvincing, look of innocence. Nicole's outburst of laughter had given David his reward, and Sister the evidence she needed to send him to the principal's office.

David hopped off the bus after school and ran up the street to a tiny Cape Cod on the lower East Side—the only home he'd ever known. A few years ago the house had been bursting with the ruckus of six children. Today David sat alone in the quiet bedroom his brothers once shared. Across the hall the girls shared the other upstairs bedroom, although only the younger two still lived at home. David had spent his earliest years in a crib tucked in the center hall closet.

David's mother, Virginia, was an eastern European Catholic, both traits deeply embedded in her DNA. His father and namesake was a diminutive German with an iron constitution. His job with the coal company required him to crisscross Pennsylvania, West Virginia, and eastern Ohio. He was always home for dinner, but his appearances at the table were quiet and brief. As soon as the family finished eating, he'd retreat to his La-Z-Boy to watch the evening news and fall asleep.

As a young man, the senior David had been a proud member of the Wagner Nine, a baseball team formed by his thirteen siblings. But as a father, he struggled to provide. Somehow he and Virginia always managed to scrape together just enough to feed their growing family and faithfully fill their weekly collection envelopes at church. In fact, in a minor miracle, Virginia had won a $325 lottery ticket, which provided the cash they had needed to close on their house.

The Wagner children grew up knowing that ham on Sunday meant potatoes and ham on Monday, split pea soup on Tuesday, and ham-and-cheese sandwiches on Wednesday. At the end of the month as money dwindled, they braced for the inevitable stench of kidneys boiling on the stovetop, assaulting their noses the moment they turned onto their street. It was one of the reasons David never invited friends home.

David's mother had been in her late forties when he was born. The girls liked to say, "Mother brought him home from the hospital and gave him to us as our living baby doll." But it was his brothers' attention he craved, especially Matthew's.

The day Matthew left for college had ranked as the saddest day of David's young life.; David was barely eight years old. The family gathered together to say the rosary as they did every Sunday. Then they ate sandwiches in the kitchen. When they finished, Matthew told David to come with him. He carried David on one arm and his suitcase on the other. He stood David on the couch in the family room so he could look him in the eye. David spotted a tiny dot of Miracle Whip in the corner of his brother's mouth and fixated on its movement up and down as he spoke, unable to hear that his hero and best friend was leaving.

Matthew and David were best friends despite their ten-year age difference. When Matthew wasn't working, he spent most of his free time with his little brother, playing at the arcades, working around the house, or watching TV. Matthew never tired of David or got annoyed with him. He talked to him like a big kid, and he was always there for him when David got hurt or felt sad. David couldn't imagine a day without him, let alone four years.

"When will you be back?" David asked, trying to sound brave.

"Not 'til Thanksgiving, buddy. College is a lot of work, and it costs lots of money to go back and forth. But I promise when I get home we'll hang out, okay? We'll go to the arcade. Play Pong. Whatever you want. And I'll take you to get ice cream. How about that?

"You're a little man now, David. You start school tomorrow. You'll make lots of friends your age. It'll be great. And you know what? I bet you'll be so busy with homework and friends you won't even realize I'm gone. The time will go fast, I promise."

David's gaze shifted from the Miracle Whip up to Matthew's eyes, which were filling with tears. Unable to hold back any longer, David threw his arms around his big brother and squeezed tight.

"Please don't leave me," David whispered through sobs. Matthew held him for a long time. Finally, he sat him down on the couch and wiped his eyes with his shirt sleeve. David had stifled his tears and let his brother go.

* * * * *

Matthew came back eventually. It was when David was entering fifth grade. Following graduation Matthew returned home to await entry into the US Air Force. Happily for David, the process took almost a year. Whenever he returned from school and Matthew got off work, the two were once again inseparable.

David would never forget the day his brother took him along to help pick out a new car. Matthew was working at a

Dodge dealership at the time, so they walked the lot side-by-side, eventually narrowing their choices down to a Polaris and a Dart.

"What do you think, Buddy, which one should I get?"

"I don't know."

"That's right, David. You never buy a car without taking it for a test drive. Great instincts. Want to take one out for a spin?"

David's eyes widened at the suggestion. "Are you serious?"

"Absolutely. Which one do you want to drive first?"

"This one," David said, pointing to a silver Dodge Dart.

"Hop in," Matthew said, opening the door for his little brother and then disappearing briefly inside the dealership to retrieve the keys and a temporary plate. He slid into the driver's seat and started the engine, revving it for effect.

Even now David could recall the exhilaration of that day, riding down the highway with the sunroof open, just him and his big brother. Matthew let him stand up in the sunroof; he rode that way until the wind dried up his spit and tears. When they got back to the lot Matthew said, "So, David, what do you think? Which car should I buy?"

"The Dart, no doubt about it," David said. Matthew agreed and they drove it home that day.

Matthew got his wings in 1976. It was the beginning of David's sixth-grade year. David and his parents drove down to Texas to bring Matthew back to await deployment. He would soon head to Europe to fly fighter jets. David especially hated sitting through the interminable school days during that time. All he wanted was to get home and be with Matthew, who was leaving in less than thirty days and would be gone for four years. David would be in high school when his brother came home again.

And what if he didn't come home? What if something happened to him? Terror coursed through his veins as he pushed the bad thoughts from his mind. David didn't say a word about his fears to his brother or anyone else; one didn't talk about such things, his mother often reminded them.

On Matthew's last night home, the Wagner family gathered for a send-off dinner. Virginia made pot roast with mashed potatoes and canned green beans. Most of the conversation focused on speculation about Matthew's assignment. Matthew either didn't know or wasn't allowed to answer most of their questions. Philip shared news of his recent raise.

As his mother sliced white cake for dessert, Philip finally engaged his youngest brother in the conversation.

"Hey David, are you getting many funerals as an altar boy? I bet I did one every two weeks when I was your age. That was some good money. What are they paying you guys these days?"

"I do a lot of them," David said eagerly. "I get ten dollars most of the time, but I got twenty for the Marcella funeral. They own that jewelry store on Peach Street. The grandfather died. I was wearing my penny loafers. People love it when you wear nice shoes."

"Good work, Bud," Matthew said, chuckling as he stretched his arm behind David to create space in his abdomen after the big meal. "Is Father John still chugging the altar wine?"

"Matthew!" Virginia said. "Don't you talk like that about a priest. Once the wine has been consecrated, Father has to drink it all; it's the rule."

"Yeah, well, he doesn't have to drink the beer he made us carry into the rectory for him. I assure you Koehler's Beer ain't consecrated."

"Don't say another word. You will not desecrate the Catholic Church in this house. I won't stand for it. I don't care if you're in the Air Force or president of the United States." Virginia grabbed her plate and huffed into the kitchen.

As the door swung closed behind her, Philip said, "Way to go, Matthew. Why do you say things like that in front of her?" Then he lowered his voice to a whisper, just loud enough to be heard. "Idiot."

"Shut up, Phil." Matthew said, looking toward his father, but finding no relief. The elder Wagner sat stone-faced with his eyes downcast. Clearly this conversation was over. "Come on, David," Matthew said, inviting his brother to retreat into the family room.

"Did he really make you do that, Matthew? Carry beer?"

"Absolutely." Matthew chuckled. "Priests are people too, you know, despite what Mother thinks. Father John is an old drunk just like Grandpa was. That doesn't make him an awful person. But in Mom's eyes, priests are as holy as Jesus Christ, and their word is gospel. That ain't ever gonna change.

"Learn from my mistakes, Davey. It's better not to talk about some stuff."

CHAPTER 2

Chosen One

This is what the Sovereign Lord says:
*I am against the shepherds and will hold them account-
able for my flock.*

Ezekiel 34:10

1978–1979
Erie, Pennsylvania

Before they could see the flashing lights or hear the din of the crowd, Nicole, Joe, and David could smell St. Florian's Festival —kielbasa, popcorn, and fried everything wafting toward them while they were still a block away. For this one week in September, they and the other parishioners took pride in bringing the local equivalent of Waldameer Park to their East Side community. The Bozelli Brothers Band would provide the evening's headline entertainment, followed by the Junior Turners dance troupe, the youngest of the week's performers. A buffet dinner was served in the gym each evening, rows of collapsible tables made festive with red and yellow tablecloths.

This year's festival featured an unprecedented number of rides, including spinning carts, the 360, flying swings, and for the first time, centrifugal cars that spun riders parallel to the ground. Arcade games, 50/50 raffles, a petting zoo, and carnival fare buffeted the perimeter. At the center stood the Ferris wheel, the visual focal point and main attraction. Nonetheless David found plenty of excuses to avoid it.

"Hey Nicole, I bet you don't know who invented the Ferris wheel," David said.

"Mr. Ferris," she said, rolling eyes for effect.

"George Ferris, actually," he corrected. "But do you know *why?*"

David had uncovered the trivia in a book one of his brothers left behind. He was excited to put his knowledge to use and worried Joe might steal his thunder, so he quickly continued. "George was from Pittsburgh, like my Dad. An engineer. He wanted to find a way to outdo the Eiffel Tower at the Chicago World's Fair. So he designed a tower you could ride.

"A million people rode it during the fair. A million. That's a lot of people, you know? Who knew you could get rich selling 'tickle bellies'?"

"Wow, David, you should win a prize for that piece of trivia," Father Jimmy said, nudging his shoulder as he joined the group. "Have you ridden it yet?"

David shook his head as he considered how to avoid the inevitable invitation, the one that would force him to face his fear of heights or risk looking like a crybaby in front of his new mentor and friend.

Father Jimmy and David had become friendly over a summer of weekday Masses. It was worth waking up early if only to escape the houseful of women. The lightly attended summer Masses were more relaxed and even fun, especially with Father Jimmy.

One day while Mrs. Lapinski was doing the daily reading, Father Jimmy leaned over and whispered that they should nickname the weekday faithful. His first suggestion was so outrageous David swallowed hard to try to contain the surge of laughter that ultimately escaped as a snort. He coughed to cover it up, but not before Mrs. Lapinski paused her reading and sent a scolding look his way. When she resumed, Father Jimmy winked and patted David on the leg. David thanked God that his mother hadn't made it to Mass that day.

Most of their time together was spent in the sacristy, preparing for or cleaning up from Mass. But sometimes Father would invite David to stay and help with some chore, the same type of handyman projects Matthew had always found for them to do. As they worked side by side, David told Father stories about his big brother and even brought the letters he received via airmail about Matthew's adventures in Europe.

"Do you think you'll join the Air Force like your brother, David?" Father asked one day.

"I don't know, probably not."

"Why not? You've got the makings of a military hero. You're intelligent and you have obvious leadership skills. I picked up on that the first time I met you."

"Yeah, but I don't like to fly; I'm afraid of heights."

"Well, how about joining the priesthood then? We could use a few good men," Father said with a chuckle.

"You sound like my mother. I'm thinking doctor."

David shared his family's baseball legacy with Father, telling him how his father had been one of the Wagner Nine. He brought the newspaper article to church and showed Father the team photo.

David was thrilled the day Father Jimmy surprised him at his home game. He smiled and waved to him in the stands. David hit two singles and a double, and struck out only once that day. After the game Father Jimmy offered him a ride home. David quickly agreed, excited to finally get a ride in that Mustang.

Father Jimmy took a detour to Dudley's for ice cream and told David to order whatever he wanted. David got a double scoop of chocolate with a sprinkle coat, and Father let him sit behind the wheel while they ate. He showed him all the bells and whistles with the attention to detail of a used car salesman.

"Would you like to come inside?" David asked Father when they pulled into his driveway at last. "My mother has been looking forward to meeting you."

"Thanks, David. I would love to, but it's late and I have early Mass tomorrow morning. Maybe next time."

"Okay, well, thanks for coming to my game, Father. And thanks for the ice cream."

"You're welcome, David. It was fun. You're definitely worthy of the Wagner Nine. Oh, and David, let's keep the Dudley's stop our secret, okay? I don't want the other altar boys expecting the same special treatment."

David had nodded. "Oh, no problem. I promise."

That was back in early August. David had not seen Father since school started. He was even more excited about the festival now because it gave him a chance to show off his status with the parish's coolest priest.

"How about we go conquer that Ferris wheel together?" Father Jimmy asked, clapping his hands together like a little kid, his face eager with excitement.

"Okay, sure," David heard himself mutter.

Nicole was headed to the swings and Joe said he wanted to buy some raffle tickets. That left David and Father Jimmy to brave the ride alone. David distracted himself by chattering about the teachers he'd have in the coming school year and his plan to get all A grades. He and Father shared a conspiratorial chuckle as "Velma" passed by, the little church lady whose pageboy bob and heavy-rimmed glasses gave her an uncanny resemblance to the Scooby-Doo character; she sat in the first pew on the left during eight o'clock Mass.

As they reached the front of the line, Father Jimmy mentioned that he had a funeral on Tuesday if David wanted to serve with him. David jumped at the chance to earn an extra ten bucks during festival week.

The next thing he knew, he and Father Jimmy were clambering into the swinging cart. The attendant locked the safety bar in place, which seemed inadequate even at ground level. David checked it repeatedly to make sure it was secure. With the first jolt backward David felt his stomach flip. The motor paused as quickly as it had started, so the next riders could board. David realized the climb to the top would be slow and agonizing.

He tried to distract himself by looking around to see if anyone had noticed him with Father Jimmy yet. Then he glanced up to see if Father looked as nervous as he was. Father stretched a protective arm across the back of the seat and David felt himself relax slightly.

The operator moved the lever and thrust the cart backward another position. The boarding process continued until David found himself at eleven o'clock on the wheel, which felt a lot higher than he hoped it would, and they still hadn't reached the top. He looked down, trying to spot Nicole, Joe, or anyone else he knew. He could still hear the festivities, but from up here they seemed a world away. David tried to think of something funny to say, but his mind was a blank.

As the wheel began moving again, Father Jimmy put his hand on David's leg. "Are you doing okay, David?"

David nodded and forced a smile, trying unsuccessfully to relax his grip on the safety bar. When at last they notched up to the top, David's head swirled with vertigo, and he found it difficult to breathe. He was trying to decide if the air was actually thinner this high up, or if he was simply terrified. He focused his gaze forward and resisted the urge to look down, but he couldn't help it, and every time he did his stomach lunged into a free fall.

He looked at the people moving like ants on the ground. That's when he noticed Father Jimmy's hand was higher on his leg than was comfortable. David figured Father was just as focused on the ride as he was, so he shifted subtly in his seat, hoping he'd get the hint. Instead, Father moved his hand unmistakably on top of his groin. David's chest clenched. His heart beat wildly. His mind raced to process what was happening, even as his body responded involuntarily.

Adrenalin flooded his veins, putting every nerve on high alert. The fried stench suffused with tobacco and cheap aftershave to assault his nose and heighten the sensation that he was about to throw up. His mouth was so dry he couldn't swallow, and his breathing became so erratic he thought he might pass out.

Reality disintegrated into snapshots: The dark silhouette of St. Florian's spire glowing crimson in the festival lights; the distorted image of the large hand on his privates; topsiders pressed against the cart's metal footrest; the arcade swarming with faceless people; a bicep with veins bulging under a black shirtsleeve; a small white hand gripping futilely to the safety bar.

But a singular image imprinted itself deep in his consciousness, one that would haunt him for years to come: the indelible expression on the man's face, the glossy eyes and thin, sneering lips transforming someone David had loved like a brother into a menacing stranger. With his free hand the man jerked David's leg wider. "Relax," he commanded.

David looked desperately toward the operator as the cart approached the bottom of the rotation, and realized it was Sal, a friend of his cousin. He pleaded in vain with his eyes for Sal to rescue him. But as soon as the cart jerked upward again, Father Jimmy renewed his touch, this time more vigorously. David's stomach lurched with the next descent, and his body betrayed him, physical release overwhelming and intertwining with terror.

David lost count of the revolutions and eventually the hope that Sal or anyone else would save him. When the ride ended, Sal stepped forward to open the cart, but Father Jimmy covered the latch and said David really wanted another ride. "No!" David screamed silently. Before he knew what was happening, the cart retreated on another round. As soon as they were out of sight, the priest renewed his assault, this time forcing David to touch him.

The world washed away and David floated above the cart, observing from a safe distance. The festival provided the perfect, tawdry backdrop, its tacky colors and stringed lights attempting to cover up what was really just a cheap playground on the poor side of town. On the final dizzying rotation of the third ride, the man's appetite finally quenched, David was startled again, this time by a rush of hot breath in his ear. "You can't tell anyone," he whispered hoarsely. "If you do I'll tell your mother."

Back on the ground, Father Jimmy stepped out of the cart and pumped Sal's hand, thanking him profusely for the rides. Then he reached back to help David down from the cart. Stepping shakily onto the ground, David glanced backward, half-expecting to see the little boy he'd left behind. In a matter of minutes the only life he'd known had been destroyed, a violent collision of pleasure and rage inflicting traumatic wounds. He did his best not to cry, but he couldn't help glancing guiltily at the people in line, wondering if anyone had witnessed the disgusting things he had done.

Just then Mrs. Lapinski broke through the crowd and made a beeline for them. David startled at the sight of her, certain she was about to humiliate him publicly.

Instead, she spoke in the syrupy tone she reserved for clergy. "Where have you been, Father? We've been looking all over for you. We need you to offer the blessing before dinner service begins." She hooked Father Jimmy by the elbow and tugged him toward the gym.

Father squeezed David's shoulder and gave him a look that removed any risk of betrayal.

David stood motionless; he literally didn't know which way to turn. He couldn't think straight. All he wanted was to get as far away as possible. But if he left now, he'd face a thousand questions from Nicole, not to mention his mother. If he stayed, he risked bumping into Father again, and there was almost nowhere he could turn to avoid the Ferris wheel spinning perilously in the distance. He walked until he saw Nicole in the food line.

"How'd it go?"

"No biggie," he lied.

"Where's Father?"

"Mrs. Lapinski. Time to bless the buffet."

They found Joe finishing off his second kielbasa, and walked together past a handful of video games posing as an arcade.

"We have to pace ourselves, guys," David said, plotting his escape. "We've got all week. I've had enough for one day, what about you?"

"David Wagner calling it a night?" Joe said to Nicole, raising an eyebrow.

"I had Mass this morning, man. I'm tired." David spoke as nonchalantly as possible.

The friends walked together until turning up their separate streets home. David lived farthest from school, so he walked the final blocks alone.

When he arrived home, he ran upstairs and threw himself on his bed. He laid staring at the ceiling for what seemed like hours, the Ferris wheel ride replaying over and over in his mind as vividly as if it were projected on the ceiling. Each time, he looked for what he had done to cause it or should have done to stop it. He heard Father's words echo the threat, almost laughable because the last thing David would ever do was tell anyone. It was close to four in the morning when he fell asleep, and as he dozed off, he prayed that God would not punish him for the horrible sin he had committed. He promised God and himself it would never happen again.

"David, hurry up, you're gonna be late," his sister yelled up the stairs. David looked at the digital clock on his nightstand with one eye open. 7:25. He gazed out the window at the sky dimmed to a gray haze by Erie's relentless cloud cover. As he came fully awake, the dark images from the weekend fled the light, and he prayed for relief from the anxiety that pinned him to his bed.

"I'm up," he said to his sister and himself.

It was Tuesday. The funeral. The realization sent him into a panic. He struggled to put on his school uniform with shaky hands and reassured himself that what had happened was a fluke. He would be safe in the sanctuary of the church. He regained his composure as he headed downstairs, and then he heard his mother yell from the kitchen, "David, come here please. Father Jimmy just called."

His heart skipped a beat. *He couldn't; he wouldn't.*

"He asked me to remind you that the funeral is at ten today. He said to be at church by 9:15. He also said be sure and wear your dress shoes."

"Yes, mother." He entered the kitchen to show her he was already wearing his loafers.

"I think you're his favorite altar boy," his sister chirped proudly. "Mother, you really should invite Father for dinner one Sunday."

David headed to the bus stop and recited his daily prayers, the ones his mother had taught him when he was a little boy. *"For all the ways I have harmed others I ask forgiveness. For all the ways I have been harmed by others I offer forgiveness."*

The words took on new weight this morning. Could reciting these words erase the black stain of mortal sin that Sister Susan had taught him about in second grade? Or had God turned his back on him in disgust, condemning him for eternity? He couldn't begin to forgive himself, so he was pretty sure God must be appalled by him too.

When he got to school, David noted with some satisfaction that he was able to stay focused and ask good questions during class. He decided things would be back to normal before he knew it. No sooner had he settled into the day than he looked up at the clock and noticed with alarm that it was 9:25. He raised his hand and told Mrs. King he had to serve a funeral. As David walked briskly toward the church, he grew increasingly self-conscious, wondering if Father would be watching for him. As he entered the sacristy, Father Jimmy stood with his arms crossed, clearly irritated by his tardiness.

"You're late," he said sharply, putting David on edge.

"Sorry," David mumbled and started to get ready.

"Here, let me help you," Father Jimmy said, taking the cassock from him. David raised his arms and allowed Father to place the robe over his head. He felt stupid and vulnerable, but he didn't want to risk provoking Father's anger further. The priest smoothed the folds of his cassock, allowing his hands to brush lightly over David's body as he did so, and then he drew David into an unexpected, but warm embrace. David was relieved Father Jimmy wasn't angry anymore and suddenly hopeful that everything just might get back to normal.

"You know you're my number-one altar boy," Father Jimmy said as he released him.

Going through the familiar rite of the Mass of Christian Burial left David's mind free to wander back over life before the Ferris wheel. He recalled the wish list of things he had wanted to do with Father Jimmy, like playing baseball and fishing off the dock. Father Jimmy was about the same age as Philip, but since he wasn't married he had a lot more free time than his hardworking brother.

David was lost in reverie when the pallbearers stood up, snapping him back to reality as they approached the casket. He stood between Father and the casket as they proceeded down the aisle. After the funeral David hung up his cassock and followed the other altar boy toward the door.

"Hey, would one of you two mind joining me at the cemetery?" Father Jimmy didn't wait for a response. "David, how about you?"

"Um, okay."

"Adam, will you please let Sister Annalise know that David is with me? I'll get him back right after lunch."

Adam nodded and mumbled to David. "Lucky dog."

David walked with Father across the parking lot toward the car. On the way to the cemetery, David found himself uncharacteristically chatty. He told Father Jimmy he was thinking of going to St. Michael the Archangel High School, rather than St. Thomas High School like his sisters.

"Why would you do that, David? I don't know anyone else in your class going there. The way the buses run, you won't get home until four thirty or five. What will your mother think of that?"

"Uh, I don't really know." The truth was he wanted to get as far away from St. Florian's as possible. "Did I tell you I'm home-room editor for the newspaper now?"

"No, David, good for you."

"Well, I could have been editor-in-chief if I wanted to. Joe is. But you know that's a lot of extra work, what with baseball and all the homework I'll have this year. And besides, I really want to try out for the lead in *Oliver Twist*."

"I'm proud of you, David. I'll tell you what, if you land Oliver I'll be at every performance."

On the way back from the cemetery, Father Jimmy stopped at McDonald's and let David choose whatever he wanted for lunch. David ordered a Big Mac with fries and a chocolate shake. They sat in the Mustang in the near-empty parking lot as the lunch rush had already passed. The air in the car quickly grew heavy with the greasy aroma as the pair ate and talked with their mouths full. David began to worry he might miss all his afternoon classes and suggested maybe they should head back to school.

He glanced toward Father for a response but all at once found himself forced back in his seat by the weight of the man's body. David thrashed instinctively, but Father Jimmy pinned him to the seat by his neck. David began to shudder uncontrollably. He was so panicked by the hand suppressing his airway that he didn't notice at first the one moving toward his privates.

Afterward, Father Jimmy sat facing forward, composing himself. They drove back to school in silence. As David turned to exit the car, Father tousled his hair. "Remember David, tell no one."

David shut the door and then glanced back as the car turned toward the church.

Father Jimmy finagled the Mass schedule so that David was by his side for weekly Mass and every other Sunday. As the weeks turned into months, David noticed that Father seemed to lose interest in the things they used to share. Now his sole focus was on finding ways to get him alone.

Quitting the altar boys definitely was not an option. And the idea of telling his mother what was happening seemed the riskiest option of all. What if she blamed him even more than he blamed himself? So he endured it the best he could and prayed it would end.

He allowed himself to be drawn into Father's lair again and again, innocently pursuing the relationship that had made him feel important and valued, while trying futilely to avoid the darker side. The premature awakening of his emotional and physical desire left David wondering if he was gay, hating himself for letting it happen, hating even more the part of him drawn to the pleasure, but most of all hating Father Jimmy for ruining everything.

David had always considered church to be his second home, finding comfort in its sights, smells, and sounds. Now those same sensations aroused foreboding, anxiety, shame, and a new emotion for David, rage.

David tried to simply accept his circumstance. He feared that to reject this one bad thing would mean rejecting the good things about his faith too. So after each encounter, David reminded himself that when the priest administered Holy Communion he took Jesus inside him. Before receiving Communion, he always made sure to pray the Act of Contrition.

Oh my God, I am heartily sorry for having offended you.
And I detest all my sins because of your just punishment,
but most of all because they offend you, my Lord,
Who art all good and deserving of all my love.
I firmly resolve, with the help of your grace, to sin no more
and to avoid the near occasion of sin.

But sometimes late at night, David jolted awake, paralyzed by the fear that he would go to Hell.

* * * * *

"David." He heard his name as he strolled down the hall toward English class.

"Good morning, Sister Susan." David leaned into the doorway of his former seventh-grade classroom. "Hi."

"Do you have a minute, David? I was hoping I might run into you."

"Sure." David walked to the front of her desk, the same way he had when Sister had caught him in one of his pranks. He had always liked her. She was younger than she looked in her nun's habit, which was just shy of one hundred; in reality she was probably only in her mid-thirties. She was a good teacher and a good sport, considering all the practical jokes he had pulled in her class.

"David, I'm, well, I'm just a bit worried about you lately, son. Is everything okay?"

He was surprised by her question. "Sure, Sister," he said quickly. "Why? Am I in trouble or something?"

"No, not at all, David, quite the opposite. I'm concerned about what's happened to my favorite class clown. You know you drove me crazy sometimes, but I always loved your spirit.

"Lately when I see you in the halls or cafeteria, you just don't seem yourself. Maybe you're just growing up." She patted his hand affectionately. "I don't know. Maybe I'm off-base, but I see a sadness in your eyes instead of that devilish twinkle. Is Matthew all right? I know you two are really close, and I know you must miss him terribly. How long has he been in Europe?"

"About a year and a half." David glanced nervously away to avoid her reading anything else in his eyes.

"Are you worried about him? David, I'd just like to help if there is something I can do."

David looked toward the blackboard behind Sister's head, filled with her always-perfect penmanship. So much had changed since he had sat in this room. It seemed like a life-time ago. Sister had always treated her students like the children she would never have, providing the right mix of love and discipline to win their universal affection and respect. Whenever kids boasted that Sister loved them most, their classmates would reply, "Sister Susan loves everyone!" And it was true.

Her honesty and concern struck a chord with David. He knew she was right. He hardly recognized the person he had become. He hadn't even thought about practical jokes this year.

He appreciated her concern, loved her for it actually, but he also knew that telling the truth was not an option. Besides, if he did tell her, what would she think of him? What could she do anyway? She'd probably start by having him expelled.

"I'm good, Sister. Everything's fine, okay? Look . . ." Anxious to change the subject, he pulled an airmail envelope from his backpack. "I just got a letter from Matthew. Want to read it? He loves Europe. He's flying fighter jets. A lot of stuff he's doing, it's top secret.

"Thanks again, Sister. Good to see you. I'd better to get to class." David waved quickly and turned to leave.

"Good to see you, David," she said to his back. "Stop again when you have more time and tell me more about Matthew, okay? I'll be praying for you, David."

"Oh, okay, thanks," David gave her a final, awkward wave and disappeared into the hallway.

* * * * *

"But I'll never see you again." Nicole plopped her chin into her cupped hands, as she sat on the steep front steps of her family's house. David had been working on demolishing the steps with Nicole's dad. On weekends they worked together to install the new walkway. With just a couple steps to go, David was planning to wrap up early so he'd have time to get ready for eighth-grade graduation.

"Why go all the way to St. Michael's, David? Come to Jefferson with Joe and me. It's walking distance."

"No can do." David worked to dislodge his last paver of the day. Nicole grabbed a worm from the newly exposed soil and threw it at David. He flung it off his shoulder and back at her and she squealed.

"Ginny's never letting me go to public high school, Nicole, you know that. I'm lucky that seminaries don't take kids my age or she'd have me shipped off by now."

Nicole thumbed through the *1979 Eighth Grade Memory Book* as David continued working. "Let's see what they have to say about you in here. 'David Andrew Wagner,'" she read with affect. "David came into the world on April 15, 1965, and will miss the closeness of everyone next year.' See? That's what I'm talking about. Why do that to yourself? 'He took part in the musical, the talent show, the altar boys, and was on the newspaper staff.'

"*Oliver Twist* was a blast," she said, recalling the musical in which she played Rose Maylie to David's Oliver. They had practiced after school for weeks to pull off two performances, one during the day for the student body and the other at night for the parents. Nicole's mom and dad came, and they even dragged her brothers under protest. She'd still be paying for that had David not been the lead.

The boys had made a point of hooting and hollering for his solo. They knew, as she did, that David's parents wouldn't make it, so they were happy to fill the gap with genuine affection for their sister's best friend. David was a fixture at their family dinner table and a member of the family to all of them. Philip came and sat with Nicole's brothers. Father Jimmy had attended both performances, along with Fathers Tom and John.

"Read yours," David said, even though he knew Nicole's profile by heart since he and Joe had written it. Nicole began:

"'Nicole opened her mouth on May 6, 1965, and hasn't shut it since! She liked the closeness among the students and teachers and will miss how much fun everything was when she attends Jefferson next year. Nicole is interested in animals, talking, and boys.' Hilarious, David. So funny I forgot to laugh."

She glared at him in mock offense before continuing. "'She enjoyed being president of student council, and took part in cheerleading, the newspaper, the musical, and chorus.' We did it all. I'm going to miss that. And I'm gonna miss hangin' with you." Nicole knew David wasn't one for emotion, but she seemed to be feeling nostalgic and a bit sad. She considered David her best bud.

He dodged her sentiments with humor. "Well, Joe and I did everything, but you weren't an altar boy, remember?"

"Always gotta rub it in, don't you?"

Nicole had made it clear she took exception to what she called "the Church's chauvinism." David, on the other hand, accepted the Vatican's perspective that since Jesus chose only men to be his disciples, he intended only men to lead the church, from altar boys up to priests.

"You know, I really am going to miss you, David Wagner." She reached over and hugged him before he could protest. "I've gotta go shower. See you tonight." She skipped up the broken walkway, stepping gingerly over the last remaining stair.

As he watched her disappear, David regretted that he hadn't gone steady with Nicole. He'd had a crush on her since fourth grade, but they were such good friends she never took his invitations seriously. Last year, when he finally got up the nerve to ask her to the Valentine's Day dance, she said no because "no one else was going." He had always wondered if that was the real reason, rejection feeding his self-doubt.

But none of that mattered now. It was time for a fresh start, and David intended to close the door on St. Florian's and everything that had happened there for good.

CHAPTER 3

Student Leader

A friend loves at all times, and a brother is born for
a time of adversity.

Proverbs 17:17

Summer 1981
Santa Monica, California

As soon as Dave emerged from the Jetway, Matthew made a beeline for him. As they embraced like the long-lost brothers they were, other passengers maneuvered by them with varying levels of annoyance. Dave and Matthew didn't notice.

"Look at you." Matthew pushed him back to arm's length and looked up at least four inches at his baby brother. "What are they feeding you these days, man? You must be six feet tall."

"Almost."

"How was your flight? It's a long way to Cali, isn't it?"

"Yeah, about five hours. I slept most of the way. It was fine, not too bad," Dave slung an arm over his brother's shoulder, accentuating his new height advantage.

"Well I'm glad you're here, man. Glad you made it. We'll have a great time. I've lined up lots of things for us to do over the next two weeks." Matthew searched his brother's face for some sign of the distress he had heard on the phone. He had suggested the visit after their last call.

Something was up; Matthew had no doubt about that. He just needed some time to get Dave to open up.

"Did you get the booklet I sent you on my new car? What did ya think?"

"Yeah, it looks cool, Matt."

"So you wanna drive home? You've got your license now, right? Maybe I'll stand up in the sunroof this time."

Dave laughed, which Matthew thought was a good sign. Maybe he just needed a break from his mother and the girls.

When they got back to Matthew's house, he and Dave quickly fell into their old rhythm. They played video games, watched TV, and drove around in Matthew's car, taking turns speeding down the desert highways near his house.

They visited Disneyland, followed by a day trip to Knott's Berry Farm. But the best days were the ones the brothers spent just hanging out.

One day Matthew got Dave to help build an overhang on his house so his wife and son could be outside without getting scorched by the hot sun. As Dave lifted a piece of plywood from the rooftop to bring to Matthew, a desert breeze caught the board, pushing him toward the edge.

"Drop it, Dave!" Matthew yelled. "Put the board down!"

But Dave refused to let go. When he finally wrestled it down, he lay on top of it, panting, holding on for dear life.

"Dave, what were you thinking? Don't you know you're more valuable to me than an old piece of plywood? You should've just let go."

"I couldn't."

* * * * *

Dave didn't have words for why he couldn't let go. Mostly he felt an urgency to please his big brother. It had been so long since they'd had this kind of time together. Matthew had been in Europe for four years. While he did write to Dave, they rarely talked by phone and he hardly ever came home. During those years, Dave had endured a living hell, caught up in an unholy relationship with Father and then left to sort out his sin and shame in secrecy and silence.

Dave wanted Matthew to see that he had grown up. He was no longer that kid brother whose "help" on projects actually required a lot of patience. He was nearly a man now, able to do things like carry a stupid piece of plywood across a roof without dropping it.

But plywood wasn't the only thing Dave was having a hard time letting go. Despite his best efforts, he couldn't get past what had happened to him back at St. Florian's, nor would it let go of him. High school was supposed to be a fresh start, but some days it felt like he had just moved from the frying pan into the fire.

St. Michael's seemed to tolerate, if not promote, relationships between male teachers and students. There was Mr. Lark, the theology/PE teacher who was homosexual and always looking to form close relationships with Dave and some of the other bookish boys. While they were technically only a few years his junior, they were still his students.

Father Hill, the senior advisor and moderator of the Social Involvement Network, was never without sophomore Jeff Johnson by his side, and there were loud rumors about Father Hill's weekend parties with the school's athletes.

Brother Anthony seemed like a potential ally. An awkward guy who desperately wanted to fit in, "Bro Anthony" was young, still in seminary, and in his first year of teaching. But just when

Dave was beginning to trust him, Bro Anthony made a pass at him one day after school.

Jokes and innuendos about such situations were commonplace among both students and faculty, but Dave never heard anyone express concern about wrongdoing, which led him to believe it must be part of growing up.

As Dave grappled with all the normal hormones and self-doubt of adolescence, he struggled to discern the proper boundaries with adults who purported to care, yet expected things he knew in his gut were not right.

He just wanted more guys like Matthew in his life—men who were strong and caring and interested in him, but who loved him with no expectation that he would do things he found disgusting and demeaning.

The past four years had left Dave feeling desperately alone; even God seemed indifferent to his pleas. Dave still attended Mass every Sunday with his mother and father. And every night he prayed for God to take away this thing, whatever it was, that sent the wrong signal to men with whom he desired only mentoring and friendship.

He wanted desperately to share all of this with Matthew, to tell him all that had happened to him, to see if high school had been the same way for Matthew, and to ask what he might be doing wrong. But Dave had concluded it was partly his fault.

He didn't know exactly what he had done, but how else could he explain that he'd become a target for so many men? If Matthew found out, he probably would be disgusted, and maybe even fearful that Dave might be a negative influence on his son, David's nephew. What if he sent him away? That would kill him.

He couldn't lose Matthew.

The brothers sat side by side on the roof, neither of them speaking for what felt like an eternity. Matthew finally broke the silence.

"So what's up, Dave? I heard something in your voice when I called home last month. Is everything okay back home? Is someone giving you a hard time? Phil maybe? I know he can be hard on you."

As he had rehearsed what he might say to his brother, Dave could almost grab hold of the relief that would come from shattering the shell that hid his secrets. Tears formed, about to crest on the wave of relief.

Matthew waited beside his brother, stalwart, steadfast. At last he leaned over and gave him a hug. Dave relaxed into the safety of his brother's embrace. No matter how hard he tried, the words would not come.

"Hey, Dave, you know what?" Matthew said, lightening the mood and letting the pressure off his kid brother. "Last time I called home, Mum said, 'Matthew, I never thought you'd be the one to move so far away.' It made me sad for her. I know it's especially tough since I'm her favorite."

"You know Mum and Dad like me better, Matt. Now that you're out here it's not even a contest."

Matthew laughed at their familiar bit. "You ready to get off this hot roof? Let's get some lemonade and cool off."

As the days passed, Dave and Matthew fell into an easy routine, just like old times, but different. Dave was no longer a little kid, and that made it better in some ways. Dave imagined what it would be like to move here, to live with Matthew and his family, to make a fresh start. Dave felt a sense of comfort and safety with Matthew that he never experienced elsewhere in his life. Even from across the country Matthew had been the one to hear his pain and try to do something about it. No one else seemed to notice or care.

* * * * *

On several occasions Matthew tried to create the space that would invite Dave to open up, but he never came close again. It tore at Matthew's heart to see his brother in pain, but he didn't want to push him away. He knew how tight-lipped the family was, and if he pushed too hard, Dave might shut him out completely. He resolved to fill his brother with as much love as he could in the time they had together.

As the time for Dave's departure grew closer, Matthew could sense Dave's anxiety. He wished he could stay longer. When they called Dave's flight at the airport, Matthew stood with him in line until it was time to board. Matthew grabbed Dave's face in his strong, meaty hands.

"I love you, David Andrew. Don't you forget it. I'm always here for you, buddy, okay?"

"I know, Matt. I love you too. Thanks for everything." David's voice cracked, as he hugged his brother and then clung to him like he had the first time they were separated. He let go, swiping at the tears edging out of his eyes. He walked quickly down the Jetway, turning once to wave, wearing a forced smile.

Matthew raised his hand high until Dave disappeared from view.

Fall 1981
Erie, Pennsylvania

"Nic!" Dave yelled across the high school parking lot. Taking long strides even for his lanky frame, Dave met Nicole as she gathered her belongings from her car. "I knew you couldn't resist me for long." He wrapped his arm around his friend. "I'm surprised you made it two years before transferring to St. Mike's. You got here at just the right time; I've sifted through all the riff-raff."

They fell in with the stream of students walking briskly to beat the bell.

"You're gonna love our group, Nic. Lynn is hilarious. Carol you remember from Presque Isle. We're the smart kids so the teachers love us and we pretty much get to do what we want. Let me see your class schedule."

He waited while Nicole unzipped her backpack and retrieved her schedule. He was thrilled that she was going to finish high school with him. He had missed her friendship and sidekick loyalty, not to mention her easy laughter at his jokes.

Deep down, he also looked forward to having the upper hand socially, at least for a while. "Charlie in Charge" his friends called him behind his back; they recognized Dave's one-upman-ship, but didn't mind too much because he was such a good friend.

He escorted Nicole to her first class, "Theology with Mr. Lark."

In the five-minute breaks between classes, they caught up on the past two years. Nicole told Dave how unhappy she had been at Jefferson, how she had struggled to make the transition from the small, close-knit community of St. Florian's to the large public high school.

"I literally begged my parents to switch," she said.

"But isn't St. Mike's so *far*?" Dave grinned. "I guess the chance to be close to me was too good to pass up."

"No doubt. It looks like you're big man on campus out here, Dave."

"Yeah, pretty much. The classes are tough, but I've made honor roll every semester. The teachers are cool. Lynn and Carol hang with the librarian. They chat her up so they don't have to go to class. She gave them her secret for creamy hot chocolate, adding coffee creamer. Gross, right? But they swear by it.

"I have to introduce you to Father Tankiewicz too; we call him Tank. He's a good friend. He's been over to the house for dinner a couple times."

"Your house?"

"Yeah."

"What? You never even had me over for dinner!"

"You're not a priest," Dave said, laughing.

Dave was the first one out the door of his last class, and he found Nicole before the hallways filled with the end-of-day exodus. As they walked toward the parking lot, he said, "We're gonna hang at Lynn's Friday night and have a few beers. Her mom will be at her boyfriend's."

"Where do you get the beer?"

"We sit in the parking lot of the distributor. We ask people going in until someone gets it for us. We do it all the time."

* * * * *

Nicole quickly felt at home among Dave's friends, even if she couldn't keep up with their beer consumption. As they reviewed the entire faculty for Nicole, Lynn suddenly stood up when they got to Father Hill.

"He hates girls," she declared.

"Who does?" Mark asked.

"Father Hill. I was just thinking about how he has that Social Involvement 'leadership team' to his house every weekend, all boys of course. Buys 'em beer and pot too, I hear. They even drive his car."

"And school vehicles," Mark added.

"You tell me how that's fair. He's the senior-class advisor. I bet if he were here right now he couldn't tell you my name, or Nicole's, or Carol's. But he'd know you guys." Lynn pointed at Dave and Mark with her beer can.

"Same old double standard. We'll be lucky to get college recommendations out of that guy. Good thing we're tight with the librarian, Carol," Lynn said, laughing.

Carol chimed in. "I heard Jeff Johnson stays there every weekend. He told me Father Hill is always tickling or *accidentally* touching them. It's totally creepy."

"Well, they're the dumb ones for going there in the first place," Dave said.

"Hey, I wish someone would buy us beer every weekend," Carol said. "I'd put up with a little tickling."

"I'll tickle you whenever you want." Dave wiggled his fingers in front of her face before digging them into her sides. Carol squealed and struggled to push him off.

"Stop, Dave," she gasped through laughter. He relented and swigged the rest of his beer.

Lynn walked to the kitchen and retrieved a new beer from the fridge. "I bet Bro Anthony would love to get in on those parties."

"Ugh, Bro Anthony," Carol said. "Remember, my mom made me go to counseling with him after my parents' divorce? Well, he was awful. She let me quit after three sessions. I can't stand the guy."

"You and me both. You know he made a pass at me last year," Dave said.

"Get out! Seriously?"

"Would I make that up?"

"Did you ask anyone to the semi yet, Dave?" Nicole said, ready for a new topic.

"No, I was thinking maybe I'd take you." He wrapped his arm around her waist, emboldened by the alcohol.

Nicole laughed and shrugged him off.

As the beer and conversation ran out, Lynn and Dave agreed to meet for nine o'clock Mass on Sunday.

Lynn's family's funeral home was just a few blocks up the street from Father Tank's place. Sometimes, when the party went too long, the girls stayed at Lynn's and Dave crashed at Tank's, since Father mostly stayed at the rectory or at his parents' house on weekends.

Tonight was one of those nights. The friends stood on the street sharing the last two cigarettes from David's pack of Marlboro Lights.

"It's a good thing Tank isn't here," Nicole said, looking in his darkened street-level window as Dave struggled to get the key in the door and Carol returned the fruits of her evening into the narrow walkway between the houses.

"He'd kick our butts for sure."

At last the lock clicked, and the girls said good night to Dave before walking back up the street to Lynn's. Dave turned on the lamp inside the front door and then decided to look for some food. He saw a note taped to the fridge.

Dave,

Welcome!

I had to go in to town. I'll be back around 11:00. Make yourself at home. Raid the refrig for the ginger ale or fruit. See you later.

Tank

January 1982
Student Government Conference, State College, Pennsylvania

The first assignment of the day at the student government conference was to write a letter to yourself to keep sealed until the start of senior year in the fall.

The group had traveled one hundred and fifty miles southeast from Erie to State College for the two-day Pennsylvania Catholic Schools Student Government Conference, along with elected representatives from other parochial high schools across the state. Dave wondered what type of leader would choose the mountains of central Pennsylvania for a January meeting. The purpose was to contemplate God's call on leaders; the other, unstated goal was to help the young men discern if God was calling them to a vocation in the priesthood.

As Dave looked out the large windows of the retreat center at the clear, crisp morning, he embraced the weekend's invitation to introspection, prayer, and bonding.

After lunch most of the student body leaders broke out into subcommittee planning sessions. A select group of boys were invited to take a chilly but scenic prayer walk on the grounds, accompanied by several male teachers, including clergy. Afterward the group gathered in a small meeting room. The only climate control was an electric heater that clicked on and off every few minutes as cold air seeped in through the single-paned window above it. The boys sipped hot cocoa, complete with stale mini marshmallows. The water scalded Dave's tongue, so he sipped sparingly on the remnant of the now-tasteless confection and listened intently.

The lay teachers spoke first, sharing how God had called them to teach and how they chose to teach in a Catholic school for much less money because they cared deeply about perpetuating the faith in the next generation. Then the priests took turns sharing their personal stories of God's call.

Tank spoke eloquently about the leadership traits he had observed in each of the boys, the faithfulness they displayed in their activities and behavior at school, and their kindness toward their fellow students. Dave marveled at how Father saw such Christlike qualities in these awkward, acne-faced kids from ordinary families living unremarkable lives. Tank said they were unquestionably the strongest leaders in next year's graduating class.

"No, more than that," he said, "you are the most promising leaders I have encountered in my entire teaching career." His voice choked with emotion as he spoke of their unique place among the ranks of young men he had mentored.

As the session wrapped up, the boys were asked to keep their meeting confidential, so as not to alienate the other students, and each was handed a prayer card for the discernment of vocations.

The next day was Sunday, and the conference ended at ten. Backpacks cluttered the wall by the cafeteria doors as students lined up their chairs theater-style. When everyone was settled in their seats, Father Tankiewicz and a handful of priests from the other schools celebrated Mass using a cafeteria table as a makeshift altar. Even in the sterility of a school cafeteria, Dave noticed how the familiar rites and hymns, lifted in unison by the young voices, infused the room with the serenity he usually associated only with the austere edifice of the church. He thought about how over the past two-and-a-half years he had earned the respect of faculty and administration, as well as his peers. The notion of losing it all and starting again in college filled him with a growing sense of dread.

After the session broke up and the last lingerers finished talking to Tank, Dave confidentially expressed his interest in a vocation. He asked Tank to pray for guidance in his decision-making. Dave saw the unmistakable enthusiasm on Father's face. Father committed not only to pray, but also to marshal whatever resources Dave might need over the coming year.

As they parted Tank encouraged Dave to consider applying to become a Eucharistic Minister. It was an emerging and coveted role that permitted a layperson to assist in the distribution of Holy Communion.

Among Dave's family and friends, considering the priesthood was as much a part of growing up as getting a driver's license. As he had listened to the priests share their stories, he realized some aspects of the calling were very appealing. Dave loved the church, and he desired the high level of respect and status the priesthood bestowed.

The voice in his head countered that he was unfit as a person, not to mention as a priest. It seemed like every accomplishment was outweighed by one of his disgusting compulsions. A week after he made honor roll for the first time, he had lost his virginity in a clumsily executed tryst with the house painter's daughter. He set a goal to make honor roll every semester even as he built a long list of conquests that included, but certainly was not limited to, his girlfriend. Serving on student leadership and on the tennis team were offset by his growing, irresistible stash of porn magazines.

Dave considered the possibility that the structure and discipline of the priesthood might actually provide a remedy to these problems. And, so quietly that he barely acknowledged it himself, he also recognized that even scant interest would win him favor during his senior year, whether he ultimately followed through or not.

February 1982

The letter arrived on St. Mike's High School letterhead. It was addressed to Mr. and Mrs. David Wagner, but Dave knew no one would be home for hours and he wasn't going to wait to see the contents.

> *February 19, 1982*
>
> *Dear Mr. and Mrs. Wagner,*
>
> *I am very happy to announce that David has been appointed to be a Minister of the Eucharist for the remainder of this school year. At an Evening of Recollection with the new Ministers of the Eucharist last night, I was truly inspired by the students' faith and eagerness to be genuine Christians. You have every reason to be proud of David.*
>
> *The new Ministers of the Eucharist will be installed by Father Hill and me at our Ash Wednesday All-School. I invite you to attend that Mass. Thank you for your son and your support of St. Michael the Archangel High School.*
>
> *Sincerely,*
> *Reverend Daniel Tank*

April 1982

It was Dave's seventeenth birthday. He loved that his birthday fell so close to Easter, both for the significance of the holiday and because it usually meant he'd have the entire Easter break to celebrate. This would be a short school week; classes ended at noon on Holy Thursday, and the break extended to the entire next week. Easter marked one of the holiest weeks on the Catholic calendar and one of the few Fridays that Dave and his friends would spend sober.

At lunch Carol, Lynn, Nicole, and Mark treated the cafeteria to a raucous rendition of The Beatles' "You Say It's Your Birthday." Nicole made Dave's favorite chocolate cupcakes. Carol gave him a card that said, "In honor of your birthday I called a radio station and requested some of your old favorites— "I left My Beer in San Francisco," "Rhapsody in Beer," "I Found My Beer on Blueberry Hill." The note inside featured Carol's perfectly rounded cursive in rows so straight Dave's eyes always searched for pencil lines.

> *Really, I can't even remember how we became such good friends, except for our famous AP English. Always remember our famous drinking spot and when you burped. Also, you staying at Fr. Tank's, and Nicole and me staying at Lynn's? Even though you always make fun of me, I think if you stopped something would be wrong. And you know without you to agree with me on my many complaints, I'd probably be a mess. But seriously thanks for being such a great friend. Without you, school would be boring! Love you always, Carol*

When he arrived home after school, Dave spied crepe paper and balloons hanging in the dining room and felt oddly irritated by his sisters' efforts. He stepped into the room with an outsider's view, noticing how the decor reflected the age and poverty of his family. The furniture was old and heavy, overwhelming the tiny room. The sagging seat cushions, thick drapes, and yellowed wallpaper contrasted starkly with the tacky birthday décor. Dave recalled the clean, cheery white walls of Nicole's newly constructed house, reflecting the youth and vibrancy of her family.

"Happy birthday, Davey!" his sister squealed from the kitchen. She ran into the room and embraced him, oblivious to the stiffness in his response. He forced a smile at his always well-meaning, but far too complacent sister. She was satisfied with her lot in life; he was not. He wanted more, and a college education represented his first, best opportunity for change.

For dinner, Dave's mother served pierogi, an eastern European dumpling filled with cheese and mashed potato. It was a family tradition, produced en masse by the women several times a year, and then frozen for special occasions like these. After dinner everyone sang "Happy Birthday" too loudly and woefully out of key, and then his mother served sliced yellow sheet cake with chocolate frosting, both recipes by Betty Crocker. His gifts included a couple of shirts and a pair of Wrangler jeans. He hugged his mother and shook his dad's hand, even though he planned to exchange the gifts for better brands next time he went to the mall.

Dave and his dad retired to the porch while the girls did dishes. He observed his father in the silence, from the creases lining his forehead to his diminishing frame. Already in his seventies, Dave's father was the same age as some of his friends' grandparents. His dad was a kind and gentle man, but also old and tired, and that separated Dave's parents from those of his friends. He understood that his father didn't have the energy to do more, but he also felt the loss of his presence more profoundly than he liked to admit.

His dad swayed back and forth on the creaking aluminum glider as the evening sky dimmed the room. A nearly empty coffee cup drooped in his hand as he dozed off to sleep. Dave lifted the cup and gently placed it on the table. Then he headed to his room to do his homework.

Good Friday was as much of a tradition in the Wagner household as Easter. The family fasted all day, and beginning at noon Virginia enforced strict silence. The TV and radio remained off as the family prayed the rosary during the hours of The Lord's Passion. At two, Dave drove his mother and sisters to St. Florian's for Stations of the Cross.

The church was quiet and austere. Dave waited with mounting anxiety to see which priest would serve. He could barely stomach the thought of having to follow Father Jimmy through the fourteen stations of Jesus' passion and crucifixion. Fortunately, it was Father John who led the faithful in a recitation of the prayers. They were printed on a handout, but the older members of the parish knew them by heart.

"The twelfth station, Jesus dies on the cross," Father intoned. "We adore you, O Christ, and we praise you."

"My Jesus, three hours didst Thou hang in agony, and then die for me; let me die before I sin, and if I live, live for Thy love and faithful service," Dave chanted in unison with the congregation.

As Father John and the altar boys knelt before the oil painting of Jesus' death, Dave and the others followed, easing onto the padded kneelers bolted to the pews in front of them. He fixed his thoughts on the image of Jesus crucified, but the voice inside reminded him that God had seen everything he had ever done, including his mortal sins. A mortal sin, Sister Susan had taught, is a grave act that you know is wrong, but do anyway.

Dave's soul may be as black as night, but he wasn't ever confessing those things out loud to anyone, especially not a priest. He had tried a few times to wrap up those great big black sins in a blanket statement at the end of his confessions—"and all my other sins"—but both he and God knew that didn't count.

He turned his eyes away from Jesus and fixated on the small altar boy kneeling obediently beside the priest, holding the crucifix Dave had once carried with such pride. He looked just like Dave had then. Why had he been singled out? Was it something he had said or done? How he wished he could go back to the way things had been before, when the world, and the adults in it, were safe; when kneeling beside a priest made him feel special and strong, instead of nauseous and anxious and dirty.

"Our Father," the priest intoned as Dave and the others stood and finished the prayer, followed by the "Hail Mary" and the "Glory Be."

"Jesus Christ crucified," Father said.

"Have mercy on us," the congregation responded.

"May the souls of the faithful departed, through the mercy of God, rest in peace."

"Amen."

The final station, "Jesus is laid in the tomb," was followed by the veneration of the cross, for which everyone lined up to kiss the plastic feet of Jesus affixed to an eighteen-inch, wooden crucifix. The priest held the crucifix flat between his hands, while the altar boy used a white cloth to wipe the feet between kisses. As if that would sanitize anything, Dave thought to himself.

Dave returned to his pew with the gravity of Christ's suffering weighing on his heart. He exited church with the women of his family, isolated by the fact that his solemnity came from the heavy burden of guilt and shame.

August 1982

It was the first day of school, and as Father Tank had instructed at the conference Dave opened the letter he had written to his "senior self."

Dear Dave,

Well, the goal I made was to already know where I'm going to school and prepare myself for it both mentally and spiritually. I hope by now I at least know where I'm going. I bet it's Gannon.

I think that it's the best thing I could do for myself, and Mom and Dad. How am I preparing myself? I'm scared now, so I can imagine what I'll be like in six months.

Last night I really felt like a failure. I was afraid to lead. Not so much afraid as reluctant. I tried to lead by example, and when that failed I tried authority, but I didn't have any. I feel better about it today.

How does it feel to be a senior? I hope there isn't too much work to go along with it. Are you still seeing Laurie? She has really been special to me in realizing my faults and weaknesses as well as my strengths. I may get disgusted and upset with her at times, but I do love her.

We talked about loving our parents. I realize how lucky I am to have my parents when I see some other kids and the problems they have with their folks. I also love my family, especially my sisters since we are closer from growing up together.

That's all I'm going to write, except for this. Try to make yourself realize that college won't hurt; it's something to look forward to.

God be with me,
Dave

September 1982

Following the conference, Dave reconnected with Brother Anthony as a vocational mentor. Bro Anthony, who had taught at the school the previous year, was now living at a friary in Delaware.

An envelope from Brother Anthony awaited him on the kitchen counter. Dave ignored it and made himself a sandwich. His mom was ironing altar cloths at church, so he was home alone. He was growing weary of this flirtation with the priest-hood, even though he had resolved that it couldn't hurt to string things out just until he got the letters of recommendation for his college applications in a few weeks.

Bro Anthony's ongoing emotional neediness annoyed him. In every letter, he requested a response and a photo of Dave. Dave didn't send his photo, nor did he intend to. Unlike Bro Anthony, who sat in a monastery with nothing to do, Dave's life buzzed with activity.

As he ate, he jotted a quick response on a piece of loose-leaf paper. After finishing lunch, he got out his application for Gannon and focused on plans for his real future.

When Nicole's dad gave Dave his tickets for the Erie Blades game, it was a no-brainer to invite Father Tank.

"This is an important time for you, David," Tank said as they waited for the Blades to the take the ice. "Lots of big decisions are coming up that will set the course for your life. Take your time and choose well."

Dave's stomach churned. "Yeah, thanks for the reminder. As if I wasn't feeling enough stress on my own."

The Blades lost 1–6, continuing their dismal start to the season. It was late when Tank dropped Dave home, so Dave didn't invite him in.

October 22, 1982

A few weeks later Dave got another letter from Brother Anthony, ironically the same day his letter of recommendation arrived from Father Hill. Dave skimmed the letter of recommendation, noting with satisfaction the section specific to him.

During the four years David has spent at St. Michael's, we have found him to be a definite asset. David is mature

*and weighs all sides of issues before making decisions. He
is willing to follow his values and ideals, even when this
is counter to the group pressure.*

*David is a very enjoyable student. Teachers remark
about his interest in learning, his insights and contributions to discussions and his overall good attitude toward
learning. David gets along well with both peers and
faculty. He is always respectful of the other person and
really makes an effort to make everyone feel important. I
strongly recommend David . . .*

"Yes!" Dave said aloud, standing alone in the kitchen. He
left the letter on the kitchen table so his mother could read it.
Things were finally coming together. He opened the letter from
Brother Anthony and barely skimmed it, already planning how
he would wind things down.

Dear Dave,

*I received your letter today and words have not the power to
express the joy it brought me. Your letters do so much for me.
You are such an outstanding person blessed greatly by God. You
make me a better person just by being you, and I realize how
lucky I am to have you as a friend. Thank you for thinking of
me and taking the time to write.*

*You have no idea how great I feel knowing you. You are
obviously touched by God in a special way. Please pray and do
what He wants; don't listen to what other people want you to
do, including myself.*

*I miss St. Mike's so much I could cry (and I do sometimes).
I feel that I let you guys down. I didn't give very much because I
didn't have that much to give, but it was one of the best years of*

my life. I learned more than I ever thought and took more than I gave. You are all such talented people you put me to shame! But I am stuck with me so thank God anyway.

If I tell you of my life and schedule here, will I be accused of giving you more propaganda? Our day here is very structured at times. We get up at 5:00 a.m. and have Morning Prayer and meditation in community, then until 8:45 in private. Mass is after breakfast. Then class until noon. Lunch and work until 4 p.m. Free time until 5:15 p.m. then another hour of meditation and prayer, 6 p.m. supper, 7:30 prayers, 8–9:30 p.m. study, 9:30 p.m. prayer, then free time until you want to go to bed. Every Thursday is a day of recollection. Saturday afternoons are free for walks or sports. Things never seem to change. Dusting is the high point of my week!

How do you like being a big, bad senior? This year will go so quickly for you. Don't waste all of it.

Well I have to go to night prayers. Please write when you get the chance. It means so much.

Know that you are LOVED *and missed a great deal.*

Peace and goodness,

Bro Anthony

"So Dad, did Mother tell you I got my acceptance letter today?" Dave asked.

"She did. That's quite an accomplishment, David. I'm proud of you. I sure hope we can work it all out."

"What do you mean, Dad? I thought we discussed this already."

"We discussed that you could go if you got the diocesan scholarship from St. Florian's."

"And if I don't?"

"I don't know, David. I don't know that we can make it work."

Dave finished his dinner fuming with frustration. He had worked so hard. He had the grades, the student leadership experience and even a recommendation from the senior advisor. Now his college dreams were going to be undone by a stupid scholarship?

The next day he walked to the parish office. Every time he visited St. Florian's he got a pit in his stomach worrying he might bump into Father Jimmy. Now he had to walk right into the lion's den.

"Hey, Mrs. S."

"Why hello, David! Nice to see you. How's the family?"

"Everyone is doing great. How is your family?"

"They're good. Getting big, you know. My daughter had another baby last month. Eight grandchildren now for us. I miss seeing your crew at church."

"Thank you. Is Father John around? I was hoping to speak with him."

"Sure, David. Let me ring him for you." Mrs. Szymanski picked up the phone and punched in a three-digit extension.

"Father, yes. David Wagner is here. He was hoping to see you for a moment, sir. Okay, thank you.

"Have a seat right over there, hon. He said he'll be out in just a few minutes."

Dave did his best not to look impatient, but he urgently wanted to see Father John and get out of there.

"David." Father John approached with his hand extended.

"Hello, Father." He shook Father's hand firmly. "Good to see you."

"Come on back, Dave," Father said, turning toward his office.

Dave took a seat as the priest made his way behind the large desk.

"You sure have grown up since I last saw you. What are you now, a junior?"

"I'm a senior, Father."

"A senior, well, how about that?" He chuckled. "I must be getting old."

Dave smiled at the priest, now easily in his seventies. "Yes, well, that's part of the reason for my visit today, Father. I have been accepted to Gannon University in the pharmacy program."

"Why that's fantastic, Dave. Just great. Congratulations."

"Thank you. Um, the thing is that, well, as you know, my family is large and money is always tight. Anyway, my parents said the only way I can go is if I can get some scholarship help. They said the St. Florian's scholarship was one I should consider. And, well, I was hoping to talk with you about it and see what I needed to do."

"Well, Dave, if it was up to me that scholarship would be yours. You're the kind of upstanding, Catholic boy we like to help. And your family is a strong part of this community. Unfortunately, I have nothing to do with the scholarship, but the good news is that you know the person who does."

"Oh?"

"Yes. It's Father Jarzombek. Do you remember him? 'Father Jimmy' to you kids. Why don't you wait right here and I'll go see when he can meet with you?"

Dave sat wondering what to do. His body reacted, first his flight instinct urging him to go. He reminded himself what was at stake and stayed put.

"David, good news," Father John said from behind. "Father Jimmy says he would love to talk with you about the scholarship.

He is free this afternoon. Can you swing by the rectory around five thirty?"

"Sure, I guess. Is there paperwork or something I should fill out first?"

"Father will have everything you need."

"Alright. Well, thank you, Father. Good to see you again."

"Good to see you too, David. Give your parents my best, will you? Oh, and tell them we appreciated their donation of the pew for the new sanctuary. That was so generous."

"Sure." Dave couldn't help wondering how his parents had managed to scrape together the money for that.

"I can't do this," Dave thought. As much as he hated the idea, he had no choice. If he wanted to go to college he'd have to find a way to get through it. Besides, it had been four years. Things would be different now. He wasn't that scared little boy anymore. He was almost a man; he could handle himself.

Promptly at 5:25, Dave rang the doorbell of the rectory. The house manager, Mrs. Grant, opened it and invited him into the foyer. She called Father Jimmy. Dave fought to calm his nerves.

When Father entered the vestibule, it was as if they were strangers. He seemed quieter and more reserved than Dave remembered, his voice soft. "Hello, David."

"Hi, Father," he said, averting his gaze.

"I thought we could grab some pizza. I brought the scholarship information." He held up a manila folder. Does that sound okay to you?"

"Uh sure, fine."

"Thank you, Mrs. Grant. We'll be back in a couple hours."

He turned to Dave. "Come on. We'll take my new car."

Dave slid into the passenger seat of the red Trans-Am. Father took his time removing the T-roof, deepening Dave's agitation.

Pizza Hut was just a few miles down the road; Dave didn't see why they had to have the top off. The new-car scent filled his nose, and he wondered how a priest could afford new sports cars so frequently. Father turned up the radio, which was tuned to WMDI, Erie's rock station. The music and the noise of the open road at least meant he wouldn't have to talk. Dave wondered why he hadn't noticed before how unpriestly the man was; he was nothing like Tank.

They walked into Pizza Hut, and Dave looked around, hoping no one he knew was there. What a humiliating and cruel twist of fate that this man, who had already taken so much from his past, now had control of his future. Father requested a corner booth in the restaurant's murky maroon interior.

As they slid into the booth Dave carefully positioned himself across from Father Jimmy, maximizing the distance between them. He stared at his hands and waited, not sure where to begin.

"So how have you been, David?"

"Fine. Good."

"How are you doing in school? How are your grades?"

"Good. Really good. I am taking honors classes in English, math, science, and social studies. And I've made honor roll every semester."

"Still playing baseball?"

"No, but I've been on the tennis team the last two years. What are the requirements for the scholarship when it comes to extracurricular activities?"

The waitress interrupted to take their order. Father ordered a large pepperoni pizza and a pitcher of beer.

"I'll have pop, please," Dave said.

"Pepsi okay, Hon?"

"Yeah, that's fine."

"Why don't you have a beer? No one will see you back here."

"I'm good. Is there a GPA requirement?"

"The scholarship was created to promote educational opportunities for worthy students from our parish attending Catholic universities. There's no specific GPA requirement. It's typically given to a student deemed worthy by his or her scholastic achievements, sportsmanship, and character. And of course, he or she must be an upstanding member of the St. Florian's parish. None of that should present a problem for you, David. How do you like high school?"

"It's good. A friend of mine from St. Florian's transferred there last year, Nicole. Remember her? We're probably the only two going there at this point."

"No, I can't say that I do. Do you know your major yet?"

"Yes. Pharmacy. I want to be a pharmacist."

The waitress put the beer and soda down on the table. Dave drank quickly, trying to find something to do other than talk to this man.

"Father, how do I apply? I assume there are forms I need to fill out? Do I need a recommendation? I got one from Father Hill and could probably get another if I need it."

"Well you can start by loosening up a little bit," Father said, pouring beer from the pitcher into Dave's empty glass.

Dave leaned back against the booth and looked around the restaurant. No one seemed to notice them, let alone sense how trapped Dave was feeling. He took a deep swig, allowing the coolness of the beer to take the edge off his anxiety. Father refilled his glass as they talked, making it harder for Dave to keep track of how much he was drinking.

The pizza came, and the conversation shifted to more innocuous topics—the Pirates' past season and the outlook for the Steelers. Dave knew he had to play along for another hour or so.

Father had the upper hand one last time, and he clearly intended to savor every moment of it. He ordered another pitcher of beer.

As he emptied the pitcher into Dave's glass, Dave got up his nerve. "Father, can we please talk about the scholarship? I can't go to college without it. It's pretty important."

Father gulped the last of his beer and nodded for Dave to do the same. He paid the check and slid out of the booth.

"Come on Dave, let's go talk about that scholarship. Do you want to drive?" he asked, dangling the keys in front of him.

"No, I'm good."

"Oh, come on. You know you're dying to get behind the wheel. Go on."

Father Jimmy was not taking no for an answer.

Dave eased into the low-slung driver's seat and fastened his seat belt. Father told him to turn north on Peninsula Drive, away from St. Florian's and home. Dave eyed the familiar landscape, trying to discern where they were headed. A few minutes later Father instructed him to follow the signs toward Presque Isle, and then to take a left. He pointed to a secluded parking lot.

Dread seeped into Dave's heart. The darkness emanating from the single street lamp at the end of the lot seeped toward the parked car. He tugged unconsciously at his shirt collar, the victim inside him bracing for the coming assault even as a voice inside him protested; he was of the age of consent now.

It's different this time. Just punch the guy if he tries anything.

As much as he'd like it to be different, he knew it wouldn't be, so thoroughly conditioned was he to enduring this demeaning ritual. And this one last time, it was his future on the line.

An hour later the Trans-Am eased out of the short driveway of his house. Once Dave heard the engine roar as it turned off his quiet street onto the main road, he stepped gingerly inside the front door, praying his parents were asleep. As he reached the stairs, his mother called from the sofa, "Where's Father, David? Didn't you invite him in?"

"Uh no. He had to get back to the rectory."

"Oh, that's a shame. I saved him some pie."

"Maybe next time, Mother."

"Did you talk about the scholarship?"

"Yes."

"And?"

"I got it."

"Really? David, that's terrific, just terrific. Father has always been so good to you."

Her words stung like a betrayal. "Goodnight, Mum."

He threw himself on his bed and was transported back to seventh grade, deeply buried thoughts, sensations, and feelings roaring back to life. But he was not twelve anymore; he was nearly an adult. How could he have let this happen? What was wrong with him? His rage turned inward, and he pounded his fists fiercely yet silently into his mattress. "Necessary evil." The hollow words echoed in his mind, offering no consolation.

June 1983

Dave waited in the East Side pub for his former PE teacher, Mr. Lark, tapping his foot nervously on the tile floor. He had stopped by St. Mike's to pick up his final transcript for college and had run into Mr. Lark. He had always been a strange duck, but Dave felt sorry for him. He was a nice man and a good teacher.

When he invited Dave to a graduation dinner, Dave didn't know whether to be flattered or concerned; truth be told, he was both. For once in his life he wasn't fast enough on his feet to think up a reasonable excuse, so he'd simply said, "Uh, sure, why not?"

As he sat waiting for Mr. Lark, the list of why-nots flowed ceaselessly through his brain. He derided himself for getting stuck in what was sure to be a long, awkward meal.

Mr. Lark appeared, standing next to the booth. "Uh, hello, Dave . . . Hi, um, sorry I'm late."

Dave stood up and shook hands with the petite, nervous little man. They both sat down and spent the first ten minutes looking over the menu. He managed to consume a half-hour by discussing the college acceptance process, his choice of colleges and major, and his plans for the summer.

"What are *your* plans for the summer?" Dave asked Mr. Lark, trying to be nice.

"Well," he began hesitantly, "I don't really know, but I'd like it to include more of you."

The shock must have been written all over Dave's face because Mr. Lark blanched and started dabbing his mouth nervously with the corner of his napkin.

"I just mean, I'm sorry. I didn't mean that, Dave." The man was stuttering. "I just think so highly of you. You're smart, handsome. I've always noticed you and admired you. I'd like to be closer friends, you know?"

Dave nodded and found himself rambling about all the things he had to do this summer, hoping to make it clear that spending one more minute beyond this meal with Mr. Lark was definitely not part of his plan. He forced himself to take a couple of bites of food, but Dave was sweating now and feeling nauseous. All he wanted to do was get out of there and away from this guy before he could make an overt pass at him.

They said an awkward good-bye shortly after the check came, and Dave beat a path out of there without caring if he appeared impolite.

Why did life exact this toll from him over and over again? Tears ran down his face as he drove toward home. It seemed like there was some kind of list and his name was on it. It was all getting to be too much to bear; too much anguish, too much shame, too much pain.

He'd rather die.

PART TWO

Denial

For whomever desires to love life and see good days
let him keep his tongue from evil and his lips from
speaking deceit.

1 Peter 3:10

Chapter 4

Pharmacist

Two are better than one, because they have a good
reward for their toil. For if they fall one will lift up
his fellow. But woe to him who is alone when he
falls and has not another to lift him up!

Ecclesiastes 4:9–10

1992
Erie, Pennsylvania

Mara hung up the phone and slid into one of the kitchen chairs
Dave's sister had left in the apartment for them. She struggled to
process the words the nurse had just spoken. *Venereal warts.* They
had just returned from their Cozumel honeymoon two weeks
ago. She and Dave had been together for two years, and she hadn't
dated anyone else since right after college. How was this possible?

She recalled the first time she had visited Dave in Maryland.
His apartment had been impeccable; even the sink and faucets
were spotless. And he was a pharmacist after all, trained in hygiene
and public health. How had he contracted venereal warts?

Must have been that girl he dated in college. Mara had never
liked her look. As reality sunk in, she worried about how to
break the news to Dave.

She had first met Dave when he and his friend Tom Monahan ended up in the same downtown bar for happy hour. Mara had the physical features and smoker's rasp of a young Suzanne Pleshette. Raven hair and a pixie cut framed her petite facial features. Pale Irish skin drew attention to her precocious green eyes. Although she was barely five foot tall and less than one hundred pounds, the mismatched strength and depth of her voice said she was not to be underestimated. It was an incongruity Dave had repeatedly told her he found irresistible.

She and her friend Susan were seated at the bar catching up on the week when Dave strolled up, ordered them drinks, and said to Mara, "I love your voice; I'm going to marry you."

She looked up from her conversation and quickly assessed him. "Oh, really? What do you do for a living? How much money do you make? What kind of car do you drive?"

He smiled confidently. "I'm a pharmacist."

"A pharmacist? I've never dated one of those before, but I've called on them for work."

"I'm Dave Wagner."

"Mara Martin."

They spent the rest of the evening in a witty verbal sparring match. Mara left without giving him her number; so she was surprised the next day when Dave tracked her down to invite her to brunch. She wasn't sure whether he was her type, but she did like his tenacity.

Dave was living in Maryland at the time. He had only been visiting for the weekend. But he began to make regular trips back to Erie to see her. He had flexibility at the moment, as he had been laid off from his job recently.

Dave told Mara that this last year had been his first time living anywhere other than the house he grew up in. He had his college roommate nearby, and his older brother, Matthew, had just visited with his wife and kids a few weeks prior. Dave shared that his brother was an Air Force pilot, so they didn't get to see each other as much as they would like. He showed her the photo of Matthew in a fighter jet that he proudly displayed in his apartment—the same one that would adorn their living room mantle after they married.

Not long after they met, Dave landed a new job in pharmaceutical sales. But a few months later, his brother-in-law helped him land a job with PackRx, a mail-order pharmacy in Erie. He had jumped at it to be closer to Mara, and soon they were engaged.

* * * * *

Mara heard Dave's car pull in.

"Hello, Wife," he chirped, as he strolled in the back door of the kitchen and kissed her forehead. "How was your day?"

"Not great."

"Why? What's the matter?"

"I just got a call from the doctor's office. It's not an infection, Dave. It's warts. Venereal disease."

"What?"

"VD, the lifelong one. They said you should go in and get treated too. "Dave, did you know? Did you have any idea you were a carrier?"

"What makes you think I'm the carrier?" Dave asked, immediately defensive. "You're the one who's got 'em. Maybe you should take a closer look at the men you dated before me." He left the room.

She remembered Mark, her last serious boyfriend before Dave. One night when they had been in an argument, he had ripped the necklace off her neck. It seemed like an accident, so she shrugged it off. A couple weeks later, she invited him over again, and while she was slicing cucumbers for the salad, he said, "My mom doesn't cut them like that." That was it; Mara broke up with him the next day. She knew she deserved to be treated better than that.

Most of the time, Dave did treat her better. And the few occasions when he had lost his temper were after he'd had too much to drink or when something else had set him off. She didn't like the behavior, but fortunately it was rare. And they were married now; Mara had been raised with a strong sense of marital commitment. Her parents weathered many ups and downs, and none of her siblings had divorced.

She committed to be a good wife, worthy of her husband's love.

She strove daily to identify his triggers and avoid doing those things.

One thing she had learned quickly was that Dave cared deeply about the opinions of others—too much, in her estimation, even though she was a bit socially neurotic herself. That made their social life a frequent battleground. Sometimes she would say or do something to be funny and then see that look in his eyes that told her she had crossed some invisible line. Of course, he would never create a scene in public. But her night would be ruined in nervous anticipation of the coming fight.

After their honeymoon, Dave and Mara had moved into a small apartment his sister and brother-in-law owned. Dave said it was just temporary and reminded Mara of his plan to be a millionaire by age thirty-five. That seemed a long way off from their present reality, but Mara admired his ambition.

A few weeks later, Dave pulled into the driveway in a brand-new, green Chevy Blazer.

"What's this, Dave?"

"It's a Blazer. And it's awesome."

"I had no idea we were buying a car. You just went out and bought it without us even talking about it? I thought we were saving for a down payment on a house."

"Mara, we talked about this. You just don't remember."

"No, Dave. I'm pretty sure I'd remember talking about a new car."

"You weren't listening then. Besides, I got a great deal. Why do you have to ruin everything? I don't complain when you go on your shopping sprees, do I? Your last clothing binge probably cost more than this car."

There it was. He knew which arrow to use and exactly where to aim. She looked away, defeated; it just wasn't worth the fight.

When they went to bed that night, Mara rolled to face the wall, still fuming about the car and Dave's denial of any wrongdoing. He had never apologized, and it didn't appear this would be his first. Dave leaned over and nudged Mara's shoulder.

"Are you awake? I love you, Wife. What do you say we make up, you know? I left a surprise for you in the bathroom."

Mara rolled out of bed. In the dim bathroom light, she saw a black, lacy one-piece draped over the towel rack. It wasn't pretty and feminine like the lingerie her friends got for their weddings; it looked cheap and tawdry. But, Dave was her husband, and she wanted to make him happy. She wanted to be loved and lovable in his eyes.

* * * * *

Dave was on the couch the next morning, perusing the sports section, when Mara rolled out in her robe in search of coffee and a cigarette. He had stopped by his parents' earlier to cut the tiny square of grass flanking their front walkway.

His dad, in his eighties now, could no longer keep up with maintenance. Each visit begat more chores for the next time. Today's list included adjusting the front screen door, fixing the leaky kitchen faucet, and tightening the basement doorknob. Dave was happy to honor his parents in this way, partly because it conjured such fond memories of days spent similarly working alongside Matthew.

* * * * *

The days grew longer and warmer. Dave and Mara decided to repaint the exterior of their duplex as a thank you to his sister and brother-in-law for giving them an affordable place to live. After work and on weekends, the two spent hours side-by-side, prepping and painting one section at a time. Of course Dave had to be in charge, but Mara didn't mind. Sunshine and a cold beer when they finished for the day made it relaxing and fun.

Mara had just climbed down the ladder to get some lemonade when she heard the phone. The caller said he was an alumnus of St. Michael's and asked if he had the Dave Wagner who had attended there in the early eighties.

"I think so," Mara said. "Let me get him for you."

"Dave, phone." She handed him the cordless.

"Hello?"

She watched his back as he strolled toward the cyclone fence bordering their postage-stamp yard. A few minutes later he rejoined her.

She handed him a paintbrush. "Who was that? Is it time for your reunion? Or are they hitting you up for a donation?"

"Neither. That guy was a few years ahead of me. Apparently he and some others are filing suit against one of the teachers for sexual abuse."

"Oh, Dave. That's awful!"

"Yeah. I knew what was going on. It didn't happen to me. I was smarter than those guys." He lit a cigarette and then swept the topic away with the smoke. He walked back across the yard to finish his cigarette.

She watched him, surprised by the harsh judgment in his comments.

1997

"Good morning, Connie," Dave said.

"Morning, Dave. Glad you're here; we are slammed this morning. We got a lot of orders overnight, so get some coffee and let's get rolling."

For the past few years, Dave had worked at Hofmeister's, a mail-order pharmacy similar to PackRx, except with a lucrative niche in specialty medications.

He liked the owner, Connie, a lot. She had taught him everything she knew about running a business, which was Dave's next goal. He was just three years away from thirty-five now, yet still a considerable distance from his financial goal. Life seemed to keep putting a crimp in his plans. In the last year he and Mara had bought their first home, a contemporary three-bedroom in Fairview, and welcomed Irish twins—Caleb, in 1995, and Margaret, just a few months ago.

Dave poured a cup of coffee and headed for the pharmacy bench, passing Connie in her office and musing about the recent change in her disposition. She had always been collaborative and engaging, but lately she'd acted aloof, almost rude. On top of that she'd given him a lousy raise in his last review, despite the business's brisk growth. She'd blamed his work ethic, but Dave knew that couldn't be it.

Dave was easily the smartest pharmacist on staff, too smart to spend his life counting pills, even innovative ones like the ones they dispensed here at Hofmeister's. He replayed Connie's feedback as he reviewed the prescriptions in the morning queue. He found the work to be relatively mindless. By the time he looked up, it was eleven. He'd finish these last few scripts and take lunch.

He started the next prescription, numbly grabbing the stock bottle, then printing the label from which he would verify the dosage and placing it on the vial. The patient name caught his eye. He looked again. *Jarzombek.* Couldn't be the same one. He sifted back through the paperwork, his hands clammy, fumbling for the original prescription. There it was: *James Jarzombek.*

Instantly Dave was back on the Ferris wheel, trapped, unable to escape. He placed his hands flat on the table to steady himself and dropped his head low, trying to catch his breath. Long-suppressed emotions broke through fissures in his shell, the pressure threatening to burst like water over a dam. He bolted for the parking lot.

"Dave, are you okay?" he heard a coworker call after him an instant before the security door banged shut behind him. He leaned back against the cinderblock wall, hoping the snap of cool air would bring him back to himself. Instead it compounded his shuddering until he no longer trusted his knees to support him. Dave slid down the wall, crouched like a junkie in need of a fix. He let his head drop toward his knees, forcing long, slow inhalations of the fresh air. After a few minutes he pushed himself off the wall and lunged for his car, struggling with the key until it finally slid into the lock.

The panic attack seized control quickly. First it sent his reflexes haywire, causing his body to react as if he were being hunted. His heart raced and his respiration became rapid and shallow. He pushed his head back against the back of the seat, tugged at his collar until it no longer touched his neck, and closed his eyes, waiting for the panic to subside.

As it finally ebbed, a new wave of emotions rushed in to take its place. They broke surface as an audible gulp, followed by a wrenching moan that emanated from the core of his being. It was the woeful, uncontrollable grief of a twelve-year-old boy, anguished, abandoned, frightened, and ashamed.

More than a half-hour later, Dave glanced up at the dash-board clock for the first time. Exhaustion swept over him as he sat ragged and raw, astounded at the power of what was buried inside him and by how it could surface unexpectedly over some-thing as simple as a name on a piece of paper. Would he never escape his past?

The very thought of everyone, or anyone, knowing those things he buried deep within filled him with a dread that made him want to die. He had never spoken a word to anyone. Now, he realized that time had not diminished his shame and never would. He could not go on living like this; that's all he knew for certain.

As tired as he had ever felt in his life, Dave started the engine. Mara was traveling for work today; the nanny would be home with the kids. As he headed home, he fantasized about suicide. Maybe he could drive off the highway or pull in front of a truck so his death would look accidental. An overdose would be harder to pass off as an accident, considering his profession. He adored his family and would never want to hurt them, but they would be better off without him.

He turned onto his slag driveway having reached no resolu-tion. He was relieved to discover Esther was out with the kids, probably at the park. They wouldn't be back until naptime. He hurried downstairs to the office he had recently finished in the basement.

He unlocked his file cabinet, retrieved a porn video, and inserted it into the VCR. He sat back on the couch, surrendering to the overwhelming need to lose himself. Later he awoke to the sound of Caleb scampering overhead; his joyful giggles made Dave smile. He put the video away, locked the cabinet, and headed upstairs.

"Dave," Esther said, clearly surprised by his appearance. "I didn't know you were here. I'm sorry."

"No problem, Esther. How are the kids doing? Good day?"

"It was a great day, wasn't it, Caleb? We went to the park. Your son is crazy about the swings. I must have pushed him for a half-hour straight, and even then when I took him out he fussed and wanted more."

"Is that right, Caleb? Do you like to swing?"

"Swing," Caleb said, pointing to the door.

"I had some paperwork to do so I decided to beat rush hour and just do it here. If you're okay with the kids, I'll finish up, and you can leave around four. I'll get dinner ready for Mara. Have you heard from her?"

"Yes. She was heading to Titusville. She said if traffic wasn't too heavy she would be home by six."

"Alrighty then." He took Margaret in his arms and kissed her on the forehead. "Caleb, why don't you get your blocks? You want to make a tower?" Dave dumped the blocks with a clatter onto the hardwood floor of the family room and stacked them high, cradling the baby on one arm. As soon as Caleb saw the tower, he toddled over as fast as his Stride Rites would carry him and knocked the blocks down, looking at his father with a proud grin.

Dave gazed at his son's cherubic face—the rosy, unblemished skin, the bright, innocent eyes, and the smile that never seemed to leave his face. He thought his heart would burst with pride and love for the one good thing he had managed to accomplish in his life: his children. As Caleb settled into the middle of the pile of blocks and started banging them together, Dave stood and smiled at Esther.

"Call if you need me." He handed her the baby and headed downstairs.

He dismissed Esther at four o'clock and was excited to make dinner for Mara. He fed the kids and gave them their baths. His time with the kids always buoyed his spirits. He loved to play with Caleb and see how he solved problems without knowing he was doing so.

Dave had bought him Tonka trucks and real wooden blocks, favorites of his own childhood, loaded with memories of hours spent alone in a world of imagination. Safe. Innocent. Full of possibilities. Holding Margaret on his lap, he stacked the tower of blocks again just so Caleb could knock it down. He wanted to create the same environment of carefree innocence and play that he had treasured as a boy, only he would protect his children throughout their lives. The importance and urgency of this cause was the best reason to make his life work.

"Hello, Wife," he said, when he heard high heels clicking on the hardwood entry.

"Dave. I didn't expect you home yet. Where's Esther?"

"I sent her home early. I made dinner. The kids are bathed and fed." Dave pushed his shoulders back and swept his arm toward the kitchen, awaiting his wife's approval.

* * * * *

Mara looked around the family room littered with blocks, trucks, and what must have been most of Caleb's toys. She always limited how many toys Caleb dragged out at one time to control the mess she'd have to clean up at the end of the day. But she saw the eagerness in Dave's face; he was only trying to help. She would just pick up once the kids were in bed.

She pecked him on the cheek. "Looks great. Alright, I'm going to go change, okay?"

"Don't change; stay the same lovely wife you are." Dave's cheery voice trailed after her as she went up the stairs.

She wondered where this carefree Dave had come from. For months now Dave had been stressed out and brooding. Mara usually made a point to arrive home first, finish making the dinner Esther started while the kids were napping, and do her best to make things perfect for him.

"Do this right and he'll love me," her familiar self-talk told her. Years of conditional love and mercilessly high standards in her family of origin had made Mara a people-pleaser of the highest degree. Yet the voice in her brain spoke harsh reprimands such as "That was a stupid thing to say." Or "Look what you did last night!"

Her friends called her the "morning after girl" because she inevitably called the morning after any social gathering to apologize for some infraction or other she perceived herself to have made. It was this fragility inside her progressive, *Women's Wear Daily* exterior that endeared her to her girlfriends.

They put the kids down by seven, following the routine Mara had established after Caleb was born.

"Routines give kids comfort," she told Dave. "It lets them know what's coming and gives them a sense of security." Although he played the carefree foil to her more rigid parenting style, this quality was one of the things he had grown to trust and love most about his wife.

The house quiet and the toys picked up at last, Mara and Dave sat down at the kitchen counter to eat, both conscious of and grateful for the home life they were building together. It was hard to believe the same playboy who threw out those cheesy pickup lines was the hardworking husband and father sitting beside her now. Mara considered him with unspoken affection.

They talked quietly and easily about their days. Dave shared that his had been pretty status quo. He fixed them both drinks as Mara loaded the dishwasher.

"So listen, Mara, I've been thinking."

She glanced up at his shift in tone.

"I think it's time for a change. I've been in Erie my whole life. I think it would be good for our marriage and our kids if I started looking for a new job, you know, somewhere else."

"Dave, where's this coming from? This is your home—where all your family is, all your friends. I'm the outsider."

She took a sip of the Bombay Sapphire and tonic he'd made for her in the on-the-rocks glasses they'd received for their wedding.

"I've told you I want to be more than a pharmacist. I *am* going to be a millionaire by thirty-five. I'm not gonna get there standing behind some pharmacy bench counting pills all day. You want to stay home with the kids, and have more? Then we've gotta start thinking about our future."

"Dave, are you looking at something specific? Are you being recruited?"

"No. If I was, I would tell you."

Even though that was far from true, Mara let it pass. She had numerous examples of Dave making big decisions independent of her. If she protested he'd turn the tables and blame her, claiming they had talked about it, even when she knew for a fact they had not. Other times, he had accused her of making a mountain out of a molehill.

"Well, why don't we look in Michigan then? At least that way we'd have my family close by. We could get a boat. I could teach our kids to ski."

"No way. I don't need your family torturing you, and thus me, at close range." She had to admit it was a quiet arms race in her family, with pressure to have the nicest house, the most enviable closet, and even the most kids. Showing up at Thanksgiving without nail lacquer was as humiliating as showing up in pajamas.

"Well, where then? How about Maryland? You liked living there. The weather's nice. It's close to everything."

"Yeah. I don't know yet. I got a call a few months ago from a pharmacy automation company. The job sounded interesting, but at the time I didn't want to move. Maybe I'll follow up."

"Where is it, Dave?" Mara said, sensing a setup. He broke eye contact, swigged the watery remains of his drink, and then munched a few ice cubes to stall. She waited him out.

"Louisiana."

"Louisiana? Where, New Orleans?"

"No, it's close to there, though. Opelousas."

"How close, Dave? I've never even heard of it."

"There's no point getting all worked up, Mara. I haven't even made a phone call yet."

"I don't know if I could live in the Deep South. It's still rebel-flag-and-gun-rack territory down there. I'd like to think about it. I don't know that I want our kids growing up in a place like that. You probably shouldn't even call if we aren't willing to move."

"Stop overreacting, Mara," he said, dismissively. "You're the one who keeps ranting about staying home all the time. This is a place where you could; the cost of living is really low."

She sat back in the rocking chair, unwilling to provoke him, especially when it was hypothetical at this point.

"Who knows, maybe we'll make some more kids. Wanna practice?" He smiled at his wife, approached her, and placed his hands on the rocker's armrests, and then bent down to kiss her.

* * * * *

They made love on the throw rug in front of the dwindling fire beneath a plush, oversized white blanket. Wrapped up together, his beautiful wife in his arms, Dave was the man he wanted to be, the one who loved and protected his family. He drifted off into a rare, peaceful sleep.

A few weeks later Connie called him into her office.

"Dave, this is difficult for me because I think the world of you and Mara. I'm afraid I have to let you go."

Her words struck him like a cold slap in the face.

"You know I've shared my concerns about your performance and your attitude on more than one occasion. I've tried to remind you of the expectations as clearly as possible. But the fact is, I'm just not seeing a change, not at the level I need. If anything, it's gotten worse lately. We're handling lifesaving, but also life-threatening drugs. I simply can't afford a mistake that could cost someone's life. You're smart, Dave, really smart. But your head's not in this game."

* * * * *

Connie paused, giving him a chance to absorb the information.

She knew he was a husband and new father. She never reached these decisions lightly. Dave was a great guy. Everyone loved him. But he had changed. He had gone from being one of her top performers to being almost a non-performer; even more concerning, he was becoming a liability risk.

She had given things time to work out, attributing it to stress at home or some other temporary issue, but as the months wore on she had no option. She had tried to communicate her concerns, but she couldn't seem to get through to Dave. He'd just grown more distant and less engaged. What truly surprised her was the look on his face. How could he not have seen this coming?

"Listen, Dave. We can talk more later, but I know you've got bigger goals and aspirations. I just think maybe this isn't the best place for you anymore. Maybe it's time to explore other options. I don't think pharmacy is right for you, to be honest. Pharmacists, well, we're kind of geeks, introverted, you know? You're not that guy. You're too outgoing. You're funny. People love you, Dave. Find a way to use that.

"You know I care about you, Mara, and your family. I've tried to be as fair as possible with your severance." She pushed a red folder toward him. "Take some time and look everything over.

"And if you need a reference, I'm certainly willing to do that. But today's your last day with Hofmeister's."

✳ ✳ ✳ ✳ ✳

Dave didn't understand. It was one thing for him to hate his job; it was another for Connie to reject him. He sat in stunned silence, churning inside, but revealing nothing. Slowly, he composed his response.

"I will review the information. I'll be in touch tomorrow if I have any questions. I guess I'll collect my things?"

As he packed up, he considered the situation. He knew Connie had been stressed out, but he had no idea she would take things this far. This was crazy. She was right about one thing: He was done being a staff pharmacist. He let his mind wander back over the past few months looking for signs he had missed. Maybe he could have kept a little tighter rein on his

Internet activities, but his productivity more than offset it. And while it was true that his overall level of anxiety and distraction had been elevated since the Jarzombek prescription, he never thought it would come to this.

As he drove home, he thought about what he would say to Mara. He needed a game plan so she didn't freak out. He thought again about the call he'd received from Louisiana. At least that would put him at a safe distance from his past. There weren't even direct flights into Opelousas; you had to fly to New Orleans and then drive two hours. He resolved to pursue that job. He had heard good things about the owner and how well he treated his people. And they seemed interested in him when they called.

Maybe it wasn't too late.

Dave told no one except Mara he'd lost his job. He rejected her suggestions that they fire the nanny and curtail spending until he found another job. Instead he began spending compulsively, just in case anyone suspected things were anything less than prosperous in the Wagner household. There was the five-hundred-dollar printer/scanner/fax, a new grill, a Cannondale bicycle, and a new Suburban. Mara had freaked out about the Suburban, but Dave wasn't about to drive a minivan, and they needed a bigger vehicle for car seats.

He initiated dialogue with Donovin, Inc., flying to Louisiana twice for interviews. By the end of October, he had secured an offer, with the help of Connie's reference. Mara loved their house, and she had done a great job turning it into a home. But he knew she would not balk at leaving behind his family and what she considered their "blue-collar ways," like vacuuming while people were still seated at the dinner table.

It had never seemed unusual to him until she made a big deal out of it. He hated how she shamed him about his family when hers was every bit as dysfunctional, only with more money to screw things up.

"You'll love Opelousas. Think of it as Harbor Springs with warmer weather," he said, referring to her hometown in Michigan. "You'll love being able to get outside and walk with the kids year-round. It'll be great."

Their first scouting visit was almost their last. Mara complained about the mugginess; then it was the man-eating mosquitoes. And when the realtor pointed out the swamp at the edge of one of the properties and warned Mara to watch for alligators, Dave felt sure they'd be on the next plane home. But he persisted and she eventually relented.

Dave moved down in November to start his job. While there, he picked out a charming, blue-planked, Louisiana-style home in the middle of town and made a down payment.

"It's a great location," he told her on the phone. "You'll be able to walk the kids to school. There's a playground right down the street. It'll be great, Mara. I promise."

While she packed and cleaned their Erie house, Dave managed to make it back just in time for the going-away party. He was the life of the party among all his college pals, singing Frank Sinatra, smoking cigars, and exercising his always-quick wit. Mara drove him home and helped him into bed, taking off his shoes and giving him a glass of water and an aspirin so he wouldn't be too hung over the next day.

* * * * *

Margaret awoke crying in her crib around six the next morning. Mara got up, made coffee, and fed her. Then she made pancakes for Caleb, got the kids dressed, and put out the few toys she hadn't packed yet. Maggie lay contentedly on her back and swatted at the mobile on her Pack'n Play. Mara busied herself cleaning the house and packing up some remaining items, periodically checking her watch and wondering when her husband would start his day.

Dave slept until noon, waking up groggy and grouchy from his hangover. He showered, repacked his bag, and kissed his family before heading to the airport for an early morning flight back to Lousiana.

Would it have been too much to expect him to stay an extra day to help prepare for the movers?

The movers arrived bright and early the next morning. The cold breeze swept in through the open doors, and box parts covered the carpets to catch dirty boot prints. It was just a house now, no longer their home. Mara bundled up the kids. Esther came over to keep them entertained as Mara directed the movers in disassembling the final remnants of their lives here. Efficient and compulsively organized, Mara had the men hopping like toy soldiers; the house was emptied and cleaned well before dinnertime

Mara paid Esther, who refused the money, instead giving her a tearful hug and scurrying to the coat closet to retrieve beautifully wrapped gifts she had bought for the kids. After saying their goodbyes, Mara packed up the kids and a few belongings and spent the evening at her friend's house. The next day, she and the kids flew to Louisiana to begin their new life.

* * * * *

Dave picked them up at the airport in the white Suburban, which Mara still hated. The next day, they walked through the house he had selected. Of course, she hated it too. Why was he surprised? All she did was complain about its age, the rounded arches of the doorways, and how much work it was going to be to fit the furniture from their open floor plan into the smaller rooms of this traditional home. Not to mention that she would have to unpack *and* decorate for Christmas at the same time.

No comment about the home's Southern charm, its proximity to town, the beautiful neighborhood, or the fact that she was finally able to quit working and stay home with their kids.

Once again, it seemed like nothing was ever good enough for his wife.

CHAPTER 5

Millionaire Entrepreneur

For where your treasure is, there your heart
will be also.

Luke 12:34

1998–2003
Opelousas, Louisiana

"Hey. Hi. Welcome! We're the Jacobs. We live next door. And, well, we just wanted to stop by and say hello and welcome y'all to the neighborhood," the woman said, standing beside her husband on the front porch, pie in hand.

"Hey y'all, I'm Bobby." The man thrust his hand out to shake Dave's.

"I'm Ashley." The woman offered Mara the pecan pie. "Be careful, it's still warm on the bottom."

Mara noted with appreciation the craftsmanship of a fellow baker, the crust perfectly scalloped and the pecans arranged in a symmetrical design. The aroma made her mouth water. "I'm Mara. This is Dave," she said, gesturing with her free hand. "It's a pleasure to meet you. I'm gonna be honest; it's a disaster in here. Come on in . . . at your own risk." She dropped her tone to a hush and ushered them inside. "The kids are napping."

"How old are they?" Ashley asked in an equally hushed tone.

"Caleb's two and a half, and Margaret—'Magpie' we call her—she's sixteen months."

"How fun! My boys are four and two. Well, we'll have to get them together to play as soon as y'all get settled. Where are you from?"

"Pennsylvania," Dave said. "We moved here for my job; I work with Donovin. Do you know them?"

"Oh sure. They're a pretty big employer in Opelousas," Bobby said.

Ashley was petite, energetic, and clearly fond of the domestic arts. Mara felt an immediate connection, hoping she might become a welcome lifeline in this cultural desert.

Dave and Bobby were telling stories like old chums in a matter of minutes. Dave opened a couple of specialty beers, singing the praises of their craftsmanship and using his well-worn bit about his own homemade brew, made using a kit Mara had gotten him for his birthday.

"Yeah, I make my own labels too, because you know beer is all marketing." Bobby laughed along with Dave.

"You know what I named my first batch?"

"What's that?"

"Wife Beater Ale," Dave said, pausing for effect, and then, "Because you can't beat a wife."

Laughter exploded as the men clanked their bottles. Mara and Ashley shared a knowing look that they were likely to be spending a lot more time together.

"Have you been in this house before?" Mara asked. "Did you know the previous owners?"

"No. They were an older couple. Friendly enough, but we never got to know them too well. Their daughter drove down from Baton Rouge and moved them to an assisted living place.

We were so excited when we heard y'all had young kids. This sweet old house is ready for some life. We're right across the backyard from you—there." Ashley pointed out the family room window. "See, that's the back of our house. Our yards connect. That'll be fun as the kids get bigger."

"It will. Do your kids go to preschool yet?"

"Oh yes, it's fabulous. You can start them at two years old. Five mornings a week."

"Well, I wasn't really thinking about starting them quite so soon."

"I can get you in our carpool. You need to come with me next week and see it. I'll introduce you to the teachers. They do a wonderful job. Jack and Edward—those are my sons—they love it. I do too; it gives me time to run some errands. Have you got a housekeeper? I can set you up with mine."

"A housekeeper? Um, no. I hadn't really given that any thought."

"Well, you need to. You're in the South now, honey. Hire some help so you don't lose your mind with these little ones. That's the secret to Southern charm. No reason to run yourself ragged trying to be superwoman; we leave that to you Yankees." Ashley laughed good-naturedly.

Sitting across from one another on the couches, the couples chatted easily until Margaret woke up from her nap. Even amid the stacks of boxes and partially settled furnishings, the house was starting to feel more like a home.

Mara enjoyed Dave most at these times. He had a way of putting people at ease, and she had to admit he was funny, even if she had heard most of his jokes before. His charm always drew a crowd, like moths to light. She watched as her husband worked his magic on their new neighbors and loved him for it.

Ashley invited them for dinner. As the day transitioned into evening, the men talked about work and hunting, while the women chattered excitedly about their children and how many more might be on the horizon. As the food, alcohol, and conversation flowed, the couples effervesced with the infatuation of new friendship.

"You honeymooned in Cozumel? We were just there on vacation," Ashley said. "Did y'all happen to go to Charlie's Crab Shack? They have the absolute best crabs ever, and that's saying something when you're from Louisiana."

"We did. It was great," Mara said. "The drinks were killer too. Dave got sunburned because he passed out on margaritas. He was red as a lobster; that German skin is not made for the Mexican sun." They laughed at Dave's mock shock.

"We should probably get going," Mara said, looking at her watch, her thoughts returning to all they still had to get done before Dave returned to work on Monday.

"Oh, have one more beer," Bobby said.

Dave reached out his hand to accept. "Oh, okay one more."

"Great." Ashley popped the top. Mara stared at Dave until his eyes met hers.

"Actually, I think I need to pass," Dave said. "I have to finish some painting Mara had me start earlier today."

"Painting? Now? Oh, let it go 'til tomorrow."

"You don't know my wife well enough yet. Tomorrow is *not* an option." Dave looked accusingly at Mara as he spoke.

Ashley glanced from Mara to Dave, who looked perfectly content to stay put and continue the great evening. Mara was painfully aware of the growing awkwardness.

"Oh well, it's fine. We know where to find you. We'll do it again soon. Thank y'all for coming on such short notice. Next time we'll plan a seafood dinner to rival Charlie's.

"I've got some great recipes I'll bring over," Mara said.
"Sounds like a plan."

* * * * *

Ashley lifted Edward onto her hip and walked the Wagners
to the door. She gave Mara a one-armed hug and promised to
stop over in a couple days. As she turned the deadbolt, Ashley
looked at her husband.

"That was an odd finish, wasn't it Bobby?"

"Who knows." Bobby shrugged it off. "I like Dave; he's
hilarious. They'll be great neighbors. She probably just needs to
get settled. You know how hard it is to move, especially with two
little ones. She's just a little uptight. Give her a couple months
in the South. We'll relax her."

"I hope so."

The Jacobs hosted a welcome party a few weeks later.
They invited five or six of their closest friends, and everyone
embraced the Wagners as immediate members of their social
circle. Opelousas had a simple charm that elevated small-town
living to an art form. Home entertaining replaced fine dining,
with family picnics or other social gatherings virtually every
weekend. The food, drink, and laughter flowed easily.

As it turned out, the Wagners quickly established their home
as *the* party destination. Dave provided the spirit and entertainment value that elevated their gatherings to epic proportions.
His larger-than-life, host-with-the-most personality paired perfectly with Mara's fanciful flair.

Mara was a natural socialite, capable of far-fetched, fabulous
party themes, with a nearly obsessive attention to detail. For
one winter event, Mara crafted a tiered network of mirrors into
a Zhivago-worthy icescape on which to present the dishes. For
Halloween she floated frozen hands made from latex gloves in

the punch bowl, and sewed Crayola crayon costumes, a different color for each of her children.

Usually the Jacobs hosted an annual Christmas party, but they gladly ceded it to the Wagners. Dave hired a pianist to play all night on their baby grand, the one he had bought in hopes that one of his toddlers would someday play. The evening ended with a caroling party around the neighborhood; it was impossibly, magically fun.

1998

"It's the lies, Ashley, so many lies," Mara said, as they finished their walk the next day.

"What are you talking about, girl?"

Ashley and Mara had walked together almost every day for the last year. They now had a well-worn, four-mile route around town, which began at Mara's front gate. It was one of the perks of the kids being in school.

Mara felt uncomfortable having them in school full-time; she preferred they be home with her. But for the sake of fitting into the local lifestyle, she had succumbed, at least for now.

"Trust me. I'm right on this. I have this gut feeling," she said, pointing to her abdomen. "He lies about everything lately. He's on the road constantly. He was never gone like this before. He used to call and check in, you know? Now, not only doesn't he call, but he also gets angry if I call him. It scares me, Ash. I don't know how to make him want to be here anymore. I just want him to love me."

"Dave loves you, don't be silly. Tell me specifically . . . what are you talking about when you say, 'the lies'? Why do you assume he's lyin' to you? The more you treat him like this, the more he *is* going to push you away. He's workin' hard, trying to provide. It's what men do. And he's doing a fine job for you,

Caleb, and Margaret, right? That comes with a price tag. He needs your support, not your naggin' all the time."

"Alright, listen. Last week he went to New Orleans for business, or so he said. He told me they all went out to dinner.

"So I said, 'Oh, that's nice. Where'd you go?'

"'Nola,' he says.

"'I heard it's good. What did you eat?'

"'Red beans and rice,' he tells me.

"Well, I look up Nola's number and call, and guess what. They don't serve red beans and rice, not even by request. I asked."

"Where do you come up with this stuff, Mara? So what? I barely know what I ate for breakfast. Not remembering what he had for dinner hardly makes him a liar."

"Okay, well then, how about this? He comes home last Friday, and as soon as we sit down on the porch he tells me he has to go into the office on Saturday.

"I ask him when, and he says, 'Same as usual,' annoyed with me, like he has a 'usual' for Saturdays.

"The next day I'm home alone with the kids all day—again. We go to the park, I nap them. Dave rolls in around four thirty, stinking of beer and fresh-cut grass and tobacco. Turns out he was golfing, not working. He'd been gone all week, but he'd rather play golf than be with his family."

"Mara, I hate to say it, but you sound a little ungrateful. Guys play golf. Guys lie to their wives about playing golf. Men need time with other men. Bobby golfs. I know he doesn't travel as much as Dave, but still. He's working so you can be home with the kids. I know it's hard, but it's not criminal for goodness' sake."

Still, Mara knew Dave was up to something. Maybe if Ashley could see how Dave treated her when they were home alone, his growing hostility and rejection of her, maybe then she'd understand why she was concerned.

"Okay well, then there is this," she said, holding up a hotel receipt she had hidden under the silverware tray.

"The Dumfries Inn?"

It was a historic, upscale hotel with a quiet reputation as a haven to upscale escorts and their executive clientele.

"I'm sure there's a reasonable explanation," Ashley said, but she didn't seem sure at all. "Not all the guests are there to partake, I'm sure. Plenty of legitimate businesspeople probably stay there too."

* * * * *

Mara couldn't sleep. As the clock on her nightstand rolled toward five in the morning, she relented and put on a pot of coffee. She folded laundry and emptied the dishwasher. She poured another cup of coffee and headed for the office.

It seemed she never slept well anymore. Maybe it was the latest pregnancy, but her growing anxiety about her husband contributed. Her mind raced with fear and accusation.

Just the weekend before, she had been out to dinner with Dave, Ashley, Bobby, and another couple. When the wife found out Dave was a pharmacist, she asked him about her tinnitus and whether it could be a side effect of taking an antidepressant. It always annoyed Mara when people treated Dave like a doctor, mostly because he ate it up. He acted every bit the MD, explaining to her that tinnitus was a common side effect, and that he had experienced the same thing when he first started taking that medication.

But Mara had no idea Dave was taking any medications, let alone an antidepressant. He must have seen a physician to get the prescription. Did the secrets never end? She asked him about it on the drive home, but he claimed she had misheard him. After he left for work the following Monday, it had taken her less than ten minutes to find the vial in his bathroom drawer.

She sipped her coffee and logged on to the computer. She had found Dave up here several late nights, and she felt the need to know what he had been up to. He kept his work computer locked down; she wasn't allowed on it at all. But this was the family PC, the one she and the kids used. She cursed herself again for her lack of computer skills. She had taken a class, but had not found time to put the knowledge to work.

After a half hour, she figured out how to open the browser history in Netscape. She got out a scrap of paper and scribbled down the websites. When she got to the sixth one, she dropped her pen and stared slack-jawed at the screen. It had to be a mistake, but as she looked down the long list of sites that followed, she became more certain about what she was seeing. Pornography sites, and lots of them. She was afraid to click on anything, in case Dave would be able to see she'd been snooping.

The shuddering emanated from her fingertips through her tender frame until even her legs were shaking uncontrollably. "Breathe." She fought futilely for control while logging off the computer.

She showered and then sifted through her closet looking for something that still fit. Her belly had popped much earlier this time. Her skin was freckled from her daily walks, and her latest haircut was too short. No wonder Dave was seeking satisfaction online.

She forced herself through the motions of a normal day—making breakfast, cleaning the kitchen, and getting the kids ready for school. Today she was grateful for school; and thankfully, it was Ashley's turn to drive. As soon as the kids were out the door, she got back online and called her friend back in Erie. At least someone out of town couldn't spread rumors here. After a few minutes of small talk, Mara blurted, "Hey, listen, I have to ask you something, okay? I found something on Dave's computer. You know I don't do computers. Don't say anything to anybody there, okay? I'm afraid Dave will find out. I don't know what to do!" Choking back tears, she read the list of websites and whispered conspiratorially, "What do you think? What should I do? I'm sick. Why would he do this? Do I confront him?"

"It's just a guy thing," her friend said dismissively, and then counseled her not to overreact. "I'd let this one slide."

It all had seemed so simple back when they were dating. Dave was funny and bright. He lit up any room he entered with his huge personality. He had a kind and easy way of engaging everyone he met. It was what had drawn her to him, the thing that bridged their vast differences. His lower-middle-class upbringing contrasted with Mara's upscale, even ostentatious one. His willingness to be outrageous, versus her near-paranoia about social conformity. His obsession with becoming a millionaire, and her innate sense of how to live like one. They should never have gotten engaged so hastily.

Here she was, stranded in the Deep South with two toddlers and a baby on the way. She was so far from family, with no safety net, no one who understood, no income of her own, and nowhere to turn. Everyone else thought Dave was great, the life of the party, and the funniest guy in the room. And he was—outside of their marriage.

All Mara wanted was Dave's love. All he wanted was everyone else's. He gave his best to his job, his friends—even the new ones he hardly knew. And now, this latest and deepest rejection: he had pursued false intimacy online over her, his flesh-and-blood wife.

Yet she'd failed miserably to convince anyone that what she was experiencing was real. It was even hard for her to reconcile sometimes. Try as she might, she could not shake off one persistent and terrifying thought.

She didn't know the man she was married to.

* * * * *

Dave was out of town on business all week, and looking forward to his annual Myrtle Beach golf outing over the weekend. Matthew would make it this year, and Dave could hardly wait to see him.

The following week he planned to take Caleb and Margaret with him to Washington, DC, to participate in a memorial race for his college roommate's wife, who had died tragically, leaving him to raise their preschool daughter alone.

Dave had deep compassion for his friend's loss. He came alongside Drew to help organize the team for the race, working tirelessly to cajole their college pals into turning out. Dave took the helm of the fundraising effort too, raising more than thirty thousand dollars, even though ten thousand of it came out of his own pocket.

Drew had always been there for Dave. He was a laid-back, quiet soul, a perfect complement to Dave's boisterous persona. Drew had been a breath of fresh air after high school, allowing Dave to redefine himself once and for all as a normal guy.

Mara wouldn't be joining him. While traveling was a challenge in her state, he couldn't help but feel that her resentment of his college friendships was the real deterrent. She was irrationally threatened by his old flames, and for some reason she also seemed to resent the time and generosity he directed toward Drew.

Dave felt like a kid again as he and his brothers rode in the golf cart to the third tee. They'd played nine holes on Friday and could easily do thirty-six today; after all it was only seven in the morning. The skies were bright and clear and the course unseasonably empty. Dave made sure he and Matthew nabbed the front seat in the golf cart.

"How's Louisiana, Dave? You teaching your kids voodoo instead of catechism yet?" Philip's sarcasm was as sharp as ever.

"Fine, great, in fact. Our company is doing well. I love my job. The kids are great, and we even found a Catholic church right there in the heart of the bayou if you can believe it."

"Don't let him get to you," Matthew whispered as they hopped back in the cart. Dave smiled and nodded at his brother. Philip climbed in behind them and swigged his beer.

"How's Mara doing?" Matthew asked. He and his wife had recently divorced, and he was well aware of the strain that kids and too much time apart could put on a marriage.

"Good, you know. She's pregnant."

"What? No way, man, congratulations! When is she due?"

"September."

"September? If you'd waited any longer you'd be handing out cigars. We really need to stay in better touch, Bro."

"Yeah, I know, but it's old hat for us at this point."

"I bet the Louisiana humidity's killing her."

"Nah. Louisiana has been good for her, actually. She walks every day with our next-door neighbor, Ashley. And even though the heat is rough I think she likes being able to get out with the kids. I'm traveling a lot. Having good neighbors is a big help."

As they packed up and said their goodbyes, Matthew promised to visit Dave after the baby was born. He had more time these days, he said sadly, now that he didn't have a wife to worry about. Matthew had struggled with his own demons following active duty, which did not help his already rocky marriage. He and his ex stayed on good terms, he told Dave, for the kids' sakes.

Dave left with a heavy heart for his brother.

"You take care of your family, you hear," Matthew said.

"I will, Matt, I promise."

* * * * *

Sunday had arrived at last. Dave was due back by dinner. Mara was anxious to see him, see how the evening would go, experience firsthand if things were as bad as they seemed in her mind. She weighed whether or not to confront her husband with her latest discovery. She couldn't stand the lies she knew would follow. But if he was going to keep denying the truth, she was going to keep pursuing it.

The day was hot; humid air wrapped around her like a wet, woolen blanket. She and Ashley sat on the porch swing, sipping homemade lemonade and trying to ignore the sweat streaming unceasingly down the backs of their legs. The kids napped inside the open windows. The ceiling fans pushed the hot air around without real relief, but offered just enough white noise that they could chat quietly without waking the kids. Mara told Ashley about her find.

"Mara, if you don't stop stalkin' that man, I swear you're going to push him away for good." Ashley placed her foot on the ground to stop the swing and looked her friend squarely in the eye.

"Leave him be, will you? Keep him happy at home and you won't have to worry about all this nonsense, okay? Please, girl, stop worrying." She patted her friend gently on the leg and restarted the swing with a push of her foot.

Mara wondered if Ashley was right. Maybe all men did such things. What did it amount to, after all? A few ill-timed rounds of golf, poor communication—that was nothing unusual in a marriage, and a little dabbling in pornography while his wife was pregnant.

The conversation took a lighter turn as Ashley suggested they brainstorm costume ideas for the upcoming museum fundraiser. Mara and Ashley both liked to sew, and planned to make their costumes around a common theme.

"How about the Flintstones?" Mara suggested.

"Great idea! Bobby was born to be Barney."

Her laughter woke Jack, which started a chain reaction that woke the other children.

"Sounds like it's time to make dinner before our cavemen get home," Ashley said. "We'll get patterns and fabric next week, okay Mar?"

As she fed the kids, Mara took Ashley's advice to heart and recommitted to being a good wife. She would make being home more appealing than anyplace else. With nervous anticipation she got the kids ready for bed. She prepared dinner and set the table on the back patio. She lit tiki torches to fend off mosquitoes. She showered and put on the one sundress that still looked flattering. She finished the look with low-heeled sandals she'd just ordered from Nordstrom's.

"Hey, Dave," she said sweetly, greeting him at the door. "Welcome home."

* * * * *

"Hey," he said, giving her a real kiss and hug, still on an emotional high from the weekend with his brothers.

"I made us a nice dinner. And, I've got a very dry martini chilling for you."

"How dry?"

"We're out of vermouth." His laugh followed her and she felt her hope flicker once again.

"Sounds perfect," he said, and then turned his attention to the kids. Dave whistled the singsong tune of "I'm Home," as he did every time he returned from a trip. As soon as they heard it, Caleb and Margaret scampered in from the playroom.

"Daddy, Daddy!" they cried, their hair still damp from the bath. They each wrapped their arms around one of his legs and sat on his foot so they could ride as he walked. After a couple steps he bent down and lifted his daughter off his foot and into his arms.

"I love you more than life, Magpie." His whispers intentionally tickled his little girl's neck as she nuzzled into him, breathing in the familiar aroma of her father, the sweet smell of alcohol mixing with the earthy, spicy scent of tobacco on his breath.

"And I love you, Caleb." He lowered his other hand to tousle his son's soft brown locks.

"Love you too, Daddy."

"Come on, kids. Let's go read some books. How about Daddy puts you to bed tonight?" They shrieked with excitement. He carried them to their room and began their nighttime routine. They brushed their teeth and then easily bribed their dad into four stories instead of the usual two.

"Just one more, pleeeease, Daddy," Caleb said.

"Alright you two, time for bed. Let's say our prayers. In the name of the Father and the Son and the Holy Spirit. Now I lay me down to sleep . . ." Dave led them through the three prayers he had said each night as a boy, concluding with, "For all the ways I have harmed others I ask for forgiveness. For all the ways I have been harmed by others I offer forgiveness."

He kissed and hugged his daughter, and as he did so he whispered the closing lines from their favorite story, *Guess How Much I Love You*, into her ear:

"I love you, Margaret."

"I love you to the moon, Daddy."

"And I love you right up to the moon . . . and back."

He did the same thing with Caleb before turning out the light.

When he returned to the kitchen, Mara poured his cocktail. He observed his wife as she moved through the kitchen, efficient, graceful, and still so pretty. He felt blessed to have his wife, his children, and his life. He offered a quick prayer of gratitude and resolved again to be a man worthy of these blessings.

"How was your trip?"

"Great! It was so good to be with those guys, especially Matthew. I told them you were pregnant."

"You *just* told them?"

"Yeah, they gave me a hard time about that."

"Matthew calls you all the time, Dave. Why didn't you just tell him on the phone?"

"He calls a lot, but I don't talk to him that often. He has his own stuff going on. Did you and the kids make it to church this morning?"

"Of course. We went to the ten o'clock, but we were a few minutes late. It's tough getting those two out of the house lately. I'm looking forward to the day Caleb can sit still. I must have gone through a whole box of Cheerios trying to keep him occupied."

Dave laughed. He looked at his wife in her sundress. She looked radiant. He felt as in love with her as the day they'd met. He just wished she wouldn't give him such a hard time about everything. Sometimes it seemed like she was impossible to please.

Mara was quiet through dinner. They chatted more about the kids and the weekend. Dave kept his weekend stories light, downplaying the beer and cigars and the stories about his brothers that could provoke Mara's ire over their "blue-collar mentalities." Despite his best effort to charm her, it was clear her mind was somewhere else.

* * * * *

"Mara, I'm trying to have a nice evening with you. What's wrong? Sometimes I just don't know what you expect of me."

"What I expect of you? You want to know what I expect from you? I expect you to come home for dinner not hung over from a weekend of boozing. I expect my children to have a father who is around for more than bedtime. I expect not to be alone in this godforsaken town all the time. I expect to be enough for you, and not to have to compete with some bimbos online."

Dave flinched. "Mara, what are you saying?"

"Oh, I think you know."

"I have no idea. What? You think I'm hooking up with prostitutes or something?"

"I'm talking about those websites, Dave. I found them on the computer upstairs. They're disgusting. Is *that* the kind of woman you want? Is that why you don't want me?"

"I don't know what you're talking about." He tugged slightly at his shirt collar.

"I'm talking about porn, Dave, pornography," she hissed the word as much from anger as not wanting to wake the kids.

"Mara, I swear I have no idea what you're talking about. If you found something show me. But I can assure you it wasn't me."

"Who else could it possibly have been?"

He returned her glare with a practiced expression that said she was the one who was irrational. He inhaled, took a deep draw from his glass, and then, still staring into the bottom of it, said, "I'm not sure what you think you saw, but let's face it, you've been under a lot of stress. And, well, you're not exactly a computer whiz."

She bristled at the condescension but didn't take the bait.

"I'll take a look tomorrow. I'm just remembering now, though, the last time Katelyn babysat I gave her our password so she could do homework after she put the kids to bed. It was the night we went out with Ashley and Bobby, remember? She's the only other person who's had access to that computer."

"The babysitter? You really expect me to believe it was Katelyn?"

"I'm not saying she's a porn addict, Mara. She probably stumbled on it by accident. It's easy to do. Did you know that whitehouse-dot-com is a porn site? Gets thousands of hits a day from people trying to find the president, for God's sake. I don't know, but there's no need to overreact."

"Overreact?!" Mara shrieked, feeling her confidence wobble. "I hardly think I'm overreacting. I don't want that trash in my house. The kids use that computer. What if they saw that smut?"

Dave patted the air with his hand, tamping her volume patronizingly.

She redirected her focus toward Katelyn. "Well, it's totally unacceptable! What if the sites are illegal? I'm going to have to talk to her about it."

"Come on, Mara, do you really think the Feds are going to swoop down because our babysitter accidentally landed on a porn site? Maybe it was a thing with her boyfriend, no reason to humiliate the poor girl. Just don't have her back. Babysitters are a dime a dozen. Find a new one. Trust me on this one. Move on."

She'd have to let it go, at least for now.

Dave deflected the conversation to calmer waters. She listened as he talked about work and how Donovin had entered buyout talks. He told her what a critical time this was for them.

But she couldn't help feeling distracted and unsettled. What a strange conversation. Why had he brought up prostitutes? To throw her off? It was something that had never even crossed her mind, but she tucked the comment away.

Sometimes it seemed like Dave lived a whole other life she knew nothing about. Unlike his previous jobs, where the families were involved, at Donovin the only person Mara knew was Dave's boss, Hugh Roth. Roth and his wife had been kind and gracious to the Wagners from the day they arrived in Opelousas. Once, when Dave was out of town and the family all got the flu, Marilyn Roth had been the only person to offer help. Mara had turned the Good Samaritan story into family lore, joking with her kids that "the only things in life you can count on are your faith, your family, and your dad's boss's wife."

As she stood to clear the table, Dave grabbed her from behind. "Come here, Wife." He kissed the back of her neck and wrapped his arms around her belly. She relaxed in his embrace; his love was all she needed to be okay. She put the dish she was holding back on the table as he led her to their bedroom.

* * * * *

Dave had been lying awake listening to Mara's breathing. As soon as he was confident she was deeply asleep he slid out to the porch.

"Sure, a lot of people smoke more than I do, but no one quits more than I do." He recalled the standard shtick he used among his friends as he lit up and inhaled deeply. A smoker herself, Mara had stopped with her first pregnancy and never looked back. He didn't mind hiding his latest relapse to avoid tempting her, at least while she was pregnant, he rationalized.

Dave was struggling with an inability to quit more than tobacco.

As he sat on the porch swing, tapping ashes into a paper cup that he would later hide in the outside trash receptacle, he replayed the near miss and cursed his carelessness. He had never imagined Mara would or could check that computer. He decided to take the DVDs he kept in his file cabinet to work, just in case she did more snooping.

It started out the same way every time, a vague yearning that gathered force until it became irresistible, overwhelming. It had been getting harder to control. Sometimes it even intruded into his workday now. The exhilaration and relief he experienced from porn were frustratingly temporary. The shame that pounded him afterward drove him back in search of relief in an endless, vicious cycle. Each time, it left him feeling out of control, a victim of his own desperate urges, like a dog returning to its vomit—wasn't that the passage he had read at church last week? That line had hit him squarely between the eyes.

Even as his mind schemed for new ways to hide what he was doing, his conscience brought him up short, like catching sight of his soul in a mirror. "Why God? Why can I never seem to stop?" He loved Mara with all his heart. He wanted to be the husband and father he strived so hard to portray on the outside. But he sensed his core rotting from the inside out. Dave closed his eyes and resolved to become the man he imagined himself to be both inside and out.

He asked Jesus to come into his heart. Yet his prayer was diminished by the voice in his head mocking him for making this empty plea for what was easily the thousandth time. He would fail again, just like all the other times. Did he really expect the Almighty to find his dark heart a suitable dwelling place after all the terrible black marks, the mortal sins that had tarnished his soul? Dave rocked gently on the swing and prayed for silence and inner peace.

Louisiana was supposed to be his fresh start: new town, new job, new friends, and new life. Yet darkness clung to him like static socks, showing up in the most unexpected and unwelcome places. Dave stubbed out his cigarette and told himself he would quit smoking, quit porn, and quit all of that nastiness.

He thought of Mara sleeping with their third child, even while his burdens allowed him no rest. He had let her down in so many ways. Why did he continue to hurt her when he loved her so much? He thought of his children asleep in their beds, so innocent. His greatest desire in life was to protect them from harm, to keep them safe from the kind of suffering he now endured. He had betrayed them all.

He had to stop this. Self-loathing weighed on his chest, making his breathing fast and shallow. "They're better off without you," came the voice from inside him, as tears rolled down his face.

* * * * *

Dave drove toward Grand Rapids Airport, breathing the rare air of self-satisfaction. He was on the verge of greatness, finally. Donovin was in active talks to be acquired, and if that happened, which was expected by year's end, Dave would receive more than a million dollars, reaching his goal more than two years ahead of schedule.

Millionaire. He rolled the word around in his mind, enjoying the free association. After a mental parade of mansions, boats, and luxury items came the one thing Dave coveted most—respect. No longer just another pharmacist, Dave was entering a new, elite category of top performers.

Next month he would travel to DC to testify before the Congressional Committee on Aging about the challenges of medication compliance for the visually impaired. And he'd just received an award from the Department of Defense, rarely given to non-military, after being nominated for his work assisting a colonel with the US Air Force pharmacies.

His father would be so proud to tell his buddies about his son. So would Matthew, especially about the Air Force connection. His college pals would be happy for him and would have to admit, at least to themselves, that he was the most successful entrepreneur among them. And Mara . . .

Maybe now Mara too would see him as a man of means, not just a kid from a family of laborers who lacked the culture and privilege she took so for granted.

Last month he had signed papers on a Florida condo near Mara's parents' winter home, using his Christmas bonus for the down payment. This morning he closed on waterfront property he purchased from her father. His father-in-law had made known his vision that all his children would own contiguous parcels along the coastline. Mara's sister had purchased the first lot at a discount, but Dave was more than happy to pay full market value. It sent a clear message that he was the son-in-law most capable of meeting the family's high financial watermark.

2000
Harbor Springs, Michigan

It had taken nine months and more than three-quarters of his windfall for Dave and Mara to build their waterfront "cottage." It now stood as the most visible expression of the family's new wealth. Dave had made it, and "Mara knew how to spend it," he liked to say.

Mara basked in the pride Dave took in her upscale taste as well her ability to devise creative, conversation-worthy design solutions to any functional challenge. The house was stunningly contemporary, yet highly efficient. The bathrooms featured c-joint plumber's pipe employed as toilet paper holders, "floating" cabinets, and faucets with spigots that turned upward to double as water fountains for the kids. Each child had his or her own color-coded towel, hung neatly on plumber's-pipe towel racks each night after baths. Three-foot-wide folding-glass panels were hinged to the shower wall, eliminating the mess of shower curtains. Mara had even ordered custom-built bunk beds that slept six—two on the top, two on the bottom, and two in trundle drawers tucked beneath.

At this point, the Wagner kids took up half the beds themselves and were continuing to fill them quickly. Caleb was now in kindergarten, Margaret was four, Audrey would be two in September, and Mara was pregnant again. In this dimension of unspoken sibling rivalry in her family, Mara was solidly in the lead and enjoying every minute of it. She'd always occupied the role of "problem child" in her family of overachievers, a chubby kid who was teased unscrupulously until she successfully enrolled in Weight Watchers during college. Now Mara compulsively managed her weight, beating it back to double digits quickly after each pregnancy, even if it meant a diet of caffeine and tobacco.

Dave had formed a consulting company, and while waiting out the term of Donovin's non-compete agreement, he planned to stay at the cottage for a few weeks. Yet even in this carefree season, Mara had trouble drawing him back into the family. He spent his days dabbling in the details of his new company or cooking up new business ideas with a couple of colleagues from Donovin.

The buyout had been bittersweet for Mara. On one hand, she was proud of Dave for reaching such an auspicious goal. On the other, she'd been denied the pleasure of sharing in the milestone. The day he got word that the deal was done, he left work to celebrate. But instead of going home, he went next door to the Jacobs'. It wasn't until a few hours and a few drinks later that he had stumbled home to invite Mara to join the party.

She pushed the memory aside, excited to be hosting Christmas at the cottage for the first time. Her family would be together with no outside distractions. It had snowed almost every day since they'd arrived, painting everything outside their window in white. Snow clung to the trees and glistened off the frozen water, wrapping their home in quiet serenity.

On the day after Christmas, the kids played with their new toys while Dave and Mara sipped coffee beside the fireplace.

"I, uh, have to go back to Louisiana," Dave said.

"What? It's Christmas. When?"

"Tomorrow."

"Tomorrow." The word sat like salt on her tongue.

"You said you'd be here for three weeks. It's not like you have a job to rush back to." Anger rose on waves of fear of abandonment, insecurity over why she continually failed to hold her husband's attention, and resentment at the infinite competition for her rightful place at the top of his priorities.

"I've still got to make money if I'm going to keep up with your spending habits." The accusation in his comment stung. "It's just a couple of meetings. We're working on requirements for our new technology."

Her shoulders sagged under the weight of her weary spirit. Defeat settled into her heart once again. "The kids are going to be disappointed." Were they not enough for him either?

"They've got their new toys and lots of cousins." He stood and strolled toward the kitchen, signaling an end to the discussion. "They'll be fine."

Opelousas, Louisiana

"Let's go," Ashley said, floating in the back door, looking every bit the Southern belle in a sleeveless shift and wide-brimmed hat.

"Go where? I've got tons of laundry and the house is a wreck." Mara looked over the family room, which Ashley often said looked better than her house on a good day.

"Lunch. You, the girls, and me. Come on. Get dressed. I'll be back for you in a half hour."

Mara huffed in false protest, but welcomed the break. She spent too much time alone these days. Two things she loved about her Louisiana girlfriends were their easy laughter and their even easier gossip, and lunch was sure to be brimming with both.

"So what did you think of the boys' Christmas antics?" Lily, the town gossip queen, asked over their Waldorf salads.

"What is that?" Mara asked as nonchalantly as possible.

"Oh, you know, that Christmas binge!"

"Oh, I did hear something about that," she lied.

Ashley eyed her warily. Mara avoided her glance, instead nodding along to keep Lily talking.

"Well, apparently Dave was the life of the party at Lester's warehouse. Those boys stayed up until five in the morning or something crazy like that . . ." She sipped her sweet tea. "And then Dave convinced them to go hunting the next day. I bet they were seeing two of everything. Probably thought they were tracking Noah's ark!" The women all laughed, and Mara forced a laugh, cautious that the horror enveloping her inside didn't reveal itself in her facial expression.

"Word is they gave up and went back to drinking. A two-day bender. I bet your man was a hot mess when y'all got home."

Mara set her fork down, confident she wouldn't be eating any more of her meal and nodded, recalling how Dave had slept most of the next two days.

"You alright?" Ashley asked, when they got back in the car. "You didn't know, did you?"

"No, I had no idea. I tried calling him, but of course he didn't take my calls or call me back. I knew he was up to something. He told me he had a meeting he had to come back for, but then he went off the grid for two days. I had that sick feeling. You see now?"

Ashley was beginning to see Mara's point. Still, she thought, it was a chicken-and-egg thing. The more Mara nagged him, the more he lied, and the more he lied the more she nagged. It just went round and round with those two.

2004
Los Angeles, California

"Living in LA these past few years has made me appreciate anything connected to home. Pepperoni bread. Pierogis! Even you."

Nicole laughed, her eyes, as usual, betraying her true emotions for her dear friend. When she found out Dave was coming to California on business, Nicole had jumped at the opportunity to take him out to dinner with her husband.

"So how are the kids?" She bubbled with so much excitement that Dave thought she might leap across the table of the restaurant to hug him again. "Remind me of all their ages."

"Caleb is my eldest; he's nine. Margaret, "Magpie" we call her, she's seven; Audrey is five, Stephen is three; and Annie is two."

"Holy cow, Dave! You're going to rival your parents if you keep this up."

"No. Mara and I agreed we'd only have as many kids as we could care for ourselves. We both had big families and the older kids inevitably got stuck caring for the younger ones. Five is the most we can manage ourselves."

"Well, that's still a boatload of kids, isn't it, Tim?" Nicole asked incredulously.

Her husband nodded. "Nicole and I are holding at two, right babe?"

"That's all *we* can manage," she said, and then turned her focus back to her friend. "We have so much to catch up on. Tell me about your job and, well, your life!"

Dave was more than happy to share the story of the buyout of his former company and how he and his buddies had used some of their windfall to fund development of a new pharmacy technology. "I traveled back and forth between Opelousas and Durham until we got funding to launch last year. Then I moved the family to North Carolina. We bought a place in Duke Forest, right by the university. You should come see it. It needs a lot of work. It's a 1960s contemporary, but the bones are good and the location is beautiful. I picked the house because a walking trail runs right behind it. Mara became a real fanatic about walking when we lived in Louisiana."

"With five kids, she has to do something to keep her sanity," Nicole said. "Dave, it sounds awesome. I am so proud of you, starting your own company. Wow."

"Yeah, I drove out to our manufacturing plant last week. They were in the middle of preparing our largest order. It was an incredible feeling to look out over the plant and see our product fill up the production floor."

"I bet! Your dad must be bursting his buttons. I can only imagine the stories he's telling at church about his son, the millionaire."

Dave nodded in agreement.

"Do you hear from Tank anymore?"

"I saw him when I was home last month," Dave said. "He is doing very well. He's not at the school anymore, of course. But he's had some good assignments."

"I'm glad you keep in touch with *him* at least."

Dave grinned sheepishly at her good-natured ribbing. Nicole had called Dave faithfully several times a year. Dave sometimes wondered why she continued to make the effort when he was such a lousy friend. He almost never returned her calls. But he had returned her call last week knowing he had the business meeting coming up in California. Now he was so glad it had worked out. Being with Nicole reminded him of the good times they had shared as kids. But when he wasn't with Nicole, it was just too hard to go back, too painful. Breaking from his past meant leaving it all behind, even Nicole. He hoped things might be different now that they had reconnected on this visit.

"Have I talked to you since the reunion last year?" Dave asked, knowing he had not.

"No! How was it?"

"It was okay. Decent turnout. I only went because I happened to be in Erie visiting my parents." That was a lie. He had taken the trip just for the opportunity to boast about his accomplishments to his former classmates. It was his way of overcoming the past—swoop in, drop his success story, and then fly back out unscathed. But as everyone shared memories, the conversation increasingly focused on the many inappropriate liaisons that had occurred between students and faculty. What had seemed unremarkable then looked quite different through their eyes as adults and parents. Dave had left the reunion after only an hour.

"They made this booklet of memories and moments, and guess what someone said was their most embarrassing moment?"

"No idea," Nicole said.

"Running into Mr. Lark in a gay bar."

"No way!"

"Way!"

"Were any of the guys there who are involved in the scandal? My dad's been sending me the articles. It's all over the news. Boys from our year and a few older and younger are coming after the diocese, claiming Father Hill sexually abused them. Didn't someone call you about that awhile back?"

"No."

"Yes, Dave, I'm sure of it. It was quite a few years ago, I don't know, maybe in '94 or '95. You called me to tell me, don't you remember?"

"Yeah, now that you say that, I guess I do. I had forgotten all about that. If it's true, it's their own fault. They shouldn't blame the diocese."

"You're kidding, right? It most certainly is not their fault; they were kids. I hate the idea of our money going to the church's legal battles. Tim and I have redirected our giving."

"That's ridiculous," Dave said. "The entire church should not suffer for the actions of a few people. You can't let it affect your commitment to your Catholic faith."

"Father Tank used to hear the teachers' confessions, remember? What if he heard that guy's? He probably did. Don't you think he had an obligation to do something?"

"Absolutely not! Confessions are private!" Dave finished his drink and ordered another.

"You sound like your mother, Dave."

"Listen, you two," Tim intervened, "You might be used to arguing like brother and sister, but I'd rather not spend the night listening to it. How about them Steelers?"

Dave followed Nicole and Tim back to their house and met their children briefly on their way to bed. The threesome enjoyed a nightcap by the wood-pellet fireplace in Nicole's living room and reminisced about old times.

Shortly after eleven, Dave stood up and said it was time for him to go. Nicole offered to call a cab, claiming they had all had a lot to drink. She had stopped drinking after the wine with dinner, so Dave surmised her concern was primarily for his sobriety.

He assured her he was fine, gave her a hug, and shook Tim's hand. "Thank you both for the hospitality."

"It was nothing, Dave. It was so awesome to see you. Are you sure you don't want to stay? We have an extra room; you'll have plenty of privacy."

"No, thanks. My meeting is early tomorrow, and the hotel is just a block away from where we're meeting. Next time, okay Nic?"

Nicole smiled at her old nickname. Dave and Joe were the only ones who had ever called her that.

"Yes, make sure there is a next time, okay Dave? I've missed you."

"Miss you too, Nic." He really did.

* * * * *

"You can go on in, I'll park the car," Dave said, as he stopped at the entrance to the medical building.

"Are you coming?" Mara asked.

"Yeah, I'll come."

"Okay."

She read *Vogue* while Dave read email on his Blackberry. She couldn't help but look at the models with envy. Five pregnancies had not been kind to her already-distorted body image. She had begged Dave for the tummy tuck. She wanted to be attractive to him, and she couldn't bear the sight of the belly weight. She was a little surprised by Dave's willingness to accompany her to this pre-surgery appointment, but she was grateful for the support. Surgery always scared her.

"Mara Wagner?"

"Yes."

"Follow me please."

Mara and Dave followed the woman in scrubs.

"Step on the scale, please."

Mara felt her face redden as she slipped off her pumps and stood barefoot on the scale, waiting for her weight to be made public—or at least known to Dave and the nurse. That was humiliation enough. The nurse scribbled the numbers on the form inside the folder. At least it was in kilograms.

Dave picked up *Cosmo* as he sat in the chair. Mara perched on the exam table in her hospital gown. Her feet were freezing, causing her whole body to shake. After a quick knock the doctor entered without waiting for a response. He directed Mara to lie back on the table and then covered her bottom half with a sheet while he lifted her gown to reveal her abdomen. Mara felt very exposed.

The doctor walked them both through the surgical process.

"While you're in there could you do an augmentation too?" Dave asked.

"A breast augmentation?" the doctor asked.

Mara lifted her head from the table to see her husband's response, and was more shocked than the doctor when she saw him nodding.

Dave chuckled. "Yeah, why not, while you're nipping and tucking anyway?" Dave had never mentioned a word about this to her. The doctor looked her way for consent. She nodded absently. The men spoke over her body as if they were building a racecar.

Mara sought comfort in her familiar mental response. *Maybe then he'll love me.* It helped her get through the day of her surgery, and the excruciating week that followed, when she was in so much pain she could barely lift her arms.

The augmentation did boost Dave's interest, at least for a while. But after a few months, things went back to how they had been. It seemed nothing ever changed.

February 2005
St. Thomas, US Virgin Islands

Dave hadn't wanted her to come. Mara begged him relentlessly to let her join the executive trip because "all the other wives were coming." If he heard that one more time . . . Dave sipped his beer at the bar in the tropical airport.

They hadn't even gotten out of the airport and already she was creating drama. Apparently she'd left her cell phone on the plane. She was off somewhere looking for it. This was exactly why he hadn't wanted to bring her. It was always something.

The airport was hot. Its corrugated metal walls and high industrial windows made it more of a hangar than an actual airport. Fortunately no one was in a hurry as the place was filled almost exclusively with vacationing Americans. Dave watched the one exception, a couple from New York, pushing their way through, the man muttering epithets under his breath to anyone who got in his way.

What in the world could be taking her so long? Either they had her phone or they didn't. He shrugged it off, swigged his cold beer, and turned on his best barroom charm with the locals drinking beside him, mostly airport employees. Their laughter drowned out the sound of his name being called, at least the first few times, judging from the tone when he finally did hear it.

"Dave!"

He turned to see his wife standing at the rail that formed the exterior wall of the bar. He gave her a defiant grin and lifted his beer. He had waited on her, so now she could wait for him. In fact, based on Mara's already-irritated disposition, he should probably order another. He ignored her glare and tried to ignore the ping of her heels striking the floor as she made her way toward him.

"What are you doing?"

"What does it look like I'm doing? Passing time while you look for your phone. Did you find it?"

"Yes, but they wouldn't let me back on the plane. It took forever."

"You're telling me."

"Dave, I'm sorry. I know. But shouldn't we go grab a shuttle? You don't want to spend our first day in an airport do you? When are we supposed to meet up with everyone?"

"We *should* have grabbed a shuttle half an hour ago, but since you made us late, I'm gonna finish my beer with my new friends."

Dave shifted a quarter turn away from his wife and re-engaged the stranger to his right. Mara stared at the back of his floral shirt for a moment before retreating to a nearby bench to wait.

Twenty minutes later Dave stood up and threw a hundred-dollar bill on the bar. As he walked past Mara, he said, "Let's go." She trailed him outside, dragging her suitcase and watching with irritation as he tried to figure out the transportation. He was too proud to admit he had no idea how to get to their hotel.

No sooner had they reached the resort's check-in desk than Dave spotted his partners out on the lanai. As the clerk shuffled the paperwork Dave raised an arm high in greeting, and then left

Mara to finish the process as he headed out to meet them. By the time she checked in and joined him, he had a drink in hand and was chatting up Sterling and Tony. Sterling greeted her first, and then his wife leaned across the table and offered her an air kiss, the sweet scent of her umbrella drink making contact first.

"Welcome, Mara!" Tony said in his always-boisterous tone. "We're so glad you could make it this time. I know it's tough with all those kids, but this is going to be an incredible week!"

"I'm glad to be here. Thanks, Tony." She wondered what Dave had told them about her absences on all the other trips.

"Hey, the girls are going to get one of those hot stone massages later. Can we make an appointment for you?"

"Oh no, that's okay, thanks, Tony. Thanks anyway."

"You sure? It sounds fantastic. A hundred stones for some hot stones." He laughed at his own joke, but not for long because Dave toasted him and downed the remainder of his drink while simultaneously waving over the waitress for another.

"Mara, go get a massage. It's good stress relief," Dave said, barely glancing in her direction, clearly still nursing his hostility from the airport.

"I'm good. I'm not feeling that well, probably just tired from the flight. I'll just go to the room and rest for a bit."

"Life of the party, that one," she heard Dave say as she headed for the elevators alone.

* * * * *

"Eggs and beer. Now that's a Pennsylvania breakfast if I ever saw one," Tony said, as he and Dave downed their second beers of the day. Mara looked at her watch and sipped on her second cup of coffee. It was ten.

She should have known it would be like this. It was the morning of day two, and the trip was shaping up to be a complete disaster. Dave was so desperate for his partners' acceptance that he tried too hard with them and had nothing left for Mara.

Her stomach churned from the stress of being so far away from her children—or was it from being so close to Dave? She couldn't say for sure.

"I talked to the concierge about renting a catamaran. We can take it out at noon," Dave told Tony.

"That's awesome, Buddy, what a great way to spend the day! Let me split it with you."

"No way. This one's on me. You can bring the booze, how about that?"

"Done. Should I call the other guys, see if they want to come?"

"Nah. It only holds six. I heard Sterling promise Kate a diamond ring. I think he and Chas are heading to Charlotte Amalie today to make good on it."

Tony laughed and finished his beer. "No kidding! Alright, let me go check on Cath and meet you down here at what, say eleven thirty?"

"Yeah. Good."

Tony slapped Dave on the shoulder and headed inside.

"Wow, so the other guys are buying their wives jewelry?" Mara asked.

"Yep."

"That's nice, Dave, don't you think? What a nice thing to do."

Dave answered with silence.

"You're so desperate to keep up with them, except when it comes to how they treat their wives."

"Screw you, Mara. Their wives are loving and supportive. You haven't laid off me since we got here. I'm going to get a shower. If you want to sail, we're leaving at eleven thirty sharp."

Too anxious to eat, she picked at her eggs and looked for-lornly over the panorama of the Caribbean coast stretching out before her. Then she gave in to her urge to call the babysitter and check in.

What had she done to set Dave off? They lived increasingly separate lives, his consumed with his company and vying for his place among his partners; hers busy caring for their five chil-dren. It was exhausting on a good day and almost impossible when she was as anxious as she was now. She was desperate for his love, and yet the more she tried the worse it got. At least that's how it felt to her.

Mara enjoyed the finer things as much as the next girl, and she was ticked off that she'd have to spend the rest of the trip listening to the other wives brag about their jewelry, while Dave left her unapologetically empty handed.

Dave and Tony were already a few sheets to the wind before the catamaran was out of the slip. Mara's sour mood was aggra-vated by having to watch her pretentious husband try to sail.

"Turn into the wind," she finally said, after watching him struggle to get the boat underway. He ignored her.

"Dave, for God's sake, will you trust me? I grew up on the water. Turn the sail into the wind!"

He looked at her and then across the catamaran to Tony with a wry smile. "I live my life to prove my wife wrong."

Mara had never felt more alone in her life. She sat back and tried to focus on the wind and the water, but even their beauty couldn't wash away the humiliation of her husband's continual rejection.

After they returned, the foursome met up with the rest of the group at a local restaurant for a late lunch. Dave and Tony were lit from their self-made booze cruise. As the party migrated back to the beach, Dave ordered a round of drinks for their party, and then for everyone within earshot.

* * * * *

Mara's glare only encouraged him; this was his turf and he would not tolerate her insolence. She'd storm out sooner or later, so why not sooner?

"Dave, I'm going upstairs. I'm exhausted," she said, looking at her watch. It was only half past five.

He glanced up from his favorite conversation with his partners: how brilliant their technology was, how they were going to dominate the market, and how much money they would all make when they did.

Mara didn't care, clearly. She didn't see how hard he had worked to make this happen. She didn't appreciate how innovative their technology was. She didn't care to know about the things that mattered to him, the things that had grown his reputation and his bank account. All she cared about was what he didn't do, or say, or buy. When he looked in her eyes, he saw only anger and judgment. He didn't need any more of that. He needed more of this. Friends and colleagues who saw him for the smart, witty, and forward-thinking entrepreneur he was. These were his peers now.

"Are you coming, Dave?" he heard in the distance.

"What?" He punctuated the "t" so as not to slur. It sounded sharper than he'd intended.

"I'm ready to go upstairs, Dave. We've had a long day. Are you coming with me?"

"Hell, no. Not until we finish tasting all the flavored rums, right Sterling?" Dave clinked glasses with his partner.

"Good night everyone. See you tomorrow."

"Good night, Mara," the group said in unison.

* * * * *

She could sense their relief at her departure. She looked back from the elevators and the wake that had closed so quickly behind her it was as if she'd never been there.

She was going home. She never should have come, she thought, as she pulled her suitcase out of the closet and began to throw her clothes in. She bolted the door to keep her drunken husband out. Then she sat on the bed and cried. She hated her husband and she hated her life. Why did he have to make everything miserable for her? She wanted out. She felt a sudden urgency to get away from all of this.

* * * * *

"Is she okay, Dave?" Tony asked, because his wife had told him to.

"Yeah. I told her she shouldn't come. I knew this trip would be too much for her. Leaving the kids is really hard on her, and she gets overly anxious." He leaned in close to Tony's head and whispered loudly. "The doctor thinks she has bipolar disorder, or disease, he's not sure yet."

"You're kidding? Oh man, I'm sorry. That's tough."

Dave nodded slightly. "It's alright. She does well at home as long as she stays in her routine. Things like this, though, they're just too much for her."

"No kidding. Well that makes sense. I hope we didn't upset her. If we can do anything to help, Buddy, anything at all."

The chatter among the rest of the group flagged as they picked up on the conversation. Dave sat stoically, a sympathetic expression on his face. "Well, I think I'd better go check on my wife."

"Yes, absolutely." Everyone seconded his decision, affirming the difficulty of his situation, the burden he bore of a wife who was so clearly unstable.

"See you all in the morning! Speedboats tomorrow, right, Sterling?"

"Absolutely. Night, Dave."

He rode the elevator alone, swaying with the twelve hours of alcohol coursing through his veins. "Beer before wine feeling fine." The old mnemonic played involuntarily as he tried to evaluate the likelihood of throwing up in the next hour. He hadn't drunk wine though. Was it "Beer before liquor never sicker," or "Liquor before beer never fear?" How were you supposed to remember this crap when you were drunk anyway?

The elevator chimed as the door opened, and Dave stood for a moment trying to decide which way his room was. He hoped Mara was asleep because he didn't feel like listening to her complaints all night; that would make him sick for sure. He put his key in the door of 729, but it wouldn't open. He tried again. The light was blinking red. He moved down the hall to 725. The light blinked green, but the door still wouldn't open. He knocked.

"Mara," he whispered loudly. No response.

"Mara," followed by knocking. "Mara let me in."

After an extended silence, he heard, "Why should I? Why don't you go sleep in Tony's room? Or pick up some floozy from the beach? You haven't wanted to be with me all day. Why should I let you in now?"

"Mara, open the door. Now." She heard the menace in his tone and obeyed. He fell into the room as the door gave way, nearly knocking her down and then using her body as leverage to push his six-foot frame back to vertical. That's when he noticed the suitcase.

"What's that? What do you think you're doing?"

"Leaving. You were right. I never should've come. This was a huge mistake. You belong with those people. I don't. And you don't want me here. I'm done, Dave. Do you understand me? I'm going home."

"The hell you are. You are not flying out of here like some deranged lunatic, not after the display you put on all day in front of my friends." He grabbed her by both shoulders, alcohol and spittle pinging her as he pulled her inches from his face.

"I'll tell you what you're going to do, Mara. You're going to unpack that suitcase. Now. Then you're going to get in that bed and go to sleep, and tomorrow you're going to apologize to everyone, every single one of them. Do you understand me?" He saw the tears spilling down her cheeks, her eyes cast downward, but it fueled rather than assuaged his anger.

"You embarrassed me beyond belief. You made a fool of yourself. How am I supposed to provide for this family when you sabotage my career every chance you get? Making a big deal out of not getting jewelry when you have thousands of dollars' worth sitting at home. What makes you think you deserve a diamond ring?"

Dave released his grip on her, spilling her tiny frame onto the bed. "I'm calling your doctor in the morning. I think we need to adjust your meds. They're making you more erratic than usual. If you don't knock it off, I swear I'll have you committed."

March 2005
Durham, North Carolina

He had been surprised all right. Dave had no idea his wife was throwing a surprise fortieth birthday party for him. Mara had rented out Starlu, one of Durham's hottest restaurants.

Everyone was there: his college friends, Ashley and Bobby from Louisiana, his siblings and their families, his partners and coworkers. Unfortunately Matthew hadn't been able to make it, and neither had Nicole, which put a damper on the evening for Dave.

In classic Mara style, the walls were adorned with blown up photos of the rat pack and a live band played Sinatra classics. He decided to make the best of the night. He and Drew and a few other college pals took turns at the microphone. Drew's harmonic voice anchored Dave's liquor-inspired riffs.

Dave could see Mara's hunger to please him in every detail of the evening, yet her nervousness only served to stir his mysterious, if bottomless, reservoir of anger toward her.

He drank himself to oblivion and passed out, facedown on his bed, around one in the morning. Now, barely conscious, he lay on his stomach listening to his children playing downstairs. He could hear Mara putting dishes away in the kitchen. His hangover made it sound like she was banging pots and pans right over his head.

Why'd she do this stuff so early? He opened an eye to check the digital clock on the bed stand: 11:26 a.m. His head split with each sound from below. He found his phone, scrolled quickly to his email, and then put the pillow over his head. Faint images from the evening flashed through his mind as he drifted back to sleep.

He awoke again after two. The banging in his head had slowed to a throb. His pulse quickened with sudden awareness. What had she spent on that party? Easily twenty grand! His rage lifted him out of bed. He struggled into the bathroom, not bothering with the light switch. He stumbled into the shower and let the hot water wash the sweat and murkiness away. He didn't know the source of his anger, but he knew the only cure.

His first time had been on a business trip to Thailand. Before that, his only experience with prostitutes had been cruising French Street to harass the local streetwalkers with his frat brothers. Now, the world's oldest profession had moved to the World Wide Web. He'd found it shockingly simple to locate websites and schedule appointments via email. In fact, he now congratulated himself for making one earlier today, right from his Blackberry—with a hangover, even. It was the only way he knew to de-stress from all the anxiety Mara's birthday fete had caused.

"I've gotta run into the office for a few hours," he told Mara as he poured a cup of slightly scorched coffee.

"Are you kidding?"

"Just for a few hours."

"No one's going to be in the office today. They were all at your party last night, and they were as drunk as you were. It's already almost three."

"As a matter of fact," he lied, "Sterling just emailed me an hour ago and he's already there. I'll be home around six."

* * * * *

Mara sat down at the kitchen table suddenly agitated by the kids' ruckus. Exhaustion conformed her posture to the chair. She'd worked so hard to pull the party together for Dave. She had been sure it would show him how much she loved him, remind him of how things used to be between them. But it hadn't worked. He'd slept off a hangover and left the house with not so much as a thank-you for all her effort. If anything he'd seemed aggravated with her. And now he was off somewhere, with someone else.

She was sure of it.

Dave had barely tried to conceal his hostility toward her lately. Last week he had ripped a bookshelf out of the wall, accusing her of lying about the amount she'd spent on it. Last month, he had given away Margaret and Audrey's combination playhouse and bed. Mara had found the idea in a craft book and hired a carpenter to make it, thinking it was a great way to turn their bedroom into a playroom. It had taken a week to build, sand, and paint. The girls loved it; Dave hated it, probably because it wasn't his idea. While he had a painter at the house estimating some exterior repairs, Dave told him he'd throw in the girls' bed for free. He gave it away right in front of Mara.

She couldn't avoid feeling he did these things just to hurt her.

And the lies had continued unabated. He'd sold their treadmill without notice. When she asked him about it, he said he'd sold it to someone at work because she never used it. But she'd never seen the money.

He invited a guy he knew to take a free vacation at their Michigan cottage. "He makes coffee," Dave told her. "He promised us a pound of coffee a month for a year to pay us back."

She'd received one box with a coffee press and a couple pounds of coffee, but that was all.

He wouldn't allow Mara to drive his new toy, a 1964 Mustang convertible, because she "wasn't on the insurance," yet he had invited her dad to drive it. When Mara suggested he insure it with her sister, whose company specialized in classic cars, he told her he had tried to call her but she hadn't returned his calls.

"He never called me, Mar," her sister had later told her. "Why do you keep believing him when all he does is lie to you?"

That was the question she pondered now, staring at a plate of his leftover birthday cake on the kitchen counter. She buried her face in her hands. What was she to do in the face of endless lies, overt hostility, and five children who needed more from their father? But it wasn't just the kids. She too loved him desperately.

She craved his love and approval more than anything else in her life. It's why she'd agreed to the breast augmentation, thrown him the lavish party, and worn those awful outfits in bed.

It's why she did most everything these days, she realized, as tears filled with regret and hopelessness rolled down her cheeks.

* * * * *

Come Sunday, Dave made sure the family all attended Mass. He was a big deal at their humble parish of St. Ignatius, having recently made a generous donation toward the school's renovation project. But in this case his philanthropy had a purpose.

"I don't want Caleb in one of those temporary buildings with some teacher we don't know and no supervision," he'd told Mara.

He'd also made a significant gift to the church's capital campaign. His financial support, along with having so many children enrolled in the school, had earned him a seat on the Catholic School Advisory Committee. There was gamesmanship on both sides, Dave recognized. His status and counsel were only as valuable as his financial contributions. And for his part, his regular attendance at Sunday Mass and active support of the church and school were his attempts to atone for his sins. He hoped that God recognized his heart was in the right place.

He gave generously to other causes as well, making a major donation to his college in honor of his best friend's father, gifting thousands to his siblings, and even making what turned out to be a bad loan for five thousand dollars to a temporary receptionist at his company who had told him a tearful story of her financial bind. Later her scam was exposed, yet Dave declined to press charges, instead forgiving her debt.

Today was Monday, his day to drive the kids to school, whenever he was in town. As usual, he led them in the "Our

Father," and shared his paternal wisdom about working hard in school and treating their classmates with respect.

"Daddy, will you be at my soccer game tomorrow?" Margaret asked from the back seat.

"Wouldn't miss it, Magpie."

"Dad, they have a sign-up today for altar boys. Can I do it?"

"No, Caleb." Dave felt his heart skip a beat at the very mention of it.

"Why not, Dad? Michael and Justin and Matthew are all signing up."

"You've got soccer."

"Please, Dad."

"Caleb, no means no. Now zip it." Dave drew his fingers across his lips as he glared at his son in the rearview mirror. Caleb knew that look in his father's eyes and said nothing further.

After he dropped the kids off, Dave's cell phone rang. It was Matthew.

"Hey little Bro! I can't believe I actually caught you. How've you been?"

"Good, Matthew, how 'bout you?"

"How was your party? I'm so sorry I couldn't make it."

"It's okay. It was good."

"It was sweet of your wife. She worked hard on that, Dave."

"Mm-hmm."

"I hope you appreciated her effort."

"Mmm-hmm."

"Dave, are things okay between you two? I got the impression from Mara that there's some strain. It's understandable with the moves, the kids, and everything. I'm here for you, I really am, but trying to track you down by phone's like nailing Jell-O to the wall."

"We're okay, I guess. The party was a nice thought, but it's a lot for Mara. She can't do anything halfway. She's been struggling with anxiety and depression, and the party just pushed her over the edge. She's short with the kids. She's harping on me. I've been trying to get her to go see her doctor more than twice a week, but she won't listen."

"What about you, Dave? What's your part? It's not all one way. You can't just point fingers at your wife without looking in the mirror too."

Dave was silenced. The truth of his brother's words pierced his heart.

"Dave? Are you really okay? You sound so down."

"Sorry. There are just some things you don't talk about, Matt. Listen, man, I've gotta go. I'm pulling in to the office and I'm already late for a meeting."

"Okay, Bud. Love you. Take care."

"I will. Bye."

Dave fought back tears. How had everything gotten so complicated? Matthew was right. The problems in their marriage were his fault too—more his than Mara's. It was the cost of his secrets; protecting them had become his obsession. Suddenly he recognized the source of his rage: He no longer saw Mara as his wife; she had become the single greatest threat to exposing his sham of a life.

May 2005

"Where are you?"

Mara reacted instinctively to the suspicious tone in Dave's voice, detectable even over her cell phone. "I'm at the deli with Jenny," she said as nonchalantly as she could muster.

"How was Stephen's birthday party?"

"Good. It was good. His teacher did such a nice job." She could feel her hand beginning to shake.

"Are you having me followed?"

"What?" How could he know? Panic set in as she glanced up at her friend. She wasn't about to get into it here. "No. Wait. Let me call you right back."

"You're having me followed." He hung up.

Mara was a raw nerve ending and she knew her friend could see right through her attempt at normalcy. She didn't care. She wrapped up lunch quickly saying she had to get to school. From her car, she tried calling Dave but he wouldn't answer. The school pick-up line took an eternity.

How had he already discovered the private investigator? What was he capable of, in his anger?

Mara's father had given her the money for the PI after she showed him an article Dave had given her on bipolar disorder.

"You're not bipolar, Mara," her father said. "Your husband's the one who's nuts."

She hadn't known how to go about hiring a PI, so she let her friend Maria take charge as soon as she got back to Durham. Maria found the guy, drove Mara there, and did all the talking during their meeting. All Mara had done was to hand him the cash.

As she drove to Dave's office with the kids chattering in the back, she questioned her decision. She was growing terrified of him lately.

* * * * *

He knew she'd come to his office. Dave angled the paper with the divorce attorneys' names on the desk so she'd be sure to see it. He heard his children's voices before they toddled in behind his wife. Her gaze swept down to the names on his desk. She looked up at him eyes filled with tears and questions. He rejected both.

He was not about to have a confrontation here in the only place he still commanded some respect. He had a reputation to maintain, one she'd already severely compromised with her past histrionics. He grabbed her, noting how easily his hand wrapped around her arm. "Let's go," he whispered. "Come on, kids," he said as calmly as possible.

Mara was shaking. He could hear her crying softly as they walked briskly down the hall. His grip tightened as they passed some coworkers. He was startled by his desire to hurt her. He couldn't get out of there fast enough. At last they crossed the parking lot to the Suburban. He opened the door and began lifting the children into the car, buckling the youngest into their car seats.

"Look at this car, Mara; it's a pigsty. You better start taking care of it. It's the last one you're ever going to get."

"We need to talk, Dave. When are you coming home?"

"When I get home."

It was after eleven when Dave pulled into the driveway.

Was she on to him? How could she know? She must have known something in order to hire a PI. He just didn't know how much. His leg jittered in growing agitation. If she knew, she would expose him. And in her unquenchable wrath, she'd ruin everything. He tapped his forehead rhythmically against the top of the steering wheel, seeking comfort but finding none. It was all spinning out of control, and Mara was close to uncovering the truth. If he couldn't stop himself, he'd have to find a way to stop her.

He stumbled out of the car and headed for the house. The door handle wouldn't turn. He tried again. It was locked. *She didn't.* He slammed the wood hard with his hand. He turned and threw his body against the door, but it wouldn't budge.

He looked around the garage. With thousands of dollars' worth of tools, surely he had something to break into his own house. Then he spied the crowbar on the pegboard above his workbench. Working the bolts out of their hinges took longer in his state of inebriation.

By the time he got the door open, he was ready to chuck it across the garage. But he wouldn't want to risk damaging his classic Mustang. He stumbled into the house and started gathering clothes, desperate to get far away from Mara as quickly as he could.

"What do you think you're doing?" she said, trailing him as he picked up his things off the bedroom floor and then headed for his closet. He spun around and made a zip-your-lip motion across his mouth.

"What does it look like I'm doing?" he hissed. "Leaving you!"

"What about the kids, Dave? You can't do this to the kids."

He was tired of her always invoking the kids. It was her last weapon against him. "You're right. Where are *my* kids? I'll take them. You'll never see them again. Not where you're going."

"They're asleep, Dave. Leave them alone. Why are you doing this?"

"Why am *I* doing this? Why are *you* doing this, Mara? That's really the question, isn't it? You're the one who hired the PI. He was awful by the way, didn't even know how to tail me without getting caught. Did you really think you could get away with this? You're nuts, certifiably nuts!"

He threw his clothes in a laundry basket, then stalked outside and slung it in the back of the Excursion.

* * * * *

Mara ran after him, out into the driveway. She was terrified
the kids would wake up, yet desperate to stop him from leaving.
As he pulled out, she tried to hold on to the car. Her arm got
caught in the door handle and she fell. He stopped just long
enough for her to free herself and then tossed his wedding ring
toward the woods and peeled out of the driveway.

She stumbled back inside, her knee cut, hand bruised, and
heart breaking. She paced the main floor before heading back
to the bedroom. There on the dresser was a business card for a
divorce lawyer.

* * * * *

He had been gone for two weeks now.

He'd called only once, to instruct her to tell the children
he was out of town on business. "I'll be back on Friday to take
Magpie and Audrey to the lacrosse tournament for the weekend. Next weekend I'm taking Caleb and Stephen. I'll pick
them up from school on Friday. Just send a bag with each of
them. Understand?"

"Okay. Okay, fine," she said through tears. "Dave, when
are you coming home?" She disregarded the pitiful tone in her
voice. She could not function without him, in part because anxiety over his whereabouts consumed her. Maybe he'd actually
left her for someone else.

"Not until you get some help." He hung up.

It seemed like morning would never come. Mara had told
herself that eight o'clock was the earliest she could call the
church.

Thank God, Father John took her call. She told him her
story, including her decision to hire the private investigator.
"You don't understand everything I've been through, Father,"
she cried. "Dave's gone all the time. I don't know where he is,

who he's with, what he's doing. He lies about everything, and whenever I call him out, he blames me for all of it. I don't know what I did. I don't know how to fix it. I don't know what it's going to take to get him to move back home."

"What do you want, Mara?" Father asked, his words slow and deliberate.

"I want him back."

A few days later, Mara pushed Stephen and Annie in the double stroller on the trail behind their house. On her return she saw Dave's shadow at a distance running toward her. She was terrified. Should she run away? What was he doing here? She looked around to make sure other people were visible on the trail, in case she was in danger. When he reached her, he made only scant eye contact before turning his attention to the kids. He squatted in front of the stroller, grabbing the metal rod on either side in a way that unnerved her. The kids squealed with delight at the sight of their father.

"Hey Annie! Hey Stevie!" He leaned in and kissed them both, then unbuckled Stephen and swung him up onto his hip. Stephen threw his arms around his father and held tight. Dave turned and walked in front of Mara without saying a word all the way back to the house. She parked the stroller in the garage and got Annie out. Mara changed her diaper and put her down for a nap, then came and got Stephen and did the same.

She noticed Dave's laundry basket, the same one he had thrown his clothes in that awful night, now filled with neatly folded clothes, sitting benignly in the hallway. Had he done his laundry or had someone else? Where had he been staying? Was he going back? She went into her bedroom to freshen up, hoping this meant reconciliation was in the air.

She washed her face and headed into the closet to change out of her exercise clothes and then stopped cold. There on her dresser sat a letter addressed to David Andrew Wagner from Hinckel & Hinckel, Attorneys at Law, Senior Partner Ted Talwell IV.

She scanned the paper. Under "Scope of Representation," she read, "Our responsibilities in this representation will include advising and assisting you in negotiating a settlement of your claims with Mara and, if necessary, filing or defending a divorce action to ensure that your interests are properly protected regarding equitable distribution, child support, post-separation support, alimony, etc."

Also on the dresser was a typed letter from Dave, dated three days earlier.

Mara,

For the past 16 weeks, there has been an unacceptable level of strain in our relationship with considerable anger and verbal abuse being directed at me. Leading up to this date our relationship was slowly deteriorating from the previous summer.

I am not able to take the constant stress of being verbally abused, accused of lying and deception, or accepting unreasonable criticism for how I conduct myself or with whom I associate. The events of Thursday, May 20 (I discovered I was being followed) led me to seriously consider our relationship and whether or not I could ever feel the same way toward you again.

I must apologize for the times I told you half-truths or mistruths. Although I feel it was justifiable I will accept responsibility for my actions, as I realize it eroded your level of trust. I also apologize for not taking a more aggressive approach in demanding you get the mental help you needed earlier. Whether or not your diagnosis is correct, you are not yourself and you need to get well.

I believe you when you say you will do anything to keep our marriage together; I am, however, skeptical that you will be able to change all of a sudden to a sweet and loving spouse. Even if you are able to keep yourself under control that doesn't mean that you are "cured."

I have consulted with an attorney who has counseled me on my rights and responsibilities regarding possible separation that would ultimately lead to a divorce. I understand it is an option to work through a mediator (in this case, a marriage counselor) to establish a set of ground rules applied to our relationship and daily living arrangements, and apply those rules over a period of time to allow us both to evaluate our relationship before deciding to opt for legal separation.

In the interest of the children, and to continue to demonstrate my dedication to your well-being, I propose a 60-day period during which we will live and operate within a certain set of boundaries, as we discussed. During this period, I will continue to live at home, but will sleep in separate quarters. I will fulfill my role as father and a partner in terms of daily responsibilities. My travel schedule will be quite full during this period, and should it cause a burden to you personally, I will re-evaluate it and make adjustments where possible. I will keep you informed of my whereabouts when traveling, and let you know I am safe upon completing travel. I will accept calls from you if I am able, and if you are trying to reach me due to an emergency you can simply leave a callback number and 911.

Additionally, I will assume control of all finances and need to have full disclosure from you about any credit cards or outstanding debt that is in your name exclusively. We will establish a monthly budget, and you will be given an allowance of $700 to spend on yourself for incidentals or luxury items.

I refuse to fund any additional cosmetic surgery or personal trainer visits.

You may resume retaining a housekeeper when available on the condition that the time freed from housework and laundry is dedicated to the care and nurturing of the children.

I agree to a weekly meeting with the marriage counselor to discuss our relationship and your progress.

My wish is that our relationship is repaired, and I am able to love you with my whole heart and soul. I do not want a divorce, but I recognize the pain of divorce is more tolerable than the pain of abuse.

I pray for our relationship and our family daily.
God bless YOU.

Mara sat in the chair, letter in hand, tapping her heel absently on the hardwood floor while she waited to meet with the marriage counselor, Alex Mead. He was Dave's pick; in fact, Dave had already met with him twice. If his letter was any indication of the picture he had been painting of their marriage, she had an uphill battle to garner any support.

But as soon as she met Alex, her spirits buoyed. His eyes were full of compassion, his demeanor unhurried, and his body language showed full engagement with what she had to say.

"Mara, as you know, I had an opportunity to spend some time with your husband last week," he began. "I think the best place for us to start would be for you to give me your perspective on what's been going on in your marriage."

Mara sat upright in the cushioned leather chair, suddenly energized. "Really? Okay, well, how much time do you have?" she joked. He laughed.

"Seriously, it's a long story. I don't even know where to begin. Maybe the best thing would be to read you the letter Dave gave me." She raised it to eye level. He nodded, so she began, indignation fusing with anger as she read the words aloud.

Alex sat, silently making notes.

"Would you say you have issues with money?" he asked when she had finished.

"No."

"Your husband implies you are somewhat of a shopaholic in his letter. He said something along those lines when I met with him."

"Hey, I spend a lot of money; I admit that, I mean, we have five kids. It costs a fortune to feed, clothe, and provide for their needs. And I like nice things, who doesn't? But a shopaholic? No, I'm not the one with the addiction."

"Well, I tend to agree with you. I asked Dave some follow-up questions, whether you had unopened shopping bags around the house, for instance, or clothes with price tags on them, items stockpiled in pantries and closets. His answer to all of those was no, so unless you're hiding all of that really well, you don't fit the bill, no pun intended.

"How are things going with your children? I'm sure all this stress has been tough on them too."

"It is, especially the fights. But the fact is he's gone more than he's home, so when he's not there I keep things pretty level and try to keep them happy and feeling secure. Dave is a good father when he's around. He loves them and they love him."

"Do you think you're a good mother?"

"Yes. It's the most important thing in the world to me."

"Dave has some concerns about your anger around the children."

"That's just part of his attempt to make me sound crazy. He sent me this ridiculous article a few weeks ago about parents

who yell at their children and how it leads to corporal punishment. I never hit them. In fact, Dave's the one who doles out
spankings. And when I try to stop him, especially when he's
yelling at Caleb, he turns and gives me that zip-your-lip sign—"
She moved her fingers across her lips. "As if I'm challenging his
authority.

"I am a good mother. I'm doing pretty much everything
because Dave isn't there. Yes, I get worn out. And yes, I probably
yell too much. It's tiring, but I'm doing the best I can."

"How do you respond?"

"To what?"

"How do you respond to Dave's letter?"

"You mean to Dave or to you?"

"To anyone."

"That I'm not crazy."

"That's what you told Dave?"

"No, that's what I'm telling you. He won't speak to me. And
he wouldn't listen if he did. If he can make me out to be the
crazy one, he doesn't have to take responsibility for his actions."

"There's a term for that, you know."

"For what?"

"For what you're describing. Did you ever see the old movie
Gaslight? It's about a woman whose husband manipulates her
to convince her she's going insane. We call it 'crazy-making' in
the biz."

"Crazy-making? I guess if the shoe fits. But I'm not crazy."

"That's the point. If Dave shifts the spotlight to you it allows
him to deflect responsibility for the problems in your marriage.
Have you considered writing a letter back?"

"No. No, I haven't."

"I think a healthy next step would be for you to respond to
Dave's letter with your own. Be intentional about your words

and mindful of the outcome you'd like to achieve because your response will set the tone for what happens next. Take back some power in your marriage, Mara, but do it with love."

She sighed and sat back in the chair. It was such an uplifting notion to think that she could have any effect on the avalanche of emotions, hostility, and accusations that had fallen down on their marriage.

"Alright, Alex. I'll do it. It's a good idea."

The next morning Mara left an envelope in the downstairs bathroom where Dave would find it when he got ready for work.

Dear Dave,

I love you. When we fell in love with each other we could feel our love for each other. No matter what we were doing we always had fun. We had passion, hugs, and kisses. We wanted to be together all the time. I used to say, "You are so good for me." I love you. I want to work through our problems and issues. In an article you once emailed me it said, "Strong families don't question whether it's best to part ways." I want to be a strong family with our marriage and family our priority (such as in the past).

My long-term goals for us are as follows:

- *A loving, caring, supportive marriage*
- *Work on patience with each other and show love to one another*
- *Nurture each other, not everything and everybody else*
- *Love and respect each other*
- *Love each other unconditionally*
- *Resolve conflicts and discuss major decisions together*
- *Express affection*

- *A marriage that is trustworthy and forgiving*
- *A strong, healthy family*
- *Raise our children together*
- *Create a healthy environment with both parents*
- *Raise our children so they may have faith, do the right thing and strive to always give their best*
- *Teach and show them to love unconditionally*
- *Spend quality time and "quantity" time together*
- *Be best friends*
- *Share and laugh like we used to*
- *Accept each other's faults*
- *Rejoice in each other's strengths*
- *Be warm and caring*
- *Be HAPPY—both of us*

For Dave
- *For you to be happy personally and professionally*
- *I will support you and appreciate you*
- *I will give you credit for the things you do right*
- *I will empathize/sympathize with your level of stress*

My short-term goals
- *We succeed in working hard to get out of our crisis*
- *Work through our present challenges*
- *We together begin to repair the damage and work toward our long-term/lifelong goals as a married couple with a strong family*
- *We feel that there is hope to regain the loss of our love*

In response to your conditions:

Sixty days is not enough time to regain our eroded trust or for me to establish a solid relationship with a new psychologist. I feel it is not adequate time for us to really work together to get the help we need from the marriage counselor either, in order to emerge from our crisis and discuss our progress. Your traveling a significant amount is another reason to extend the 60 days. Last week you had mentioned our trip to Michigan in the "middle" of our evaluation period. Believe me, it would be nice to go, but our marriage, our life and the healthy lives of our children are what matter most . . . always. And should come first. Because of the short timeframe you've given me and the amount of work we need to do together, I suggest seeing Alex Mead two times a week and extending the time period.

Your intent to take over the expenditures/expenses leaves me no independence, and it shows me that you don't trust me. The outstanding debt on my cards is for the kids' clothing, and I think it should be paid out of the household budget.

I would like to look at my allowance. It doesn't seem reasonable to me. You have never complained about my clothing or home goods purchases in the past. Maybe we should look at past bills and come up with a different number (or is this just a 60-day requirement?).

I do want you to fully participate in your role as father. I always have. I guess this would include coming home at a reasonable hour, sharing family meals, and helping to tuck the kids in bed. Both the kids and I need you home and involved in our day-to-day lives more than you have been in the past.

I have faith that we can work really hard together and that our marriage can be repaired and restored. I am willing

*to work as hard as possible. The problems ahead of us are com-
plicated and result from many things. We both are responsible
for the slow deterioration of our relationship and for our crisis.
I, too, love you with my whole heart and my whole soul. I am
praying for God to direct us and help us in this time of crisis
and always.*

I love you.

M.

September 2005

Dave woke up hung over and still fuming over the public
scene Mara had made the night before. Her jealousy and verbal abuse were at an all-time high. He was out of patience. The
sight of her handwriting on another envelope only stoked his
anger.

Dear Dave,

*"How thick does my head have to be?" you asked. Thick, I guess.
I've realized and now know that my so-called obsessions are
troublesome. They caused severe trouble last night. My inability
to deal with them caused you trouble and pain. I now know
and didn't see before (or want to admit it).*

*I never intended to act and deal with my anxiety the way I
did and I want to thank you for attempting to help me, though
at the time I didn't even recognize your love and care.*

*I am able to understand and identify the precursor to "that"
behavior and take the cue to halt the next step from happening.
You said it before I did . . .*

I've given you space because I love you. I've not badgered you (excusing my inexcusable behavior) because I love you. I'm getting better because I love you.

I'm trying to focus on what I can do to make us right and our family right. The truth is I hope I can earn your trust again. I want you to love me the way you used to. I want you to trust in what I'm going to say and how I say it and in how I am going to act and/or react.

I intend to be the person I once was. The person you fell in love with.

I am learning tools to cope with my frustrations and emotions. What I've learned is that there is more work to do.

I know that it seems like two steps forward and one step back, but I am still working on it. I know I need to work on it.

I am asking you for your continued love, support, and effort.

M.

Dave tossed the letter aside. Did she truly believe her morning-after apologies could erase the damage done by her drunken accusations the night before? How much humiliation was he expected to bear? He did his best to keep a high wall between his work and family, yet Mara somehow managed to come crashing in, and every time it turned into an unmitigated disaster.

As soon as she had got a couple drinks in her, the inappropriate questions began. This time, to his coworkers, followed by accusations, confrontations, and tears. Thank goodness Tony had been there to drive her home. Dave would have been content to let her walk the five miles in her godforsaken, three-hundred-dollar heels.

2006

Five million dollars.

That's how much Dave and each of his partners would receive in less than a week. If money covered a multitude of sins, Dave had just been washed clean. Yet even as he celebrated at the James Joyce with Tony at what should have been the high point of his career, he found himself fighting feelings of fear and loneliness. What was the point of living if he couldn't feel pleasure at a time like this?

Since Tony was now divorced as a result of his own relationship with alcohol, he was only too happy to have a drinking buddy and roommate. When Dave had left Mara the first time, after the PI incident, they commiserated about wives and marriage. And when Tony traveled for work, he instructed Dave to "make himself at home" at his place, with a wink and a nod that said he understood a guy had to do what he had to do with a crazy wife at home.

Dave was growing increasingly isolated away from Mara and the kids, and he found himself struggling to get through each day. He hadn't told his family about their most recent separation. His mother was advanced in her dementia, and his father's health had grown progressively frail.

He couldn't remember the last time he had spoken to his friends. While he would have loved to share the news of his latest achievement, it would be too hard to navigate the more delicate aspects of his life. He felt particularly guilty about Nicole and Matthew. Both had continued to call him faithfully, yet he had actively avoided speaking with either of them. They knew him too well and there would be no hiding from the truth.

His sister had left him a message when Nicole's brother had died; it must have been about six months ago. He had meant to call her, but never did. He had known her brother well; he was someone who had been there for Dave many times, including at *Oliver Twist*. But something held him back. His guilt over not calling created a wedge that made it impossible to even think about picking up the phone now.

Several times he thought of calling Tank. As Dave had told Mara in one of their counseling sessions, "You can't be mad at Tank; if it wasn't for him I wouldn't have my faith." But he was so busy with his church responsibilities. And if Dave couldn't face the truth with his other friends, he certainly wasn't going to call his priest friend and lie.

A waitress carrying plates bumped into Dave's bad shoulder as she passed by, bringing him back to his present companion, Tony, who was quite at home with his beer and unaffected by Dave's silent ruminations. Dave clinked his mug against Tony's.

"To five million dollars."

CHAPTER 6

Mr. Nice Guy

He who commits adultery lacks sense; he who does it destroys himself. He will get wounds and dishonor, and his disgrace will not be wiped away.

Proverbs 6:32–33

July 17, 2007
Harbor Springs, Michigan

"What time will the guys be back?" Ashley asked, placing seven paper plates around the Wagner's kitchen table. She paused to look out the long, large windows at the bay, not twenty yards from where she stood. The Wagners' cottage was beautiful, and she was so glad to be with her old friend again.

"Who knows," Mara said. "Probably six. They had an eleven o'clock tee time, but the course is crowded this time of year, and you know Dave and Bobby aren't coming back without stopping by the lounge."

Mara stirred the cracked-pepper cream sauce for the penne, a favorite of the Wagner kids. The hot dogs would take just a couple of minutes. *Always the planner*, Ashley had thought, when Mara outlined the plan for them to feed and bathe the kids, and then send them to the downstairs rec room for a movie, so the two women could enjoy a few minutes of quiet time together. The kids had already had a big day playing on the rocky beach and swimming.

Mara fixed two Bombay Sapphire gin and tonics, and then raised her glass in a toast. "Thanks for coming, Ashley. It's so good to be with you and Bobby again."

"Of course, Mar. We miss y'all. It's not the same without you next door."

Ashley had almost cancelled the trip. Bobby's father was in the hospital again. She felt terrible about leaving him. But Mara had been so upset whenever they talked by phone lately that Ashley was determined to get up here and get a better handle on what was going on.

She felt better just being here. In her mind, Mara always had a tendency to exaggerate things. Dave seemed happy. He was so proud of the cottage—although Ashley didn't consider a million-dollar home a "cottage"; but she did love it and was glad to see them doing well. Their kids were great, but Ashley had no idea how Mara kept up with all of them with her husband gone so much.

Therein lay the source of Mara's discontent, in Ashley's opinion. She had too much on her plate. She was exhausted and, because she didn't work outside the home, she had nothing to do except conjure up suspicions about her husband. Ashley hoped she'd have an opportunity to talk with her and remind her how good she had it, and how she should spend more time being grateful and less time worrying.

"Well, we better start fixin' dinner for the boys or it's going to be a long night for all of us after all that sun and beer," she said, half-joking.

"No kidding." Mara flipped open her *Barefoot Contessa* cookbook to the pork recipe she had started with her first cup of coffee well before dawn.

The women fixed dinner for the grownups while the children ate, the kitchen effervescing with chatter and laughter. Later the kids settled in to watch *Aladdin* in beanbag chairs downstairs in their PJs with heads damp from the bath. Things grew peaceful at last.

Twenty minutes later the women heard the Excursion crunching down the gravel road. The couples enjoyed a beautifully prepared meal on the patio, recollecting good times.

As Dave bragged about his recent success, Ashley could see Mara recoiling. Maybe it was her social sensitivity, always on high alert. Or maybe it was her empathetic heart, one of the traits Ashley most loved in her friend. Mara would understand how Dave's words landed on the Jacobs, whose financial fortunes has not been as bright. Ashley had confided in her earlier that day about her decision to return to work. Mara discouraged her, based on her belief that women should be home with their children, but in this moment, Ashley could feel her friend's solidarity as she stepped outside her own prejudices and into her friend's pain.

"We should check on your dad," Ashley said to Bobby. Bobby pulled out his cell phone and pressed send on the recently dialed hospital number.

"No service." He tried again to no avail.

"We have terrible coverage out here," Dave said. "Here, try mine." He handed Bobby his Blackberry. Bobby walked off the patio and into the driveway so as not to disrupt the conversation. A few minutes later he returned.

"He's doing fine right now," he said to Ashley. "Nothing's changed."

The girls cleaned up from dinner, and then they all sat around the table chatting in the easy, comfortable cadence of old friends. After an hour or so the guys announced they were heading down to the beach to smoke cigars. Dave left his phone with Ashley in case she wanted to check in at the hospital again. As soon as they disappeared from view, Ashley seized the opportunity. She crossed her legs and turned to her friend.

"So how are you doing, Mar, really? Are things between you and Dave any better?"

Mara took a long drag on her cigarette and leaned in conspiratorially.

"It's actually gotten worse. He's gone all the time and he doesn't answer my calls, sometimes for days. He was in Vegas for a tradeshow a couple months ago. I called and called, no answer.

"I left a voicemail, 'Dave, it's me. Call me as soon as you get this.' Nothing. Finally, I was going crazy; it had been two days. So I texted '9-1-1' to signal an emergency. He called back two minutes later.

"I say, 'Where have you been?'

"He says, 'I just got your text, what's wrong?'

"I say, 'I was desperate. I couldn't get ahold of you.'

"He starts swearing; he's so angry, Ashley, as if I'm the one who's in the wrong.

"He yells at me, 'Don't you ever do that again, do you understand?'

"He turns it around, do you see? I know he was with somebody out there. I know he's cheating. I know it here." Mara pointed to her gut.

Ashley listened sympathetically, but her stomach dropped as she realized it was the same old thing. She could feel Mara's pain and wanted to believe her, yet she struggled to reconcile her friend's perspective with the Dave she and Bobby knew and loved. He always seemed so laid back and non-reactive, even to Mara's endless diatribes, like the one at dinner tonight. She couldn't help but think Mara was creating a self-fulfilling prophecy, pushing her husband away with her never-ending suspicions and paranoia.

As she listened, she stared absently at the table and then out at the water, wondering if her husband was engaged in the flipside of the same conversation. Dave was a lot less forthcoming than his wife about their problems, but he had shared his concerns about Mara's mental state with Bobby in the past.

As Ashley watched her this weekend she could see why. Mara was as thin as a rail, smoking like a chimney, and living on caffeine. It appeared that her sleeping was erratic too; she had been up by four each day, flitting around the house, which prickled with her high anxiety. It had to be affecting the kids. Ashley stared unseeing at the table until her thoughts were interrupted by the sudden realization that Dave's phone was still there.

"Mara, Dave's phone." She lifted it in her hand. "Let's check it. If he's up to something, maybe we'll find out; and if not, you can finally relax a bit."

Ashley punched in the passcode to the Blackberry and navigated to his inbox. She felt guilty prying like this, but rationalized that if she could help alleviate Mara's worst fears, she would be doing Dave a favor, well worth the minor violation of privacy. She scrolled through the emails, huddled with Mara around the dim, blue light.

"I'm not seeing anything here, Mar."

"Yeah, it's too clean. Check the deleted folder."

Ashley followed Mara's instruction. She rolled the button and clicked "Deleted," then began to scan the "From" field on this new list of emails. After more than a minute of scrolling it was clear Dave hadn't bothered to clean out that box in some time.

"Wait. What's that?" Mara stopped her.

"What?"

"That." Mara pointed to an email domain, "@eros.com." She glanced toward the beach suddenly afraid of getting caught. "Quick, send it to your email. We'll look at it tomorrow."

Ashley obeyed.

"Now go back into the sent box and delete your email, and then go to "Delete" and remove it altogether. The last thing I need is for him to find out we were snooping."

Ashley marveled at Mara's ingenuity.

"Ashley, I'm sick. You know that can't be good. Maybe it's more porn like what I found in Louisiana, remember that?"

"Let's go to bed, Mara. I'm exhausted. We'll look at it tomorrow."

"I'm sick. I need to know what it is. How am I going to face him? I'm scared, Ashley."

Ashley wrapped an arm around her friend's bony shoulder and for the first time started to see that perhaps she was not so crazy after all. "Don't be scared, Mar. Dave's not going to do anything to you. If it's porn you can deal with it. He'll be so embarrassed that you caught him—again—it might be enough to get him to stop. Let's get some sleep."

The women hugged goodnight at the bottom of the stairs before Ashley headed to the second floor and Mara to the master suite on the main floor.

"How'd you sleep?" Ashley asked the next morning, finding Mara in her usual spot in the kitchen with a half-empty pot of coffee.

"I didn't. Want some coffee?"

"Sure, thanks," Ashley said, reaching for a mug in the cabinet. "What do you want to do? The kids will be up soon. I know you're jumping out of your skin. I don't know when we'll have time to look at it again."

"Ash, I took Greek mythology. I know Eros. I know what this is. Do you have your phone? Forward the email to Helen. We'll tell Dave and Bobby we're going to the store. They can watch the kids; we'll go over there to check it out."

"Good idea, Mara. You are scary good at this stuff."

"I have to be."

Ashley walked upstairs and returned with her purse. She dug until she found her own Blackberry. "What's Helen's email?" Mara gave her the address.

"There, it went." Ashley covered Mara's hand with her own. "Mara, I'm sorry you have to go through this, truly I am. We'll figure it out, okay? It'll be okay."

"My kids, Ashley. What about my kids? I don't know what I'm going to do." Mara put her head in her hands, and Ashley watched her tiny shoulders wrack with sobs. She looked so fragile, like a bird on a wire, so easily broken. Yet if her own worst suspicions turned out to be true, Mara had been far stronger than Ashley had given her credit for.

An hour later the women were dressed and heading out the door. The kids were still in their PJs, eating cereal downstairs with Nickelodeon blaring in the background, while the dads nursed their hangovers and sipped coffee on the couch.

* * * * *

Richard and Helen Culver were neighbors and friends. A decade older than Dave and Mara, they had become surrogate parents when the family spent time at the cottage, embracing their children like grandchildren and popping by often to help Mara with anything from groceries to minor repairs, especially when Dave was gone. Helen opened the door anticipating Mara, but saw immediately that it was more than a social call.

"Good morning, neighbor," she offered gently. "Come on in." She looked at Ashley for some hint of what was going on. "Can I offer you ladies some coffee?"

"No thanks, Helen," Mara said.

"What's going on, Mara?"

"I don't know," she said, trying futilely to keep anxiety and fear out of her voice. "We need your help. Ashley sent you an email this morning that we need you to look at."

"An email? Okay. Let's go to my office," she said, leading them to the back of the house. "Rich," she called out, "Mara, Ashley, and I will be in my office for a little bit, okay, Hon?"

"No problem," came her husband's voice from a distance. "I'm headed down to work on the boat."

Helen turned to the women. "Have a seat." She closed the door and then sat down across from them. "Now, why don't you catch me up on what's going on."

Mara looked at Ashley, who offered a recap. "We don't know yet. I'm sure you know that Mara has had her suspicions. Last night we did a little snooping on Dave's phone—not right, I know—but we were hoping we'd find nothing and put Mara's mind at ease. You should have an email from me. We didn't have time to check it out, but it's from the domain eros-dot-com, which sounds suspicious, obviously."

Helen nodded and logged onto her computer. "Want me to print it out?"

"That'd be great," Ashley said.

Helen printed three copies and the women read the email. If not for the address, the email read like an appointment request.

"Can you look it up online? What comes up if you type in "www-dot-eros-dot-com?" Mara asked.

"Let's see." Helen's fingers betrayed her apprehension. She mistyped the address twice before finally getting to the right page. When it loaded, her breath caught. Mara and Ashley peered over her shoulder.

"Oh my God, oh my God, oh my God," Mara chanted as tears choked off her ability to speak.

Ashley looked at Helen, hoping she was missing something.

"It's an escort service," Helen said, trying to remain calm. "Mara, you need to confront him with this."

"No, no, no." Mara shook her head vigorously, her body trembling from the shock. "I can't, Helen. I can't." She became more and more hysterical.

"You stay here," Helen told Ashley. "I'm going to call her brother."

A half hour later Mara's brother, who was a local physician, arrived with her anti-anxiety medication in hand. He and Helen spoke in whispers in the kitchen, and then he phoned Mara's Michigan psychiatrist, who agreed to meet her later that day.

As the medicine took effect, Mara began to regain her composure. Her brother left. She knew he was cynical about what he referred to as "her meltdowns." This wasn't the first time he'd been called in to help. Dave was quite effective at casting her as a "nut job" even with her own family. Mara wondered what he might have said to her brother about her mental health to reinforce his negative perception.

Helen sat in front of Mara, holding both her hands in her own. "Mara, look at me. You need to confront Dave with what you found. Trying to keep this inside will kill you."

"You don't understand," Mara said, her pitch rising. "I can't tell him. He'll have me put away."

"He's not in any position to cast judgment. You need to get the truth out in the open, get him to face his part in what's happening in your marriage."

"I am not talking to him about this. Neither are you or Ashley or my brother or anyone else. Do you understand?" Her tone was urgent, approaching panic. "I'm going to deal with this my way on my terms."

Mara had exerted her will for now at least. Helen and Richard were like second grandparents to her children, and she knew from experience that she could count on their support in many ways. But they didn't know the Dave she knew and what he was capable of.

Mara remained rigid, unmoving, as Helen withdrew to a chair.

July 2007
Durham, North Carolina

Bill Beam waited in the conference room. The grandeur of the twenty-foot-long conference table and the high backs of the overstuffed chairs made Bill feel shrunken like Alice in Wonderland. The furnishings were lavish. He recognized the vase stuffed with a robust, fresh floral arrangement as a Simon Pearce. The mandatory legal tomes lined wooden shelves along the far wall. Bill wondered if any of the firm's lawyers had pulled even one of these books out to reference for a case, or if they were purely for show.

That type of extravagance was something Bill and his wife would never understand. They had created a good life and decent living operating their private investigation firm. They operated on a core belief that people were fundamentally good, despite the fact that they typically encountered them at their very worst. Most of the people they had investigated were regular folks caught up in the consequences of their bad choices. It was the nature of the human condition.

"Bill." The voice jolted him from his reverie; it was deep, confident, controlled.

He rose and extended his hand to Mara's attorney. "Bill Beam."

"Gilbert Richards. Good to meet you. I understand you're the investigator hired by Mrs. Wagner."

"I am. I've been on her case since last fall, late September to be exact."

"Are you aware that Mrs. Wagner is pursuing legal separation, likely to be followed by divorce?"

"Yes, I'm aware of the separation." Bill was surprised by the mention of divorce. He'd never gotten the impression Mara wanted that. She was different from the other wives he'd worked for. For one thing, Mara had the goods on her husband at a level even Bill had to admire. She'd come to their first meeting with calendars, phone bills, and credit card bills that together created an impressive paper trail for her case.

But Bill didn't sense she was pursuing her husband's money as much as his heart. She still loved him. She was angry, hurt, and emotionally distraught by his apparent lack of affection or fidelity, but she seemed more interested in winning his love than in getting "a good settlement."

In his experience, attorneys didn't always work in their clients' best interest when it came to matters of the heart. He voiced his opinion about Mara's motives to the attorney.

"My job is to secure the most beneficial financial and custodial arrangement for my client," Gilbert said. "I'm interested to hear what you've learned so we can decide what to include in our filing."

"How much time do we have?" Bill asked, the natural storyteller in him aroused by the facts of this case.

"As much as we need." The attorney glanced at his watch and then toward the investigator's overflowing case binder, telling him Bill's words were less than truthful. "How did you and Mrs. Wagner get connected?"

Bill sat as tall as he could in the enormous chair and prepared to report on his work. "I'm pretty sure she Googled me. I wasn't her first PI. She'd hired another back in 2005 when she first suspected her husband of cheating, but her husband busted that guy's tail in short order. According to Mrs. Wagner, Mr. Wagner got so angry he threatened to divorce her right then and there. That investigator's approach was a bit more cynical. He actually told Mrs. Wagner that her husband was only doing what all husbands do. She definitely didn't share his point of view.

"At our first meeting she gave me a lot of background. We talked about how long she had been married—fifteen years—and that they had five children; that they lived in a beautiful, million-dollar home in a secluded neighborhood on the outskirts of Durham, which Mr. Wagner purchased in . . . let's see . . ." Bill thumbed through his notes in the binder. "Late 2006."

"Then we discussed her husband's work routine. She told me he had founded his own company, that he had made a lot of money in a couple of deals. She indicated that when he wasn't traveling he worked from the company's offices, although he was no longer involved in day-to-day operations. She also said he's been leading an R&D project for the past several months. I got the impression of a hard working, successful businessman. At that point I was curious to learn how he was even finding the time to get into trouble, but people do manage, don't they, Mr. Richards? Otherwise guys like you and me would be outta business," Bill laughed, while the attorney nodded flatly.

"She was highly emotional and her information came out scattershot. But over the course of two hours she managed to cover most of the important details. It was clear Mrs. Wagner was intent on getting to the bottom of whatever her husband was involved in. To tell you the truth I felt sorry for her. She seemed like a nice lady, and here she was with five young kids and a husband up to no good.

"So I asked her what she knew about his behaviors. The short story: she and a girlfriend found an email on his phone; stop me if you already heard this."

"I did hear it from her, but I'd like to hear it from you."

Bill recounted the email discovery and how Mara had decided to keep the information secret.

"She hasn't told a soul for more than a year. I think it's mostly from fear of how her husband might react. You can tell the secrecy has taken a toll on her; it's got to be tough keeping up appearances in the face of such difficult truths.

"Anyway, I began with a deep dive on the paperwork, thanks to my wife, Erica, who is much better at that stuff than I am.

"I have to tell you, Mr. Richards, I've been in this business a long time, and I have never met a wife who was wrong in her suspicions by the time she hires an investigator. These women have to call a stranger—like myself—and spill their whole personal story. It's not as simple as, 'My husband is up to something'; they have to answer a lot of personal questions about their sexual history, relationship ups and downs; the entire marriage becomes evidence. I know that's rough," Bill said.

"I knew right away that Mara was right in her suspicions, she had the goods on him. She just needed help to document it. Her first thought was that he was seeing someone from work; that's what she suspected.

"Before I followed him I was looking at a pretty clear paper trail, between his phone, travel itinerary, and money. He'd make a series of phone calls during a concentrated time period, usually beginning around ten or eleven in the morning, and then no calls for a few hours. He would withdraw three hundred to a thousand dollars and then disappear, literally falling off the grid. For a businessman on a weekday, that seemed unusual.

"It was easy to do a reverse lookup of the phone numbers and determine that he was calling an escort service. Eros. He found the prostitutes off that site, not Craigslist. He formed a loose habit of Tuesdays and Thursdays.

"There are more than a dozen tabs here," Bill said, lifting the cover of his binder, "each representing a different lookup, a different escort. Most are local, but some are out of town, probably on his business trips."

"Were you able to follow him to any of these appointments?" the attorney asked, shifting in his seat and looking through the glass wall of the conference room, signaling slight impatience to the investigator.

"Yes, I was getting to that. The second part of my engagement involved following him. It took me a week or so to pick him up. I'd show up in the parking lot of his office in the early afternoons and he wouldn't be there. I'd ask his wife, and she'd assure me he was at work. Finally I decided to tail him from home, so I picked him up when he left in the morning. Turns out he was at the office for only a few hours; that's why I had been missing him.

"At first I thought, 'Oh he's a successful businessman. He'll be at the office all day, working hard,' you know? Yet he's only there for a very small window of time. It seems like his daily activities are more consumed with making calls, setting up escorts, and going to teller machines. He pretty much stops into the office and then leaves.

"The first time I followed him he drove out to North Raleigh, to a house in a nice neighborhood, about forty-five minutes from his home. I made the turn off Highway 401; by the time I turned around and came back, the front door was opening.

"The woman was in a negligee. He walked right in like he was walking into his own house. He didn't even have time to knock. He just parked in the driveway and walked right in.

"Some people, you watch them from the pick-up point and they're scanning, looking around, paranoid. They're on the lookout for their wives or someone they know. Some people are almost professional that way. They come in a parking lot and sit to see who pulls in with them. A light turns red and they'll just go through it to see if anyone follows them. Dave didn't do any counter surveillance; he was so confident his wife was clueless."

"You've been following Mr. Wagner for a few months now, right? I'm sure you have some impression of his character, his personality, things we should know in preparing to depose him."

Bill was on a roll now. He was a professional people watcher at heart, with a keen ability to pick up on subtle nuances, honed over many years of experience. This was the aspect of his job he knew set him apart.

"Right. It always amazes me how much you can learn about a person by following him. I guess the thing that stands out for me is that Mr. Wagner just seems so normal. He doesn't seem the type, and I've seen a lot of types. Some people you follow you realize are angry; maybe they're angry drivers, flipping people off, things like that. Mr. Wagner acts like a nice, normal person. It's just that he's doing this escort thing during the day. When he's in town he still gets home when he is supposed to get home. They even go to church every Sunday."

Gilbert Richards jotted notes as the investigator spoke. "I assume you have some photos from the North Raleigh location. Did you ID the woman so we can check her record? And were you able to confirm she's an escort, that this isn't just an affair?"

"Yes." Bill patted the binder. "We took photos of her going into the house, and they match images we have of her under her alias, Avery, on the Eros website. I staked out her house after Mr. Wagner left, and two or three more cars pulled in that day. The routines were identical: she opened the door in lingerie, usually a glass of wine in hand, and then the men quickly disappeared inside for an hour or so. The time between visits is short; I'm surprised they don't bump into each other. It's a busy place, I'll tell you that much," Bill said, shaking his head.

"The other escort we tracked goes by the name Kaelin on the website. This girl lives in a sketchy part of Durham; meets clients at area hotels. She's a pretty shady character. Her rap sheet is a mile long, some terrible stuff in there too—child sexual abuse charges and the like. I have to tell you, this is a first for me. Most of the people I follow are blue-collar guys who maybe hook up at a bar after five, or some guy who takes advantage of being out of town for work and gets an escort. This is the first time I've seen someone make it part of his weekly routine. Guess most people don't have the money, for one thing."

Gilbert noted the heft of the binder, now with interest. "This is good stuff, Bill. So we know he saw these escorts, but we have to be able to prove that he paid for sexual services, because he'll deny it; you know that."

Bill sat thoughtfully for a moment, recalling the guy he'd busted cheating on his wife with a twenty-two-year-old. He recapped the story for the attorney. "I worked a case where the guy and his wife, both in their sixties, were worth more than fifty million dollars. He was so cocky during his divorce hearing. His wife was accusing him of adultery. His lawyer claimed he was camping in the mountains at the time in question. He had told his wife he was going to the mountains and then sent an associate with his credit card to create a paper trail. Through two days of testimony this guy was confident he wouldn't get caught.

"Everyone was thinking, 'The PI is a moron, he followed the wrong person.' The lawyer kept saying, 'Are you sure you followed the right car?'

"Then finally her lawyer put me on the stand and walked me through a video I had taken of the husband and his girlfriend at a topless beach in Belize, frolicking in the water. He got hammered hard; the judge was ticked the guy had been lying throughout the hearing. The wife got more money." Bill chuckled.

"We could try that route. I could try to get video," Bill said, quickly adding, "That may be a little easier with the one at the house. It's going to be tougher with the one at the hotels."

Gilbert said he loved the approach. But he agreed that it could get messy and would probably take more time than they had. "Let's just force the escort to admit it. Tell her we're going to go to the IRS. That should get her to cooperate."

"Alright." Bill nodded. "I'll get their legal names and be back for subpoenas."

* * * * *

Two days later, Bill was back in the conference room. Getting Avery's legal name had been a piece of cake since she owned her own home. He picked up the subpoena and made an appointment using Dave Wagner's name as a reference.

She had booked him three days out. Bill worried Avery might mention the referral to Dave given that much time. That would be one weird conversation. She played a game where she wouldn't give him her address until fifteen minutes before the appointment. These girls were always wary of law enforcement.

Now Bill could hardly wait to share the story with the lawyer. He sat on the edge of his seat, his leg bouncing with anticipation.

"So I pull into the driveway and head for the door," he began, as Gilbert took his seat at the head of the table. "I'm looking in the window. Candles are burning. I knock on the door. She comes with a glass of wine, in a negligee with her breasts visible, like she just got out of bed. 'Honey, sweetie, baby,' she says, dripping with sweetness.

"She had her rap down, she was so comfortable. I had the subpoena in an envelope. 'I have this for you,' I say.

"'Not now, just set it on the table,' she says.

"She must've thought it was cash. She wanted me to come inside as quickly as possible. I didn't want to go in the house or my credibility would be ruined. She'd claim we'd had sex. I was trying to get her close enough to take the paper. As soon as she was I said, 'Here, Diane, this is yours, take it.'

"When she heard me say her real name, her face changed. She reached out for it, and I said, 'This is a subpoena from Mrs. Wagner's attorney.'"

"Good work," the attorney said, looking pleased. "What about the other one? Have you made contact with her yet?"

"Not yet. I'll start today."

* * * * *

"Hi, Kaelin. My name's Bill. Dave Wagner recommended me to you," Bill lied to the voice on the other end of the phone.

"Um, I don't do recommendations," she replied, sounding cautious.

"I completely understand. It's just that Dave's a good friend of mine. And I'm only in town here for a couple days. Do you think you could make an exception and see me? I'll pay five hundred."

"Sorry, man. Can't help you."

"Five hundred, *before* add-ons."

The money got her attention; he knew it would. But she was cagey; probably scared he was a cop.

"No. Can't do it. Like I said, no referrals."

"Okay, I mean, I guess I could call someone else," he said, his voice trailing off. Bill was an experienced angler, and he knew he had to reel her in slowly or she'd jump off the hook and disappear. He waited, letting the bait glimmer before her eyes.

"Alright, meet me at three." She named a hotel.

Bill arrived half an hour early, waited for her to pull in, and got her license plate. Then he hopped in his car and headed back to Gilbert Richard's office to run her tag and get her legal name for the subpoena. The next step would be the toughest; he called her cell phone from his car.

"Hi. It's me. Bill. I am *so* sorry. I can't believe this, but I can't make it today. Can we possibly reschedule?"

She unleashed a string of profanities he had never heard arranged quite that way. Then he played his last card.

"I'll pay double."

Silence. Then finally, "Alright, a thousand dollars. Same time tomorrow. I'll call and let you know which hotel I check in to."

"Okay, but can you give me a general location?"

"Capital Boulevard," she said and hung up.

He went to Gilbert's office and had the subpoena an hour later.

His phone rang at 2:47 p.m. the next day. She gave him the hotel and room number.

*****

"I swear, it was almost the exact same thing," Bill said, detailing the encounter the next morning to Gilbert. "She steps back from the door in her bra and panties. 'Oh I got this for you, honey. Hey baby.' Almost word-for-word the same as the other girl. I try to hand her the envelope and she says, 'Just set it on the table.' She wanted to get me in that room as quickly as possible. Just like Avery.

"I say her legal name and then, 'No this is a subpoena.'

"'What do you mean?' she shouts. 'That's not me!' Then she grabs it. 'That's not me; I'm not going to court.'

"I tell her, 'What do you think, I just picked someone out in a hotel who's having sex with Dave Wagner? If you don't show, they'll report you to the IRS.' I turn and walk back toward the elevators.

"Then she steps out in the hallway and yells, 'Hey, wait a minute. You mean I just rented this room for nothing?'" Bill couldn't contain his laughter at the absurdity of it.

Neither could Gilbert. "Unbelievable."

Chapter 7

Stoic Husband

For nothing is covered that will not be revealed, or
hidden that will not be known.

Matthew 10:26

December 2008
Durham, North Carolina

As they pulled down the private road toward his cousin's house,
Brody and Alison mused over what lengths Mara might go to
this year. It was their fourth year celebrating Christmas Eve dinner together, and the gatherings always looked like something
straight out of *Southern Living.*

The soft yellow glow of Christmas lights invited them into
their warmth as they pulled into the driveway. When their three
little ones scampered out of the minivan and into the house,
Brody knew he wouldn't see them again until it was time to go.

On the first floor, a large open floor plan encompassing the
kitchen, dining area, living room, and master suite was the antith-
esis of the labyrinth that led through the rest of the house. Brody
still couldn't navigate the other floors without getting lost.

Mara was busy as ever with meal prep, but quickly flit-
ted over in apron and heels to kiss the kids and hug everyone

warmly. David showed up a few minutes later, martini shaker in hand, smiling broadly and clearly ready to celebrate.

Brody admired the detail and near-perfection of the space. While he and Alison loved their more typical suburban lifestyle, it was impossible not to appreciate his cousin's extravagant lifestyle, accentuated by Mara's impeccable flair.

Savory aromas from the gourmet meal mingled with natural pine from a fresh-cut Christmas tree David had cut down with the kids the weekend prior. This is what Christmas smells like.

He noted how Mara had expertly wrapped the tree lights so intricately the wires were barely visible; better than his pre-lit artificial tree, he thought with amusement. Artful, expensive Christmas decorations expertly adorned the space. The effect was exquisite, and yet the house still felt welcoming and even kid-friendly. He didn't know how she managed that balance, but she seemed to do it every year.

Brody wasn't unaware that this outer perfection covered a multitude of sins, so to speak. In past years these gatherings had often been rife with conflict, usually started by Mara. He hoped this year might be as relaxing as it looked.

By they time the kids had been fed and the four adults were seated for dinner, Brody, David, and Mara were on their third martini; only Alison had abstained, sipping lightly on a glass of wine, having accepted designated-driver responsibilities. So far the evening had been memorable for the wonderful meal Mara had pulled off yet again and for David's high spirits, which lit the room and left Brody's sides hurting from laughter.

They sat in satisfied silence in the glow of the diminishing candlelight. Brody noticed Mara's attention was fixated on her husband's cell phone, which sat innocuously on the edge of the table. The first sortie came without warning.

"Who ya gonna call this Christmas, Dave?"

Dave met her gaze but made no response in words or expression.

"Who?" The word slurred to twice its normal length.

Brody watched her stack dinner plates without breaking eye contact with her husband, as if cleaning up this mess would somehow offset the new mess she was about to create. Brody stole a quick glance at his wife, her eyes filled with trepidation.

"Come on, David, why don't you tell them who you called last Christmas? Who will it be this year?"

"Maybe whoever is in the *office voicemail?*" She curled her fingers into air quotation marks and sarcasm dripped off her words.

Brody watched his cousin; his face betrayed no emotion. He wondered how Dave maintained control the way he did. Why did he put up with this? Mara seemed to seek safety in numbers and often, even without the additional fuel of alcohol, used their presence as cover to vent her insatiable paranoia toward her husband. He pitied her and resented her all at the same time. It seemed impossible to enjoy a visit with his cousin without this tension.

He eyed Alison. She instinctively caught Mara by the elbow and eased her toward the kitchen with a gentle whisper. "Here, let me help with the dishes." Mara wobbled in her heels, plates clanking precariously.

Brody picked up his martini glass as well as Dave's. "Come on, Dave, let's see what the kids are up to." His cousin followed silently. Brody replenished the shaker quickly before heading down the stairs. Mara was whispering loudly to Alison as they left about "the lies." He owed his wife for sure.

After checking on the kids, who were sleepily watching a movie, he and Dave opened the doors from the lower level to the veranda. Outside, the crisp, cool evening was chilly, but the air and sky were clear. Brody unstacked a couple of chairs and refilled his cousin's glass before they sat down.

Peace.

* * * * *

"How can he just sit there like nothing's happened?" The secrets she'd kept bottled up for so long were eating her alive. She wanted to tell Alison the truth. Brody; he always looked at her like *she* was the crazy one. Everyone thought she was crazy. Dave had told them she was. As much as she wanted to tell them what really was happening, who would believe her? And then Dave would finally get his way; he'd put her away somewhere, away from her kids, and he'd get away with it all!

The weight of the secrets was exhausting her. It had been nearly a year since she'd learned of the prostitutes, and still she had told no one, nor had she confronted Dave about it directly—until tonight; she'd come so close to speaking the truth.

Who you going to call? What she'd wanted to add was "Avery? Kaelin?"

Fear, her bodyguard, bade her silent. But she wondered if Dave had seen through her words, if he suspected what she knew. She began shaking involuntarily at the possibility; Alison put a protective arm around her. Mara was unsure whether it was sympathy or pity, and at the moment she didn't care. Any simple kindness was a temporary salve to her nonstop pain.

The hum of the dishwasher was the only sign there had been a meal. The room had been restored to its pristine appearance. Alison told Mara she needed to round up the kids, and a few minutes later she and Brody departed. "Call if you need me," Brody had whispered in her ear as they hugged goodbye.

"What's wrong with you, Mara?" Dave hissed as soon as they were gone.

It was enough of a spark to reignite her fury. She whipped around to face him, looking square into the eyes of a man who was a stranger to her.

"Me? I'm not the one with the secrets, Dave! Who's on your office voicemail, huh? Why don't we give it a call right now and see?" She held his phone tauntingly in the air.

He quickly snatched it from her hand.

She turned and ran up the stairs to the nanny apartment off the kitchen. She found the laptop that had been driving her mad and brought it with her to the kitchen. "How about this, Dave?" She held the laptop high. "See this? This computer has been locked down for fifteen years. Why?"

He moved toward her slowly, foreboding in each step. She clutched the computer to her chest, backing away, her fear masked by rage. "Why? Why?" she chanted repeatedly. She dodged his attempt to grab the laptop.

He stepped back. "I don't need this abuse. I'm leaving."

She watched as he headed toward the garage, suddenly wondering if the kids were still awake. She followed him into the garage. He was sitting in her brand-new Acadia. Her rage flared.

"I'm leaving you," he said, and started the car.

Before she had time to think, she had darted to the car, reached in the passenger's side, and pulled the keys out of the ignition. "Not in my car you're not," she said, emboldened now by her rare show of courage.

Dave got out, passing her as he headed into the house and closing the door before she could follow. The lock clicked. She walked around to the back of the house, her heels sticking in the dirt with each step. From the porch she knocked on the French doors. "Kids. It's me, Mom. Let me in. Open the door." She could see them sleeping inside and didn't want to alarm them.

She repeated her plea as she checked the double set of doors. Fortunately one was open.

Mara found a phone. "Brody, Dave's leaving. I need your help. Please. Can you come back and talk to him?" Her hysterics roused the children, who began to follow her, some fearfully holding on to her.

She walked toward the master bedroom closet, holding the phone to her ear with one hand, the computer under her other arm. Dave was grabbing clothes and tossing them toward a suitcase.

The kids were crying now, their terror rising on the tenor of hers. "Don't go, Daddy, please." Their pitiful pleas broke her heart. She hoped Brody could hear the pain his cousin was causing.

"He's leaving me, Brody. Come talk to him. Please."

"I can be there in a half hour. Try to settle down. It'll be alright."

She watched Dave turn his attention to the kids. He spoke to them calmly, as if he were leaving on a business trip. They stifled their cries, clinging to his every word. Annie crawled into his lap and snuggled against his chest. He rubbed her back as he reassured them he would see them in just a day or so, and that they needed to get to bed and not worry about a thing. Caleb sat tall, bravely wiping tears from his face.

Mara would never understand the man's talent for behaving so convincingly in front of others, while reserving such rancor and hostility for her alone. As he returned to the closet, she hung up on Brody and instructed Caleb to get the little ones back upstairs, promising to be up in a few minutes to tuck them back in.

As Dave was bent over, zipping his bag, Mara inadvertently grabbed the neck of his t-shirt while pleading with him not to go. In her panic, she had forgotten his old, unspoken rule about not touching his neck.

Without warning, Dave flung his arm around and knocked her backward. With the force of the blow, Mara lost her balance, and the back of her head banged against a low window sill. Immediately she felt the blood and touched her hand to the wound.

Now she looked up at him in stunned silence. He gazed at the blood on her fingers. Then he picked up the phone from the floor and punched some numbers.

"Yes, my name is David Wagner. I want to report a domestic dispute. My wife is intoxicated and she attacked me physically in my sleep. I pushed her off of me in self-defense, but she is continuing to behave aggressively. Can you send the police please?" He hung up and tossed the phone back on the ground.

"I'm leaving." His spittle hit her like venom along with his words.

As soon as Dave's car was out of the driveway, Mara called her parents in Michigan. "You've got to come," she cried, hysterical. "Please. Dave's left me."

"Okay. We're coming."

Mara would later recall this as the first time her mother had simply said yes to her request. She hung up, relieved to know help was on the way.

Next she called Brody back and told him not to bother coming. Maybe now he'd believe her.

A little while later, Mara received another call from Brody, checking up on her. Exhaustion was rolling in like waves, her body relaxing with the realization Dave would not be back, at least not tonight. She assured Brody she would be fine, but when she heard a knock at the door, he agreed to hold on.

As she stepped into the family room, she saw uniformed men shining flashlights through the glass panes. "It's the police."

"Okay, call me back if you need me." Mara smoothed her clothes and opened the door. She invited them to step inside and closed the door behind them. They questioned her husband's whereabouts and took a report about the altercation, noting details about her head wound. She agreed to contact Emergency Medical Services.

When the EMS had finished treating Mara, the police prepared to leave. They instructed her to call if her husband returned, and encouraged her to seek a restraining order.

* * * * *

Mara's parents arrived by the afternoon of the following day. Although her mom couldn't resist making a dig about her smoking, they were otherwise helpful and supportive.

On day two, her mother whisked the kids away on what she called "Granny's Mystery Trip," giving Mara and her dad some much-needed time together.

With Dave out of the house, she finally felt safe to confide in her father about everything that had been happening: the prostitutes, the fights, her increasing isolation, and her fears about what Dave might do if he found out what she knew.

Her father was irate. In a rare display of emotion, he expressed genuine concern over her wellbeing. "Do you realize you've been emotionally and verbally abused? Mara, honey, you need to follow through on that restraining order." He sat by her while she called her attorney and sought protection from her husband.

Mara phoned a locksmith, and by the end of the following day the locks had been changed. She slept soundly knowing her father was within earshot in the nanny apartment, shotgun by his side.

The following day, with her mom's help, Mara put what remained of her husband's clothes and personal belongings in bags on the front porch.

Another day passed without incident. Then Dave showed up unannounced. Mara's father became livid at the sight of him. After insisting Mara go to her bedroom in the back of the house, he approached the front door. From her room Mara could hear him yelling to Dave through the heavy glass door.

"Mara has filed a restraining order, Dave. This has gone far enough. It's in your own best interest to collect your things and get out of here as quickly as possible. I suggest you make arrangements to stay somewhere for a while, until you and she have a chance to make some longer-term decisions."

Mara couldn't hear Dave, but a few moments later her dad informed her he was gone and she could come out.

The kids were feeling the strain of their father's absence, and Mara's mother encouraged her to talk with them. After dinner Mara drew the kids into her bedroom, where they instinctively piled into the bed like they had done in happier days.

"I know you all miss Daddy." They eyed her intently, nodding their heads.

"Your dad and I, we used to be best friends. Now we're not. Understand? Sometimes when you and your best friend are not getting along, you have to take a little break from each other. Like you and Jamie did, Stevie—remember that? That's what Daddy and I are doing. We're taking a little break. Do you understand?

"But we're working on being best friends again. I love you and Daddy loves you. To the moon and back. Okay?"

The kids nodded in unison, not really understanding. Yet they seemed to relax into her assurance. That was good enough for now.

A couple days after her parents left, Mara received a certified letter.

Dear Mara,

I want you to know that I am totally committed to working things out. I have honored your request to move out and have made arrangements for a three-month lease in a furnished apartment.

I'm not sure how best to pick out a counselor this time. Perhaps your psychiatrist could give you a referral?

At this point I believe lawyers to be a detriment and I refuse to engage in any discussions with and/or between counsels. Please be careful with the advice you apparently have been given—I'm concerned it may not be given in the spirit of helpfulness, and they will be prone to advise in their best interest, not ours nor the kids.

Let's plan to meet soon so we can formalize a plan on:
- *Counseling*
- *Visitation*
- *Rebuilding our relationship*
- *Saving our marriage*

I love you very much!
Dave

Every time Mara felt life reaching a somewhat predictable rhythm, Dave threw her a curve ball. A few weeks after his letter arrived, he called and invited Mara to come inside to see his apartment when she dropped the boys off for visitation, a temporary arrangement they had worked out through their lawyers.

She noted with condescension how, left to his own devices, his style had reverted to what he had known growing up:

magnets splattered all over the refrigerator, the counter looking like an electronics display with the toaster, blender, and other small appliances cluttering the workspace; and worst of all, her pet peeve, a dirty dish towel hung over the dishwasher handle. She bristled.

She couldn't fathom why Dave wanted her approval so much now, proudly showing off the cheap artwork and furniture that looked like it had been purchased at Bed Bath & Beyond.

He asked if she'd had a chance to review the separation agreement. She had, but could not bring herself to sign it.

She tried changing the subject. "Not yet. I'll try to get to it before our counseling appointment." But by the time they met up in the parking lot for the appointment, she still hadn't signed.

Dave copped an attitude the moment he saw her. "I don't know why I agreed to this," he grumbled. "You're the one who needs to go. This guy will see right through you. Do you really want to discuss your erratic behavior? Your wild spending habits? Your mood swings? I don't know why I let you manipulate me like this. You know what? I'm not going." He turned and walked briskly toward his vehicle.

Mara ran after him, appalled by her damnable neediness, even in the face of his endless assaults.

July 17, 2008

"For the record, we're here today in the matter of Mara Wagner versus David Wagner, deposition of defendant, David Wagner. And, Mr. Wagner, I've already introduced myself, but my name's Molly Murray. I'm one of the attorneys representing your wife, Mara."

"Uh-huh." Dave tugged at his collar and then folded his hands self-consciously on the conference table. He took in the lavish styling of his wife's attorneys' offices. Even the air was laden with rich leather and the heavy aroma of the lilies in the centerpiece. Dave tried to estimate what this circus was costing him per hour. These offices. Two attorneys and a stenographer on her side. No doubt Mara had purchased a new outfit or at least new shoes for the occasion; he looked but could not recall if he had seen the ensemble before. His own attorney's expenses were being covered by the company, thankfully. His partners had more than a little self-interest in keeping his wife as far removed from the business as possible.

Dave offered a joyless grin to Ms. Murray as he prepared for Mara's latest legal ploy. She'd had the subpoena served to him in a pre-Memorial Day crowd in the middle of the courtyard of his apartment complex, where he had been living since their separation following "the Christmas incident."

As if that were not humiliation enough, Dave was now expected to endure who-knew-how-many hours of questioning, which he'd ultimately have to pay for, just so that Mara could get what? More money? More custody? She would get neither. He should have made good on his threat to have her put away when she started all this craziness. He stared at her profile as she deliberately resisted eye contact. His attention shifted back when he realized Ms. Murray was asking him something.

". . . And you understand you are under oath and your answers are being recorded?"

"Yes."

"Are you under the influence of alcohol or drugs today?"

"No."

"Okay. Please state your full name for the record."

"David Andrew Wagner."

"And if you'd please, describe for me your education, beginning with your undergraduate."

"Well, actually, I have a bachelor of science in pharmacy. It's a five-year program, not necessarily considered post-graduate, but a five-year, comprehensive program." For the next ten minutes, Dave detailed his work history with pride.

"Tell me in just a couple of sentences about each of your children. Personality, what they're like." Dave loved his kids more than anything in the world, so he knew he would knock this one out of the park, along with any thought Mara might have of challenging his custodial rights.

"Okay. Caleb is, I think he's very bright, he loves to read and has a very scientific- and engineering-type thought process. But at the same time he possesses literary skills, so he's kind of, people are usually one or the other, but he has very strong verbal skills. A very loving child entering his, you know, his preteen years.

"Margaret is very creative, very artistic—and by artistic I mean through dance. She's a very talented dancer. Very caring and has, you know, shown a lot of ambition in her desire to get her babysitter certificate.

"Audrey has a very bright sense of humor. She has a very carefree attitude. She's doing well in school, takes horseback, and has a real love of animals. She's going to continue horseback riding. That's something she has really taken to and has done very well at. And I think she has some difficulty being isolated as the middle child.

"Stephen, he's a character." Dave laughed, picturing his youngest son. "He's got a great sense of humor, as well as being very funny. He's pretty adventurous. I think that's just the influence of having some older brothers and sisters. And he's done well in school. I think, you know, all the reports I get are that Stephen is very kind to other kids at school. He and Annie have a unique relationship.

"Annie is just adorable. She's got a funny sense of humor. In fact, about two days ago she had me laughing out loud with a play on words she was trying to pull off. It was very funny. She's bright as well. She shows a lot of creativity in her play. She's done very well in school as well, and she's very caring and affectionate and loving."

"What would you say are your strengths as a father?"

"Well, I think that I create opportunities with the kids in one-on-one situations that allow us to enjoy the time together. I think I can foster activities that, you know, kind of encompass family play. Sometimes that's difficult because of the differences in age, but I think we enjoy our time together. I know I do and the children do," he said, clarifying the 'we' he meant. "I think I have a reasonable approach to discipline and a consistent approach. And I'm affectionate toward them, as they're affectionate toward me."

"How about weaknesses? What would you say are your weaknesses as a father?"

"Well, I think sometimes reacting to a situation before pausing and understanding exactly what has fueled the fire," he said, measuring his words. "You know, you hear somebody's been in trouble or you hear somebody got hurt or somebody yells, and you jump to a conclusion, which I assume is a common reaction by a lot of parents."

"How about Mara's strengths as a mother?"

"Undoubtedly very affectionate, fosters creativity in the children, and I think she is always looking to create an activity or situation for them that helps them expand their creative abilities. For special events and holidays she decorates and has the kids help her. For Halloween and St. Patrick's Day, holidays you wouldn't normally make a big deal out of, she creates situations that make it very special."

"What about her weaknesses as a mother?"

"I think, like all mothers, she gets frustrated when the children don't behave or don't listen. I think, as I described my weakness, sometimes there is an overreaction to behavior, and I think time gets away from her, in terms of taking on a project and not realizing how much time and effort and energy it's going to take away from the kids, even though the project might be for the kids." He looked toward Mara as he spoke, remembering the endless arguments they'd had over her tendency to overcommit and run everyone ragged in pursuit of her impossibly high standards.

"Can you think of any other weaknesses you want to tell me about her and her mothering abilities?" Ms. Murray asked.

"I'm concerned about some recent events I know of related to Mara's consumption of alcohol," Dave said. "There have been some situations where I'm concerned about her, and actually, it's mostly her interactions with me that created situations where it's, you know, loud yelling and just potentially violent and dangerous. So unfortunately these events have happened.

"That's what happened the day that I left the house. That was a result of one of those altercations, and it's happened a few times since I left as well," he said, assuming Mara had already presented her side of the recent events behind their latest separation.

"Has that ever happened in the presence of the children?"

"Yes."

"And when was that?"

"Well, it happened December twenty-seventh. It happened prior to that at the house, I can't recall the exact dates—but I almost called 9-1-1. It happened less than a week prior to that as well, in front of the children. It happened one evening when I took the family out to dinner. We went to Kanki, and upon returning from the restaurant I was leaving, and Caleb was going to spend the night with me and it happened again."

"In general would you say that Mara is a good mother?"

"I think she's a great mother."

"Let's talk then about the time before the two of you separated in December of 2007 when you were living in the house. Would you say she was getting them fed and dressed appropriately?

"Yeah. I was contributing to that significantly as well, cooking dinner, shopping, picking kids up from school, things like that. Usually I'd drop the kids off at school and then drive to my office, and Mara would pick them up, but then, you know, as time went on, I contributed to the driving and grocery shopping, running errands, things like that. I'd drive them to dance and pick up from dance, take Audrey to horseback. I coached Stephen's soccer team, and I coached the other kids' soccer teams as well." He ignored Mara's eye roll as he took credit on the record that she was never willing to give him.

"Describe the current custodial arrangement you and Mara have."

"Well, prior to them being up in Michigan for the summer, I would take all five of the kids every other weekend, and take the boys one evening during the week, and take the girls another evening during the week. That was more facilitated by the kids' schedules than anything else."

He was gaining energy now as he spoke of his children. Being a father was the one area of his life where he knew he still excelled; one need only look as far as the children for evidence of that. His confidence lifted his posture and strengthened his voice.

"Is there anything else you want to tell me right now about the issue of custody?"

Feeling a growing sense of control, he seized the opportunity. "Well, you know, I think that with regard to the separation, we need to share joint custody of the children, and I've been in agreement that Mara would remain the primary caretaker; in other words, the children would primarily live with her."

"And so you're comfortable with that right now?"

"Right now, I am, yes." his words conveyed the gravity of his assessment.

"And when did you last have sex with a prostitute?" His insides jolted as if touched by a live wire, momentarily disorienting him.

"I'm sorry?" He sputtered, grasping for precious seconds to regain his balance following the ambush, forcing his adrenaline-drenched mind to process the situation.

"Do you want me to repeat it?"

"Oh, I heard you. I've never had sex with a prostitute." *Where's this coming from? What do they know?* He needed to keep his wits about him to minimize potential damage from whatever crazy theory Mara had cooked up this time.

"Okay. And by 'prostitute' I mean someone you would pay to have sex with or engage in other sex acts. Do you understand that's the meaning of prostitute?"

David's anger sparked. His well-honed instinct for denial had barely let him acknowledge to himself how entrenched these behaviors had become. Being confronted here, so publicly, was simultaneously insulting and surreal. He felt himself detaching, retreating to a safe distance away from all of this.

"I do." *Maintain composure, Dave.*

"And, you know that 'escort' is another term often used for prostitute?"

Surely she's joking. She's just on a fishing expedition. "Okay, I'll take your word for that." He worked to contain the sardonic smile threatening to crawl across his lips.

"Have you ever had sex with someone you would refer to as an escort?"

"No."

"Have you ever engaged in any other type of sexual contact with someone you would refer to as an escort?"

"No." *You've got this. They don't know anything. Stay calm.*

"Is this a copy of your Microsoft Outlook calendar?" Dave glanced passively at the piece of paper the woman slid in front of him.

"It appears to be because it has my travel schedule."

Dave racked his mind for where she might be heading with this new line of questions. While he maintained a meticulous calendar, he was too smart—and his wife too nosy—for him to record anything that might incriminate.

"And let me direct your attention to July 17, 2007. What does it say on that date?"

"'Dave to RDU late morning. Two o'clock. St. Ignatius Catholic School Advisory Committee.'"

"Are you a member of that committee?"

"Yes, I am." A hint of pride escaped. *Who do these people think they are anyway?*

"And the calendar indicates that you were getting to Raleigh-Durham International Airport in late morning on the seventeenth; is that correct?"

"That's what it says. I don't recall my exact travel schedule." He looked out the window at the impossibly blue sky and almost artificial-looking white clouds so typical of the Carolina sky; he longed to be anywhere but here.

"Were you coming home for the purpose of attending this meeting on your calendar?"

Reluctantly he turned his attention back to the attorney and her endless questions.

"Actually, the purpose of my trip was to attend a development meeting on the eighteenth at work. I know that we did have a meeting at St. Ignatius. But the development meeting was . . . at the time we were trying to put together a team of engineers for our new venture, and I was attempting to recruit internally."

"Well there was no advisory board meeting that day though, was there?"

"I'm sorry, on the seventeenth?"

"Do you recall what time your flight was into RDU on July seventeenth?"

"No."

"And where would you have gone after you left the airport?"

Dave shifted in his chair, the quiet squeak of the leather betraying his discomfort. "I don't remember."

"Did you see anyone on July seventeenth?"

"You know, I really don't recall if the school meeting was in person or was a conference call. I think it was a conference call, but I'm not positive," he hedged. "I know I was in the office with two of my business partners prior to my development meeting on Wednesday."

Stop talking so fast. Just breathe.

"So you went to your office that day, the seventeenth?"

"I believe I did. But again, I can't recall." *Careful. Don't back yourself into a corner.*

"And you spent the night at your house that evening?"

"Yes. I slept there."

"And did you do anything that evening with anyone in particular?"

"No, I don't recall."

"Who is Avery?"

Another jolt surged through him. *No! This can't be happening.* "I don't know anybody by that name."

"Can you identify this photo?" Molly Murray held up a black-and-white photo of an attractive blonde, clearly taken under surveillance. He felt trapped. He tugged at the shirt collar restricting his airflow.

Deep inside something nudged David to drop the charade. The lies sounded hollow even to him. If only he had time to think, weigh his options. He tried to envision what the truth would look like, feel like; could he even remember a time when he hadn't lived with the lies?

A small voice beckoned him to the light of truth. *Yes, there would be consequences, but they must be less than the weight you've been carrying.* The burden of it all was wearing him down and wearing him out. *If only I had time to think.*

"No." He retreated on impulse.

"Did you ever have sexual intercourse with Avery?"

"No." *Too late to change course.*

Dave's attorney interrupted, "We'll object to the question. I think you're asking him to admit whether he's committed a crime or not."

"So he's taking the Fifth on *Avery?*" Ms. Murray asked, smiling as she lingered over the name.

"Yeah," Mr. Talwell said.

Ms. Murray turned back to Dave. "But it is your testimony that you don't know who this lady is?"

"I do not know who that lady is."

She pointed now at a phone bill. "Read the telephone number that was dialed from your home on July 17, 2007."

Dave complied.

"And there's the same telephone number at the bottom right of the website for Miss Avery. Did you call Avery from your home telephone number?"

"Well, it appears that a phone call was made from that number, but I do not know this person, Avery."

"Can you identify this document for me?"

"It looks like an email string."

"From whom to whom?"

"It says from Dave Wagner to Avery."

"And you sent this email to Avery on July 17, 2007?"

"I don't recall doing this, no." Another tug at the collar. He settled back into his familiar morass of deception.

"Your testimony is that you have no recollection of whether you sent this email or not?"

"That's my testimony."

"So you don't deny sending this email?"

"I don't know that I did."

"The email asks her to call you on your cell phone to set up a time?"

"I just don't recall."

"Well, does the email say that?"

"Yes, the email says that."

"And what did she respond back to your email—or this email?"

"'Not available, already booked. Happy to see you tomorrow,'" he read flatly.

"And what's the response? That you were pretty open in the afternoon, to pick a time, let me know when you're available? Is that what the response email says, basically?"

"Yes." Why had he taken the risk of emailing? He felt naked, sitting exposed and alone in this room of people. His mind turned involuntarily to the stenographer. Was she judging him with every denial of his that she recorded?

"Were you in contact with any other escorts at that time?"

"You know, I'm really confused here. I don't know," Dave said, seeking relief first from Mara, who stubbornly refused his gaze, and then from his lawyer.

"Do you want to take a break, Mr. Wagner?" Ms. Murray asked.

"No. We can keep going. I'm just not sure, I don't understand," he repeated, frantic now to escape the questions, the room, his wife's demeaning treatment of him, and most of all these humiliating revelations.

He needed to clear his mind. On the inside, his war waged anew, the pull to end the lies and denial tugging strongly on the carefully constructed shell he had built and then reinforced over so many years.

Ms. Murray pressed on. "Other than Avery, who I've been asking you about, were you seeking contact or appointments with any other escorts on July seventeenth or any other time?"

"No." *Please, God, no more.*

"Now I'm going to show you a name written here on a piece of paper. It's K-a-e-l-i-n. Have you ever seen that name before?"

"It doesn't look familiar."

"I'm going to hand you a document marked *Exhibit 7*. Can you identify this for me?" Dave felt the pain shoot through his clenched jaw as he picked up the printout of the web page with a photo showing the prostitute splayed on her stomach looking behind her, and a second of her flexing on a pole, scant clothing underscoring her offer.

"It looks like something that was taken off a website."

"And how else would you describe it?"

"I don't know," he said, deflating. "It seems to be information about an escort."

"Do you recognize this woman?"

"No," he said, flimsy denials flowing as freely as the questions now.

"Have you ever tried to contact this woman by phone or email?"

"No."

"Did you ever have sexual intercourse with this woman?"

"Objection," Mr. Talwell interjected.

"She called your home number at 1:41 p.m. on July seventeenth, isn't that correct?"

"Seventeenth? I don't recall," Dave said.

"Do you know your cell phone indicates this same number was called from your cell phone on July seventeeth?"

"I don't know that either." He was spent. Defeated. *Would this never end?*

"And assuming I'm correct, how would you explain that?"

"I don't know if I have an explanation for that," Dave said, unable to stem the increasing hollowness of his own replies.

"Did you meet with her on July 17, 2007?"

"No."

"If you could look back at *Exhibits 4* and *7*, tell me what Avery or Kaelin charges per hour for her services." Dave looked at the photos of the women he had patronized weekly over the past several years, and read their published fees aloud as if for the first time.

"It says three hundred dollars."

"If you could look *at Exhibits 8, 9* and *10*, whose account is this?" Ms. Murray handed him several pages of his own bank statements.

"It's a joint account for David and Mara Wagner."

"If you could look down the page to the transaction that took place on July seventeenth."

"Uh-huh."

"And do you see an ATM cash withdrawal on July seventeenth?"

"Yes, from South Square, Durham."

"And for what amount?"

"Three hundred dollars."

"Tell me the withdrawals that took place on July seventeenth, eighteenth, and nineteenth of 2007."

"There were four three-hundred-dollar cash withdrawals."

"You made those withdrawals?"

"I did, yeah."

"So in three days you took out twelve hundred dollars in cash?"

"I did."

"And what did you use that cash for?"

"Well, I was in preparation," Dave said. "I was going to Rhode Island for a golf tournament on the twenty-third and our plan in advance was to, we were planning on going to the Foxwoods Casino after the golf tournament. The maximum amount you can withdraw at any time was three hundred, so I was taking out money in preparation for that visit."

"And did you continue that trend after the nineteenth of July?"

"What trend is that?"

"Taking three hundred dollars or more a day out of bank accounts?"

"No, I did it in Durham because there are no Wachovia banks up there."

Mr. Talwell requested a lunch recess, finally, and Dave slumped back in his chair. Mara passed him, her in-season, open-toed pumps clicking her disdain as if in Morse code. Despite the buffer of her lawyers, she leaned toward him and whispered hoarsely, "I hate you."

He didn't blame her.

Dave sat at lunch like a child awaiting reprimand from his parents. Ted Talwell spoke first.

"At the risk of stating the obvious, this isn't going well, Dave. Did you have any idea something like this might be coming?"

Dave shook his head.

"We have to get out of this line of questioning. That means owning up to something without offering too many details. We need to rebuild your credibility, fast."

He outlined what he wanted Dave to say when they reconvened. Dave nodded, his thoughts far removed as he considered the implications on the rest of his life. What if his partners found out? What about all the employees who looked up to him? The kids—oh God!—had she told them? He needed this deposition over with so he could get Mara alone and find out what she knew, and what she planned to do with it. He didn't put anything past her, especially in her state.

Upon returning to the hearing, Mr. Talwell began, "I'm going to withdraw my objections to the questions based upon the Fifth Amendment and withdraw my direction to Dave not to testify, and Dave wants to provide some additional testimony to clarify his earlier testimony if he might do that."

"Figure out how to start," Dave said, stumbling for words. "I've been thinking for two hours. First of all, the testimony that I gave earlier was not entirely accurate. I apologize for that. I apologize for wasting your time and being dishonest.

"In July of 2007, I did contact through a . . . I found names on a website on the computer and I contacted two women, although they didn't look, it wasn't that name and she didn't look like in those photos. On the website they were listed under a section, I believe it was masseuse. I knew it was wrong, and I can't justify my actions, but I did contact those women. I did make appointments to see them. I did not perform any sexual acts on them. They provided a hot oil massage or a lotion massage, and ultimately the session ended in, with the female . . . I'm ashamed to say I got carried away and let her . . . touch me. Mara, I can't tell you—"

"The truth?" Mara finished his sentence.

He ignored her barb and pressed on as he had been directed.

"I can't tell you how sorry I am for lying to you. I'm ashamed of what I did. I'm sorry for the pain I caused."

"I'm ashamed of you too," she said with disgust—whether at the revelations themselves or his futile denial, he couldn't say for sure; most likely both. She looked tiny and frail behind the large conference room table, and for the first time in a long while, he felt sorry for her.

"And I hope you can forgive me. I'm sorry."

"Is that it?" Ms. Murray asked.

"That's it."

"Have you ever accused your wife of being crazy?"

"I don't know if those were the exact words, but yes."

"And did you ever accuse her of being crazy when she questioned whether you were being unfaithful to her?"

"I don't know if that's exactly how I would put it."

"How would you have put it?"

"I don't know, paranoid, you know."

"With the exception of the two *massages* and other activities that you described between July seventeenth and nineteenth of 2007, have you ever visited another woman for a massage or for any other reason that ended with a inappropriate contact, as you described earlier?

"No. Sometime around October, I did make, I had a shoulder injury and I was being treated for it. I was trying to find a therapeutic massage therapist, a legitimate one, and I did make contact with a woman. I think it was either through the Yellow Pages or it may have even been on Craigslist, where I ultimately found a legitimate massage therapist, and she stated that she was licensed. She was working out of a temporary studio. And when I went there it wasn't legitimate, and I wasn't, I was still ashamed from the activity that summer, what I had done, that I was just, you know, very, very wary that it wasn't appropriate, so I left."

"I'm going to give you another page from Avery's website," Ms. Murray said, pushing the page from Eros Guide Carolinas toward Dave slowly, so everyone had time to see it. A photo of Avery dominated the page, her blonde hair covering one eye, squatting sideways, wearing only high heels. Now do you really expect anyone, especially a judge, to believe that this lady is just a masseuse?" Her words, laced with sarcasm and disdain, held an implied threat of a contempt charge.

"No. She's obviously not just a masseuse."

"And do you see anything on this exhibit that says that she does massages?"

"It doesn't say that."

"How did you find the two ladies that you met with during the July seventeenth-to-nineteenth time period?"

"Somehow online."

"But you went to your computer with the intention of finding these types of ladies?"

"Yes."

"Had you ever done that before?"

"I had looked at websites like that before, but I never, you know, I had never acted out on it," he said, hedging, in case his web history was somewhere in the lawyer's stack of exhibits.

"And you testified that the lady we've been referring to as Avery, that you met her at her home in north Raleigh; and the other lady, where did you meet her?"

"At a hotel in Crabtree Valley."

"How did you refer to her when you met her in person? Did you call her by name; if so, what did you call her?"

"I don't recall. I think I said, 'Hello, I'm Dave.' Didn't really talk to her by name."

"Will you take a look at plaintiff's *Exhibit 13*, all four pages, please, and let me know when you're done." Dave saw "Comprehensive LITE Criminal Records Search" at the top of the page, and perused the rap sheet for Diane Diaz, the woman he knew as Avery. The first listing from 1999 read, "IDSI person less than sixteen years old." He read down the page: Statutory sexual assault. Incest. Endangering welfare of children. Indecent exposure. Contact/communication w/minor—sexual offenses. The litany repeated itself over more than two years and four pages. A wave of nausea washed over him, and he looked up again at Ms. Murray.

"Now, do you realize this lady that you met with for a massage has been charged with endangering the welfare of children, statutory sexual assault, possession of a controlled substance, corruption of minors, etcetera, etcetera?"

"Yes."

"I want to, I need to ask you again about sexual intercourse and sexual acts during certain timeframes. So it's going to sound like I'm repeating myself, but I am going to give you different time periods.

"Did you have sexual intercourse with a woman or anyone other than your wife after the date of marriage and before July 17, 2007?

"No."

"And did you have sexual intercourse with anyone other than your wife on July seventeenth, eighteenth, or nineteenth of 2007?"

"No."

"Now you realize that we know where these ladies live, and we know their real names."

"I realize that." In fact, this had not occurred on him, he'd been too rattled by the endless expositions of the past hour to consider such possibilities.

"And that we're going to take their depositions, and we're going to be asking them the same questions that we're asking you?"

"Okay. I understand."

"Have you engaged in any sexual acts with anyone other than your wife since the date of separation on December 27, 2007?"

"No."

* * * * *

Dave,

You tell me that you don't feel "safe" when I'm drinking? Do you have any idea what that does to me? I had three glasses of wine in a five-hour period, but you don't feel "safe"?

Let ME tell YOU about feeling safe . . . (and this is why I drink):

I don't feel safe communicating any of my feelings to you.

I don't feel safe telling you anything for fear of your criticism and disdain for all that I do.

I don't feel safe when you lie to me about little things.

I certainly don't feel safe about all the lies about the bigger things.

I don't feel safe knowing you've slept with prostitutes.

I don't feel safe when I look back at our marriage and realize how often you lied, how often you probably cheated, how basically everything about our marriage was a lie.

I don't feel safe when you go to work every day for fear of whom you are flirting with, leering at, or sleeping with.

I don't feel safe knowing you had porn disks at your workplace. And because of all the other lies, I don't believe your explanation of them—did he watch them with someone at work?

I don't feel safe when you go out to lunch—are you flirting with the waitress?

I don't feel safe when you travel—are you sleeping alone?

I don't feel safe when your cell phone rings and you walk out of the room to take the call—what's he hiding from me now?

I don't feel safe when you surf the net—are you looking at porn? Are my children going to see something on your computer that they shouldn't?

I don't feel safe knowing you've had a "locked-down" computer for the last fifteen years.

I don't feel safe knowing that you've never been able to share your feelings, thoughts, or secrets with me.

I don't feel safe when I think about all the things you keep from me and have kept from me.

I don't feel safe knowing that you've not told your family about our separation.

I don't feel safe knowing that you claim your story for yourself—to be told to my family when your time is right. It's my story too—I've lived it, although unknowingly, and I too have paid a heavy price because of your story.

I don't feel safe knowing your tendency to keep secrets is so deeply ingrained in you.

I don't feel safe when you emotionally and physically abandon me, when you threaten to leave me, when you insinuate that I'm not doing my job as a parent, especially in light of the fact that I've done it ALL myself up until two years ago.

I don't feel safe when you put your hand up in front of my face, when you try to silence me, when you make the motions for me to zip my lip, as in "Shut up, now."

I don't feel safe whenever I hear:

"Mara, you didn't hear me!"

"Mara, you don't remember."

"Mara, you weren't listening to me!"

"Mara, I'm going there whether you like it or not."

"Mara, why don't you do it this way?"

"Mara, I don't feel safe around you!"

"Mara, don't call me while I'm gone."

I don't feel safe when you make a major decision on something without consulting me or without asking for my opinion; and when I question you about your decision you say, "Mara, we've already discussed this!" even though you only mentioned it to me.

I don't feel safe when you are on business trips and don't call or answer my calls for days at a time.

I don't feel safe when I use the same bar of soap that you've used.

July 23, 2008

Dave sat down to write in his journal. It was one of the commitments he had made upon re-entering counseling with his therapist, Dr. Lowe; a condition Mara outlined in order to continue working on their marriage following the deposition.

July 23, 2008 marked a new beginning in my life after I thought it was actually going to be the end of my life.

I woke that day before five, experiencing a terrible anxiety attack. These attacks had become increasingly more intense over the past three days. Monday morning (21ˢᵗ) I couldn't shake some of the things Mara had said to me Sunday night. My feelings of hopelessness were at an all-time high. She was in a position to expose and embarrass me for all the horrible things I had done, take the children out of my life, and leave me without ever forgiving me.

To my dismay I couldn't stop conjuring up ways to kill myself—OD, car wreck, gun, jumping, etc. I felt as though I was in a trance. Finally, I got the courage to call Mara. I told her how I have prayed to Jesus to come into my heart. I told her the whole truth would be told to her—I promised her that. After the call, my heart felt lighter as I determined to do the right thing.

I decided to try to make a calendar for the past several years of the terrible things I had done. I tried to document all the things I was going to tell Mara, but it became an agonizing task—how many times, where, etc. I was so ashamed, but at the same time angry—why did I do these things? My self-hatred was at an all-time high. I barely slept that night, woke up at five with horrible, paralyzing anxiety.

I tried praying for inner peace, but my physical being was in control—I was trembling from head to toe, nauseous, sweating.

My mind was focused on only one thing. SUICIDE. I went through all the different methods in my mind, focusing on the ones that could possibly be ruled accidental like stepping into the path of a truck while changing a flat tire or an accidental gun discharge.

Around one, I realized I had been sitting there for almost eight hours. At this point, I was resolute on what I would do. After showering and getting dressed, I went to sit in my recliner and began to debate if I should go to my appointment with Dr. Lowe. I thought I should, but an urgency to end my life took over.

I dreaded it because I knew I would have to tell her about my disgusting behavior and my sham of a life, after going to her for so long and trying to answer the wrong questions.

After leaving my apartment, I passed the school. and recalled Mara's plan to call the bishop and see that I would not be allowed anywhere near the school or be able to volunteer for anything at the school because of my horrible actions. I began to tremble and decided to drive directly to the house, get my shotgun, and blow my head off.

When I sat down in Dr. Lowe's office I started by telling her what I did in July 2007, how I had lied in the deposition and how I've been lying for so long. I thought about the lies I had told her in therapy and said, "You know how I told you I was never abused as a kid? I told you a story about how I think someone tried something but nothing really ever happened? I lied."

Then out of nowhere, and for the first time in my life, I told her about an event that unfolded in 1976 or 1977 and has stayed with me since.

Dave wrote down his memories of the inciting incident on the Ferris wheel, and how it had trapped him in an endless cycle of sexual sin, shame, and contempt.

I know many of the things she said after I finished telling my story made sense and actually made me feel better. When I left, I couldn't believe that one hour earlier I was on my way to end my life. I slept well that night.

July 24, 2008

When I woke up Thursday my anxiety level was almost non-existent. I prayed and then decided to see our church pastor, Father John, to tell him what had happened and ask him to hear my confession. When we met at church I began to sob. I had never cried like this in my life. Slowly I got my story out. This time, however, I remembered details—images, details of surroundings, colors, and smells.

I realized that the images I had recalled to Dr. Lowe were as if I were watching a movie of an event from a close perspective, with me as the narrator. Now I was seeing through my own eyes as a child, teenager, and adult. The emotions were intense as I spoke; it felt as though the tears were coming from my heart as I sobbed deeply. Father John gave me an inspirational talk, then heard my whole confession. I could feel the Holy Spirit in the room. It was the first time I ever really and wholly participated in the sacrament.

July 25, 2008

I had an afternoon appointment with Dr. Lowe. Prior to going I found a website of an organization called SNAP, the Survivor Network of those Abused by Priests. It contained helpful information, accounts of other victims, a paper called "Survivor Wisdom," which I printed and attached to this journal. I also ordered some books from their recommended reading list; one was about stories of victims who were able to recover. The other was written for spouses of men who were abused as boys. I ordered two copies, hoping to give one to Mara.

Upon arriving at Dr. Lowe's I broke down like I had with Father John. I told her that now I was seeing the scenes as if I were in them, not as an observer. I also told her about Father Hill and the stories of abuse at St. Mike's. I began to understand how I've been trying to minimize my abuse—saying I wasn't raped, sodomized—"he just touched me,"—but she pointed out how I was terrorized.

I began to remember the Ferris wheel ride and how scared I was. "You can't tell anyone." "I'll tell your mother." He told the operator (guy who worked for my cousin) to let us stay on, three complete rides, nothing I could do to get off the ride—trapped on there.

I went into detail about the night at Pizza Hut, how he offered me beer, how I wouldn't take it. He drank two pitchers and on the way home wanted to go for a "ride." I was driving his brand new Trans Am—red turbo T-roof.

Dave sat for a long time considering what to write next. This was different from the rest of his story. Then he had been a kid of eleven or twelve. Here he was of the age of consent. Unable to admit the truth, he wrote:

I drove it straight home and got out. Mom asked me why he didn't come in. I told her he had to get back to the rectory for something. Dr. Lowe told me I was being solicited. I had never thought of it that way. I remember thinking I would have hit him if he tried to touch me.

All of the things she was saying made sense to me. I felt even more relief. She encouraged me to keep journaling and warned me that unwanted memories would start coming back. I left feeling better than when I had arrived. She wanted to make sure I was safe. I told her my plans and promised I would call her if feelings of desperation returned.

I was exhausted. I figured that I had only slept about fifteen hours in the past three days. I spoke to Mara; she was upbeat, and talking to her made me feel much better.

July 26, 2008

I awoke at five a.m. in a terrible state of anxiety. I recalled how he had touched me, looked at me, how he made me touch him, the smell, the look in his eyes.

I lay there for two hours, prayed to make the anxiety leave me. I finally was able to get out of bed and get ready. I made coffee and felt my prayers being answered. I sat on the stoop and said my prayers of gratitude.

Later I went back on the SNAP website. Reading the stories made me feel better and not so lonely.

July 27, 2008

I slept! I was looking forward to going to 11:15 Mass, praying Father John would say the Mass; he did. I heard the prayer with a high level of clarity. I got emotional three to four times, but choked it back. I was debating about going to Communion, but remembered that I had confessed and knew I needed Jesus inside me.

I saw Father John afterward and we hugged. I almost started to cry; I felt so good after.

I decided to go to the house and start cleaning the garage. It was hard, so many reminders of the recent past. It struck me that the garage represented my life: a mess. I began to feel physically ill, but forced myself to continue. Pledged to get it cleaned out and organized before Mara returned. I threw away eight or nine bags of garbage and felt a small measure of accomplishment.

I spoke with Mara and had an emotional moment when I shared the garage analogy. I forced myself to eat. I wasn't hungry, although I hadn't eaten all day. I reflected on how I felt after church; I said prayers of gratitude and healing. I can only hope to recover and that Mara will forgive me.

That night in bed I remembered Mr. Lark and the "graduation dinner." I began to get angry.

The same thought recurred to him:

Was there a "club" and my name was on some list? My thoughts turned to if and how I should report him. I couldn't have been the only one?

July 28, 2008

I researched the timing of when I had dispensed the drug to Father Jimmy. When I saw his name on the prescription I had verified it was really him. I remember feeling sick, going to my car and crying. I realized that after this my performance and attitude came into question by Connie. Soon after, I began to pursue employment with Donovin.

I discussed all of this with Dr. Lowe. We talked about how this may have been "running." After starting at Donovin I don't recall thinking of this again. The move to Louisiana was supposed to be the beginning of a new life far away.

I am overwhelmed with guilt over what I did to Mara and my family. I prayed and then decided to go for bike ride. I felt good afterward, even with my second flat tire. I was tired and went to bed.

July 29, 2008

No Dr. Lowe today. I went to work and was very engaged. Mara and I talked about pain and forgiveness. I am realizing how events impacted our relationship, how I acted and was so wrong, how if I had only been able to be honest with myself. . . . I wasn't right for so long and I knew it.

One of the books came and I was able to read and semi-comprehend the words. Somehow I have a new perspective and hope that I can get myself right. The book makes great sense of my actions. Realizing how terrible they were hurts deeply, but I have confidence that by exposing that part of me I have been reborn.

Writing the journal makes me feel better. I ate a whole pizza for dinner.

July 30, 2008

I woke easily and had no bad dreams. I got ready and went to work. On the way I remembered that one week ago I was spending the whole morning planning my end. Thank you, God, for saving me.

I was busy at work again. Saw Dr. Lowe at two. We continued to discuss the manifestation of my "shock" event and some specific occurrences that I continue to remember. The phenomenon of "dissociation" continues to amaze me, how I became a spectator to my actions, unable to stop myself, and hating that part of me afterward. We talked about stress and the chain of events that sent me further into a downward spiral.

It is becoming easier to talk about, and I left encouraged. Dr. Lowe points out my discoveries and awakening. She says how important it is to accept what happened and how to handle it as part of my recovery and healing.

We talked at length about how to open up to Mara, and how to understand the effect it may have on her. I am so anxious to get up to Michigan tomorrow and see her and hold her, and to share what I have been denying for most of my life. I miss the kids SO much and can't wait to hug and kiss them.

Finished laundry, packed and paid bills. I am going to bed. I pray for inner peace. I pray for my children that nothing will harm them in their lives. I pray I can be a good father, and I say my prayer of gratitude for Mara saving my life.

July 31, 2008

I knew when I woke up today it would be a challenging day. I was nervous to see Mara and the kids. This would be the first time since the awakening of awful memories.

I flew to Michigan. When I arrived I was so happy to see the kids at the airport, so happy to be alive. I could sense Mara's anxiety.

We returned to the house, and she and I went to the beach. I said what I had practiced so many times, but it didn't seem to come out the way I thought it would. As she should be, Mara was upset. I deserved it all and more. I don't deserve the understanding she has given me, but I am thankful for it. The pain of my experience tore at me, but not as much as the pain I have for hurting her.

I know self-hatred has to be dealt with and turned to self-understanding. We continued to talk on the deck about Father Jimmy and Mr. Lark. Mara was surprisingly familiar with clergy abuse.

She took the three older kids to an overnighter and packed her things to stay at her sister's. I felt so sad and lonely when she pulled away, but Stephen and Annie quickly got my attention, and we went to the beach to play. We built a road system for their trucks. As fun as it was, the pain lingered as I felt all the regret for not taking control of my life and for what this has done to them.

I am constantly reminding myself that this is a new beginning, and I will never do anything to harm them or Mara again. We ate dinner, and then went to the beach for s'mores. The sunset made me cry. When we got back to the house a voicemail from Mara raised my spirits like only she can.

We are going to bed. Again I pray my prayers of gratitude, my prayers for forgiveness, and my prayers that I can get through all of this and be the person God created and intended me to be.

August 1, 2008

I slept until eight this morning with Stephen and Annie kicking me all night. I had energy when I woke and did a bunch of chores. I made an effort to make things just right around the house. I talked to Mara, and she said she'd bring the kids back by car so I didn't have to pick them up by boat. I was glad to hear the kindness in her voice.

Before we hung up she asked me a series of explicit questions about my transgressions. Another anxiety attack began, but I was able to control it with focus and breathing.

Harbor Days was fun for the kids and I loved watching them enjoy the games. We went to lunch and then to the rides. When I saw the Ferris wheel, I could only think of the safety of the children and we all stayed together (to their objections).

The sight of the Ferris wheel evoked Dave's memory of another incident with Father Jimmy, the event in the McDonald's parking lot. As he relived the sights, sounds, and smells of that day he felt a constriction of his breathing, only this time it wasn't a panic attack; it was being done to him. Father Jimmy had his hand on Dave's throat. He had forgotten all about that. He wrote,

> *I realized with clarity and no anxiety why I don't like my throat touched (right hand pinning me to seat of the car).*
>
> *I spoke again with Mara, and she was more agitated than before. I decided to go check on her and the kids. I found her going through my phone (I had given it to Margaret to use in case of emergency). I have nothing to hide and will show her everything, but I took some verbal abuse for about twenty minutes. I knew I needed to get back to the other kids. I'm so sad and hurting, but at the same time I am better able to stay calm, accepting the truth and making it good enough. No more will I look at it any other way.*
>
> *I put the kids to bed and asked God for his strength. Now I am going to bed. I will make arrangements to stay somewhere else tomorrow and let Mara stay here. She is right; it isn't fair that she has to be the one to leave.*

August 2, 2008

Magpie stayed with Mara at her sister's, and I woke at 3 a.m., and then again at 7. My heart was heavy with

*the pain I have caused Mara. I had my coffee (miss the
flavor of the machine from home).*

*I was surprised when Caleb woke up at 8:30. He
and I sat on the sofa, shared a throw and talked. He
was talkative, and that made me feel good. We talked
about school, guitar, lacrosse, and the fish! He asked me
to make him chocolate-chip pancakes and I obliged. I
was happy to feel our bond again. Stephen woke up next,
then the girls.*

*I started trying to call Mara at ten and stayed busy
between tries. I was so afraid she didn't want to talk
with me. Caleb went to play, and I took the three youngest to the beach while I looked at the sailboat. I wanted
to fix it so Mara could use it before she left.*

*As I was checking my phone to see if she called, Mara
appeared over the dune. She wanted to talk and we sat
on the lower deck. I was paralyzed with shame and guilt
and couldn't find the right words. I wanted to express my
sorrow, shame, and guilt, but I don't think I did.*

*We talked some more but words weren't working for
me. Mara was getting ready to leave and she asked for
a kiss. We embraced, and she turned to leave. I broke
down. I felt a rush of hurt inside that I couldn't control.
I am SO SORRY and glad that I can feel that.*

Dave knew he could have been more forthcoming with
Mara; why was it so hard for him to say "I'm sorry"? Mara had
asked about his mother and why he never told his parents what
was going on. Dave recalled the story of the scholarship and
recounted it to Mara, this time with anger that his parents had
found the money to donate a pew to the church rather than

toward his education, a decision that had subjected him to Father Jimmy once again.

> For the first time, I shared how I began to resent my parents for not giving me a true "safe" place.
>
> Mara and the kids left for a party, so I went to work cutting grass and cleaning up. I felt good about the work. Margaret surprised me; she was setting up a scavenger hunt and was planting a clue on the swing. She told me she loved me, and I got emotional again.
>
> How blessed am I to have such a beautiful daughter to give me love when I feel so badly about what I did? God's grace!
>
> Later I went for a sail. I said prayers of gratitude for the beauty of the water and the grace of God that has been bestowed upon me. I came back, cooked, and ate two cheeseburgers, and decided to finish my journal in case the kids wanted to go by boat to see the Harbor Days fireworks later. In case they don't, I've readied a fire. I hope Mara has a peaceful night, and I pray for our family and us both.

August 3, 2008

> It was 8:50, and I realized Mass was at ten. I got the kids up, fed them breakfast and got dressed. We made it to the church on time, and there were six seats in the front row. The gospel was about the feeding of the 5,000 with five loaves and two fish. I looked at the banner behind the altar and saw the image as symbolic of our family: five loaves + two fish.

I was reminded of how I had once told Mara that God must have a special plan for me. At the time I knew how fortunate I was, despite all of my sinful ways. Now I'm thinking that this journey and my awakening are going to lead me to wholeness; I really mean allow me the opportunity to be a true follower of Christ and child of God.

After coming home and making lunch, the kids and I went to the beach. Finally, after not hearing from Mara, I walked down the beach and found her sitting in front of her sister's house reading the book I gave her. She was in a good mood and seemed positive about the book.

The kids were restless, so I rounded them up and we went to fuel the boat. We anchored and went exploring. The kids and I all had fun.

I felt at peace, said my prayers, and went to bed. Although I hope otherwise, I know that we may never be together, which hurts deeply. I can only continue to do what's right and get myself healed, but nothing can happen until I make that happen first.

August 4, 2008

Dave was scheduled to fly out in early afternoon. He wanted to see Mara before he left, hoping she would see his remorse and his commitment to make things right. If only she would say something, anything, to give him some hope of restoring their marriage. But it wasn't to be.

Instead, she had seemed anxious and short with her words, her anger still apparent. She refused to stay at the house the entire time he was there. Aside from the one kiss, she had acted repulsed by him, pulling away any time he even tried to touch her hand or shoulder.

Now, as he prepared to leave, Dave prayed Mara would show up, tell him she still loved him and that she wanted to work on rebuilding their life together. His phone rang; it was her. But she only wanted to know what time he was leaving, saying she had to pack her things and would talk to him when they were all back in North Carolina.

While waiting for a cab to take him to the airport, Dave wrote a letter to Mara in his journal—a letter she'd never receive.

Dear Mara,

Today the feeling of hopelessness never left me, and now it is proving to be real. I am so sorry and I want you to know that no matter what you say to me, I can't possibly feel worse than I already do.

The shame and guilt are overwhelming. The anxiety I live with probably will never leave. I want you to know that I never did the things I did because of you.

Yes, I treated you poorly, but in some ways I'd like to think that I tried to treat you as you deserved more often than I hurt you.

Please know that I mean it when I said I will do no more harm. I pray that I can keep my pledge to God that I will not do anything more to hurt you or the kids again.

With my deepest love,
Dave

CHAPTER 8

King of the Selfie

For I am convinced that neither death, nor life, nor
angels, nor principalities, nor things present, nor
things to come, nor powers, nor height, nor depth,
nor any other created thing, will be able to separate
us from the love of God, which is in Christ Jesus
our Lord.

Romans 8:38–39

March 27, 2009
Durham, North Carolina

It was rare to see lights on at the company headquarters this
late, and even more rare that the light would be coming from
Dave's office. As he slid behind his desk, he glimpsed his
phone; another missed call from Matthew, but still nothing
from Mara.

He stared at one of the photos he had just removed from
the cork board behind his desk. It was a photo he had taken of
himself—wide smile, squinting eyes, his face slightly puffy from
too much rich food and too many cocktails, his hair cropped so
close it never needed combing, and the V-neck tee that camou-
flaged him as a typical suburban dad.

For years he had made a habit—no, an art—of taking photos of himself on disposable cameras left unattended at social events. This one was from the company's first trade show. At the time, he and his partners rode on adrenaline and ego, the rocket fuel of many startups. They were confident their technology would change the world; that giddy cockiness was visible in his smile that day. How many like it were preserved in photo albums of friends and strangers from high school, college, and myriad weddings he and Mara had attended over the years? David smiled ruefully to himself at the thought.

He placed the snapshot in the cardboard box beside his desk, along with a stack of other pictures taken during his tenure: The epic paintball war. Vegas trade shows. "Strategy sessions" with glasses lifted high. Meeting former president George H. W. Bush at an industry event.

Other than his children, this company was his crowning achievement. It had made him a millionaire for a second time, yet not to the extent he had imagined.

Even before the ink was dry on the acquisition agreement, however, he had found himself ushered into a new, somewhat marginalized R&D role. He had done his best to embrace the positive aspects of the opportunity, including fewer demands on his time and less pressure.

Even as the rest of his life spun out of control, work provided a rare haven. It was one place where he still liked the way others saw him—smart and credible as one of the only pharmacists on staff, witty and compassionate in how he engaged employees, and an effective leader who set direction without micromanaging execution.

Or so he'd thought until today. He reflected on his surprise meeting earlier that afternoon with the vice president of human resources.

"Dave, as we looked for places to drive efficiencies, we were forced to take a hard look at your R&D project," the man he had helped to hire had said. "Quite frankly, Dave, management views the project as a bit of a cash suck at this point. The inability to provide a launch timeframe for last week's board meeting kind of put a nail in the coffin of this thing. At about the same time it came to my attention that your contract was up for renewal. And, well, I'm sure you can understand how, as difficult as it is, this makes sense for the business. The best interest of the company is to reallocate cash into, uh, revenue-generating activities."

Dave had sat silent. He was shocked and dumbfounded.

The suit in front of him magically slid a separation agreement from a manila folder poised on the corner of the desk.

Dazed, Dave glanced unseeing at the document, trying in vain to decipher the words on the page. On page two, he saw that his sizable stipend would end in two weeks.

Two weeks.

His heart skipped a beat; he was running out of cash.

"My attorney will need to review this contract, of course." Dave fought to maintain composure while he scanned the document for other potential bombshells. "I mean, this is pretty abrupt. I think it makes sense to allow a couple of months to wind the project down. Don't you agree?" He laid the agreement down on the desk and looked at the unflinching exec.

"Dave, your attorneys are with the company's firm, so not only are they on board, but they'd be in a conflict-of-interest situation to offer you counsel. If you decide to go that route, you'll need to seek outside counsel.

"The bottom line is that this agreement is valid for three business days. If a signed copy is not returned by Monday, this offer goes off the table. While we certainly respect your position as a cofounder, legally at this point you're an independent contractor; so you don't have true employee rights.

"Listen, Dave, I know this is tough, I assure you it's nothing personal. If cash is a concern—"

"No, no," Dave interrupted. "It's not like that. I'm fine. I'll be fine." He pushed himself out of the chair. His legs felt like jelly. "Okay, well, I'm going to get my things together, I guess . . . while no one's here."

"Dave, remember, I will need your signed agreement by Monday." Dave had reluctantly taken the document and headed for his office.

Now here he sat, alone, dusk dimming the familiar space. He was scheduled to undergo a second shoulder surgery on Monday. At least he still had health insurance; he'd better reread the agreement to make sure. From his desk, the severance folder stared at him like a betrayer, and a wave of nausea washed over him.

He felt tired, so tired. Was it really just a week ago that Mara had found out about the money? He'd gotten a notice that two hundred thousand dollars had been withdrawn against the second mortgage he'd taken on the cottage. He'd called her, furious.

"What do you think you're doing, Mara?"

"My lawyers advised me to do it. They're asking a lot of questions about our finances that I can't answer. Where'd all the money go, Dave?"

"What do you mean?"

"I mean where did all the money go? Our bank accounts don't have nearly what they should. What did you do with all of it?"

"There is no money." He stated the truth flatly.

Silence.

"Sorry I let you down." It was the only thing he could think to say. She'd hung up on him without a word.

Now he began to count his losses; they streamed through his consciousness like grimy black sheep.

His wife.

His fortune—gone in less than five years. In fact, he'd leveraged the houses and other assets, so he was negative to some number he'd not had the fortitude to calculate.

His friends—he'd lost them one by one, as his lies demanded ever-increasing secrecy and isolation.

His business. He'd been a cofounder. He'd been on the inside. Yet as of today he was firmly on the outside, a "former" member.

As he tallied it, his life was a total loss. And he was a complete loser.

Following the humiliation of the deposition last summer, Dave had vowed to stop the escorts, the drinking, the porn, all of it. But his resolve lasted only a few weeks. Soon after, he'd found himself right back where he'd started, and even worse off. He had drained the last of his reserves, as well as everything and everyone around him, all to hide the disgusting things he had done and continued doing—as recently as yesterday.

He was hopelessly enslaved to his denial.

If anyone who still claimed to love him had any idea who and what he really was, they would despise him as much as he despised himself. Much like Mara did now. He couldn't forgive himself any more than he could stop himself.

With every passing minute, he became more convinced: He couldn't live this way any longer. The familiar voice re-emerged in his mind, whispering the last remaining path out of the pain, the one he had fought so hard to ignore, but that persistently re-emerged, sure to succeed where the others had failed . . . *suicide*.

Dave packed a few more belongings in the cardboard boxes. He removed the wedding photo Mara had framed for him, insisting he display it prominently in his office. He took down the photos she'd had framed of the kids, along with drawings they had made at school, and of course, the requisite "#1 Dad" Father's Day card.

Next he sat back behind his desk and reached into the very recesses of his bottom drawer, removing a handful of DVDs. His agitation grew as he shoved them into the bottom of the box with disdain. Dave stood up, abandoning the task, grabbed the single box, and left the office.

When he returned to his rental house, he went straight to the kitchen, retrieved the large bottle of Grey Goose vodka from the freezer, and poured himself a martini. The drink was a martini only by the Y-shaped glass he used; the contents were straight vodka. He downed it standing at the counter and then poured another. He took a pain pill for his shoulder, which was throbbing from the stress of the afternoon.

Dave grabbed leftover takeout from the fridge and reheated it in the microwave. Martini in hand, he made his way to the sleek, lime-green recliner Mara had given him for his birthday during better days. Sitting on the side table was *Out of the Shadows*, a book about sexual addiction his therapist had recommended, and the first thing he'd read on the topic that resonated. He paged through it while he ate, rereading some of the passages he had highlighted.

> [Sexual] addiction taps into the most fundamental human processes. . . . The central losses are the addict's values and relationships. The phenomenon of

multiple addictions is not surprising given the nature of addiction . . . overwork and alcoholism are often part of the addict's life.[1]

Well, at least work wouldn't be a problem now, he thought sardonically. He flipped back a few pages.

A moment comes for every addict when the consequences are so great or the pain is so bad that the addict admits life is out of control because of his or her sexual behavior.

Millions read the steamy news accounts and, despite their own prurience, make severe judgments about people . . . who visit prostitutes, who commit homosexual acts in public toilets, or even who have affairs. A smaller audience—but much larger than most imagine—read each line fearing that the same public exposure could happen to them and judging themselves with the same unforgiving standards the public uses.[2]

Dave recoiled as he recalled the panic attack he experienced the morning after the Eliot Spitzer story had broken last year. He reread the clipping he kept tucked in the front cover of the book.

The $4,000 question in the Eliot Spitzer case: Why did he do it? Spitzer, alias 'Client 9' to authorities, resigned after he was caught on a federal wiretap discussing payments and arranging to meet a prostitute in a Washington hotel room in February. The adultery in these times is not as scandalous as the hypocrisy, incongruity, and self-destructive recklessness of it all.[3]

The writer's searing analysis struck a nerve. The similarities were haunting. He had looked futilely for answers in that article and many others that he clipped and read compulsively.

It was just four months after the Spitzer case that Mara had deposed him, using similar email evidence to expose his secrets. A few weeks later, US Senator Debbie Stabenow publicly acknowledged that her husband, Tom Allen, had paid a prostitute one hundred and fifty dollars for sex in a Troy, Michigan, hotel. Privately Dave had taken pride in not being as "cheap" as Allen with the escorts he'd found during his family's vacations in Michigan.

He swigged the last of his drink and slouched in his chair, as his shoulder continued its rhythmic throb, dulled by the medication and alcohol, yet still inflicting its just punishment for his many sins.

For years he had tried to convince himself that all the secrecy was to protect Mara and the kids. As his addiction progressed, however, self-preservation became an all-consuming taskmaster, usurping his energy and ability to see beyond himself to the deep pain and need of those he loved.

Dave stared out the window at the darkening sky. It was almost night.

A wave of vertigo crashed over him, and suddenly he found himself back on the Ferris wheel. He'd never left. He could see that now. Each consequence since that fateful day had taken a seat over time like so many grim passengers on a never-ending cycle of abuse, contempt, and shame. Denial kept it all locked in place, spinning around and around, increasingly out of control, until, Dave realized, terror gripping him, it was on the verge of derailing altogether.

He sought desperately for some way to stop the madness. He tried to envision coming clean, completely clean, with Mara.

He would have to confess everything. Would she understand, or would she find him even more disgusting and contemptible than she already did? Maybe she would use the truth against him to keep him from the children.

His children. They were the only good things he'd managed not to lose. If not for them, he would have ended it all last summer following the deep humiliation of that deposition. He recalled their last outing together, how their laughter, hugs, and joy filled so much of the emptiness inside him. How often over the past few years it had been just enough to keep him going. His love for them flooded him as tears flowed down his cheeks.

Even if he could persuade Mara, the coming financial melt-down would be swift and severe. His monthly stipend was less than his monthly debt service on the houses, the cars, the equity loans, and other obligations. Having already leveraged both houses, he was without a safety net. He would have to file for bankruptcy.

A millionaire at thirty-five. Now broke . . . and broken. How could he face a community who saw him as something he clearly was not, and never would be again? He would be the talk of the town, but this time for all the wrong reasons.

Face it, Dave. It's hopeless. You're hopeless—a bad investment.

He closed his eyes. As the pain medication worked its way through his system, intensified by the alcohol, he could feel his physical pain dissipate. Or was it simply dwarfed by his insurmountable emotional and psychological suffering?

Tonight all was still, but tomorrow was an abyss he would be forced to step into, and every remaining day a free fall. There would be no light with the dawn this time. Only darkness.

Dave wished he could see some way out, for his children's sake. But now the whisper was gaining power, pointing seductively toward the only remedy for his pain.

Suicide.

He tried it on and this time, unlike in the past, it fit. He could feel it. Escape. Rest. Relief.

He had fantasized about it many times over the years, whenever the shame and regret threatened to pull him under. Back then, there had been areas of relief—the business, his expensive hobbies and lifestyle. Now things were different. There was nowhere else to turn for comfort.

He began strategizing, enjoying having his sense of control restored. Each time he played it out in his head, he grew calmer. Resolve took hold, and Dave could feel his spirits lift. He had a plan. Relief was around the corner.

He glanced at his watch and was shocked that nearly three hours had passed.

Fatigue swept over him, and he slept soundly until dawn.

Dave awoke with horrible, paralyzing anxiety. He felt ashamed, but even more, he felt so angry. Self-hatred battered him like waves upon the rocks. He tried praying for inner peace, but he was in agony. He trembled from head to toe, sweating through his clothes. As nausea ripped through his insides, he fought to keep from throwing up. He pushed back in his recliner, tears running down his temples.

The pain would be over soon, he reminded himself.

As the morning's attack of renegade adrenaline waned, Dave pushed his chair into a seated position and eased himself up with his good arm. He headed to the kitchen for pain medication, so he could shower and head out to get the kids.

After all, it would be his final outing with them.

* * * * *

On Sunday morning he left a message cancelling his Monday therapy appointment.

"Hi Dr. Lowe, it's Dave Wagner. The weekend went well. We had a lot of fun with the kids, stayed busy, and actually had a really good time, so I'm doing okay. I realized I have a conflict for our appointment tomorrow because I'm scheduled for that endoscopy on my shoulder. I will need to reschedule."

Dave was pretty sure this was the first time he had avoided a late-cancel fee in his eight months of therapy; he smirked at the irony. He hung up the phone and sat down at his kitchen table to review his plan one final time.

His shoulder surgery was scheduled for Monday morning. Mara had agreed to drive him—although he'd had to guilt her into it. Afterward, she would bring him back to his rental house to recover alone.

The end was close. The thought infused him with a rare calm.

* * * * *

Dave showered and then waited for Mara. He sat on the stoop outside in the waning darkness of the morning so she wouldn't have to get out of her car. He wondered if she had ever noticed or appreciated the little things he did like this to show her consideration. Mara pulled up at seven, right on time.

Dave got in on the passenger side. "Good morning. Thanks for taking me, Mara."

"It's fine." She sipped her coffee.

An hour later, Dave donned a nondescript hospital gown and lay in one of the outpatient surgery center's gurneys. Mara sat in the chair beside him.

"Good morning," the nurse said, pushing back the curtain. "I'm Nancy, and I'll be your nurse for this morning's procedure. Can you confirm what we are operating on today please?"

"My right shoulder."

"And have you had anything to eat or drink since midnight?"

"No."

"Have you been tested for Hepatitis?"

"Yes."

"Have you been tested for HIV?"

"Yes."

"Both tests were negative?"

"Yes."

After a few additional questions, the nurse began to prep him for anesthesia, detailing the morning's schedule as she did so.

Dave turned to Mara. "If anything happens to me, call Vince Romano." Vince was an old college friend and an attorney.

"What are you worried about, Dave? The procedure or the recovery? You've done this before."

"I'm tired of living in a shell."

Dave registered the confusion on Mara's face.

At least he had gotten these points across to her without raising too much suspicion. He closed his heavy eyelids and dozed off. A few minutes later the medical team came in and wheeled him to the operating room. The anesthesia was kicking in and he began floating away. *Is this how it will feel?*

The surgery took an hour, he was told. After another hour, Dave had been cleared to go home, and Mara walked him to the car. Still groggy from the anesthesia, he mostly slept on the ride home. When they got back to his house, Mara offered to make him lunch.

"No, it's okay. I have to go to the grocery store later. I don't have any food."

Acting put off by his rejection, Mara coolly grabbed her things.

"I'll check in later, Dave." She spoke without looking up, fishing for her keys in her purse. "Remember we have lunch tomorrow."

He nodded.

"And we still need to talk about your plans with the kids for Easter. It falls on your birthday this year, you know? They get out early on Holy Thursday for Easter break. I'll let you know what time, okay? All right. Call you later."

Dave pushed his recliner back and immediately fell asleep. He woke up hungry and padded into the kitchen. His cell phone rang on the counter as he stared into the near-empty refrigerator.

"Hello." He opened an otherwise-empty cabinet and removed bread with its wrapper twisted and tucked under the loaf, a shortcut that had always peeved his wife.

"Hey, I just wanted to see how you're doing." It was Mara.

"So far, so good." He tossed the bread in the toaster to mask its staleness.

"Did I wake you?"

"No, not at all. I'm just making a sandwich."

"A sandwich? I thought you said you . . . I would have done that for you, Dave. Okay, well, you should have food in your stomach. I'll see you tomorrow, okay?"

"Okay, Mara. Love you. Goodbye."

After Dave ate, he rinsed his plate and left it in the sink, then wiped down the counter and headed to the bedroom to sleep off the anesthesia. Even though it was far more comfortable than the recliner, sleeping in his bed made him feel alone. When he awoke, it was dusk. The room and its sparse furnishings were cast in black and white, and shadows crossed the hardwood floor.

With a subdued sense of calm, Dave reviewed his plan once more. Anxiety, his constant companion, had disappeared. For this small blessing he offered a quick prayer of gratitude.

He leaned over and switched on the lamp. He picked up the bottle of pain pills from the nightstand; he wanted to stay well ahead of the pain. It sat atop two books, *Out of the Shadows* and *When the Man You Love Has Been Abused*. He had meant to give that one to Mara, but had never quite gotten up his nerve.

In the bathroom, he washed his face and brushed his teeth. Next he removed his watch and laid it on the counter beside his cell phone and wallet. He stared in the mirror for a long moment. From the outside, he looked like the same old David, a few wisps of gray hair at his temples, slight crinkles at the corners of his eyes, but with a hint of boyishness still visible.

How could it be, he wondered, that this shell of humanity he'd been given could betray so little of the devastation inside?

He flipped on the backyard lights and began hauling in firewood, one log at a time using his good arm, until he had enough to build a decent fire. After inserting a starter log into the center of the stack, Dave held a lit match to it until it caught.

Meanwhile, he retrieved the leaf blower from the garage. Dave had always taken good care of his equipment and tools—everything in its place and well maintained. He checked the gas level in the blower. Nearly full. He set it by the closet across from the entry to the garage.

He walked to the kitchen and poured some vodka, then capped the bottle and slung it under his good arm so he could carry both it and the glass into the living room. He sat down on the couch, staring at the fire and refilling his glass until the vodka bottle was empty. As he stood, he nearly lost his balance. He staggered to the bedroom and stashed the empty bottle in his dirty clothes hamper.

Back in the family room, the fire burned well now. Although it was a little late in the season for a fire, Dave determined it was unlikely to attract the neighbors' attention. He yanked his throw rug closer to the brick hearth, and then used the stoker to pull a couple logs loose. Two fell out of the fireplace, landing close to the rug.

If the rug caught on fire eventually and spread to the couch, he had reasoned, it would help make his death look accidental. It might appear he had gotten confused and turned the wrong way when looking for the exit.

It was time.

Dave opened the closet across from the garage entry door. He had settled on this plan because it was quick and painless. He started the leaf blower and stepped inside, pulling it into the tiny space with him. The motor's hum was deafening. He leaned back against the door and slid slowly to the floor.

The alcohol and medication had done the job of dulling his senses and his flight instinct, but nonetheless Dave's breathing quickened as reality took hold. He tried to focus on slow, deep breaths—deeper and deeper, to hasten the carbon monoxide's effect.

Even in this cramped space, Dave felt more free than he had in years. Free of the shell he had hidden behind for as long as he could remember. Free of shame. Free of self-hatred. Now, there was only an expanding sense of peace and calm in the midst of sadness that it had to be this way.

Images emerged in his mind's eye. Faces and moments, like pages in a scrapbook, rich with laughter, joy, and love. His mother and father, his brothers and sisters. Untarnished memories of growing up.

Now it was the day he met his wife and first declared he was going to marry her. Now, their wedding day. He once again welcomed each of his children into the world. Felt his overwhelming love for them, free of guilt. Next, a panorama of moments around the dinner table. Playing on the beach. Gathered around the bonfire, laughing. Worshipping together in church.

The images floated away as gently as they had come. As he released each of them, he released the pain, the sadness. What remained was only a strong desire for rest. He yielded to it.

As David had done all his life, before he slept, he prayed.

He prayed for his children, that nothing would harm them in their lives.

He prayed for peace.

He prayed that death would not be painful for him or for anyone else.

For all the ways I have harmed others, I ask for forgiveness. For all the ways I have been harmed by others, I offer forgiveness.

AFTERWORD

Search me, O God, and know my heart; test me and
know my anxious thoughts. See if there is any offen-
sive way in me and lead me in the way everlasting.

Psalm 139:23–24

This is Mara.

When Dave didn't show up for Margaret's soccer game, I
started trying to locate him. I drove to his rental house. I was
terrified of what he would do if he found me there. I discovered
his wallet, cell phone, and watch lined up neatly on the bathroom counter. His car and bike were in the garage. I saw remnants of the fire and found the vodka in the hamper. . . . Deep
inside I knew something was horribly wrong, but mercifully, I
did not find him.

Growing increasingly frantic, I called 9-1-1. The police
came and searched the house until they located his body.
When they brought him out in a body bag, I longed to see
him and hold him one more time, but the police would not
allow it.

My friend, Maria, met me at home. Someone else was picking up my children from school. I will never forget what Maria
said to me: "The next hour is the most important of your life.
You have to tell your children that their dad is dead." From that
moment on, it was all about my children.

I would like to tell you I grieved like Jackie Kennedy; dignified, regal, beautiful in her pain. I didn't. My grief was ugly, excruciating, anger-filled, and lasted well beyond what is appropriate in polite circles. I remained entrenched in a cycle of pain that would push all but a few people away from me and my kids as if it had centrifugal force.

Within days of Dave's burial, the consequences he died to escape began rolling in like a tidal wave, displacing my initial grief with anger. I had known about a few of the prostitutes, but I had no idea the extent or cost of Dave's addictions. I had known that he borrowed against our Michigan home, but I'd later learn he'd been living off that cash to survive. I didn't know that he'd been severed from his company until I found the letter among his things.

Every aspect of our lives unraveled swiftly and thoroughly. First his truck was repossessed. Then our North Carolina home was listed for short sale to avoid foreclosure. I had to go back into his rental house, pay off his lease, move his things out, and sell them. Some wonderful friends helped me get through all this; others, who I thought were my friends, took advantage of me. For example, one friend from church offered to sell the contents of my storage unit; he never gave me the money. Many of our things went missing during this time, but I was too blinded by my pain to see or care.

The cash I had taken at my attorney's suggestion, along with the sale of some stock, were all I had to live on for the next five years, and much of it was consumed by attorneys' fees and creditors. Dave left a small life insurance policy, which was put in a trust for the children.

The kids and I entered bereavement counseling. Everything they tell you not to do in the first year of grief, we were forced to do. We left our home in North Carolina and moved to my hometown in Michigan. We lost our vehicles, our belongings, our friends, our school, and our church community—everything about our lives *before*.

No Justice

I submitted the evidence of David's abuse to his home diocese, including his journal entries and medical records. I traveled there a few months later to participate in a hearing. The accused priest was proven to have served in the parish at the time the alleged abuse occurred. Ultimately, he was removed from service, but remained a priest and continued to receive financial support from the diocese.

The mere act of speaking out on behalf of David's suffering, as well as the suffering my children and I endured as a result of his abuse, was an important first step in our healing process, regardless of the outcome.

What Am I Not?

While Dave was alive, the question that drove me to the brink was "What am I not?" *Yeah, I'll get a boob job. I'll make sure our kids are clean, dressed cute. I'll volunteer. I'll make you look good.* Yet none of it was ever enough to win his love. *What am I not?*

Slowly I began to see that Dave and I had been trapped in a cycle of abuse, enablement, and codependency, a cycle that his death ended as abruptly as a high-speed collision into a brick wall. I became consumed by my anger—all I could focus on were his wrongdoings.

I would remind myself to focus on how the kids were feeling, but meanwhile I continued raging against him. My mind became my worst enemy, endlessly recounting the prostitutes, the wasted money, the cruel things he had said to me. I spent years reliving a nightmare I hadn't fully understood I was trapped in until he died.

My drinking started to become a problem as our marriage was falling apart; now it took hold with a vengeance. *It blocks this. It blocks that. I won't feel it. I don't have to deal with it. I don't have to live the next three hours.*

My family staged an intervention and sent me to an inpatient rehabilitation facility for six weeks. My children, reeling with grief over the loss of their dad, now had their fear and sadness compounded by being separated from me. Abandonment is one of the lingering issues that haunts them to this day. The in patient program was a complete and utter disaster; in fact, I believe it exacerbated my addiction, heaping fuel on the fire of my already consuming feelings of powerlessness, resentment, and victimization.

I Was Right.

As the years unfolded, the only reason I wished Dave was still alive was so I could tell him, "I was right and you were wrong."

"I'm ashamed of you," he used to tell me. Or, "How could you think that?"

"You're psycho."

"You're overreacting."

All the things he used to say to me, I now longed to scream back at him. I wanted him to be alive because I was right; I just hadn't known it until he died.

Ultimately my own journey through addiction has given me sympathy for Dave. Now I can relate. They say in Alcoholics Anonymous, "Don't take that first drink," because alcoholics can't stop. I now see how it is the same for the guy who gets online to look at porn; after a while, that's no longer enough, so he goes to a prostitute. It just keeps escalating; all the sneaking, the driving around, the money, the time.

A Good Mom

Whatever it cost me personally, I stood up and took care of my children.

I walked the walk. You can't raise a salutatorian by being a drunk. My oldest daughter was class president and won a pageant scholarship with her poise and manners and accolades. My other daughter was a state skiing champion and the youngest player on her varsity soccer team. She couldn't have done all that if her mom was just a drunk.

My younger son is an incredible musician; he's in marching band; he played varsity golf as a freshman; he served on Michigan Youth in Government. My youngest daughter plays soccer, participated in the junior pageant, and is an outstanding student. They've all overcome a lot, and I did my best to ensure they always had what they needed, especially my love.

Even on my worst days, my kids came home from school to a family dinner; it was only afterward that I'd drink, fall asleep, and pass out.

I didn't just attend their ski meets, I rode the bus to every practice and competition. I never missed a soccer game. I did it all . . . until I didn't want to do it anymore.

Then I would go to the soccer games and feel so alone. Every other mom and dad were there together—at least it felt that way to me. I'd drive to the away games alone. As the kids grew into teenagers, it got harder to do things as a family; now we had three varsity soccer games instead of one. I began to resent it. I didn't set boundaries. It took the joy out of what I was doing.

Last year was the first time I missed one of my kids' events because of drinking. It was in March, two months before my DUI. I didn't want to be there for my youngest; I just wanted to stay home and drink. I was so tired.

No Aha! Moments

Since that time, things have been getting better, slowly. When I got stopped for the DUI, all I could say was, "My kids, my kids, my kids." That night I had an encounter with God, as many people do sitting in a jail cell—how cliché! As I was being eaten up by anxiety and worry over my children, I heard God's Spirit speak to my heart: *What difference does it make if you are sitting in this jail cell or passed out in the next room?*

That was the beginning of my journey to recovery and wholeness. It's not been about one aha! moment. I've relapsed. But now my fear—of the disease, of the hard work, of jail—has left me. I fear it for my kids, but not for myself. Last Saturday I thought, "God, I know you have given me great gifts. I have the gift of intuition and the gift of strength. I'm a strong person. Why can't this be easy?"

And that's when it occurred to me: *If this isn't easy for me, I can only imagine what Dave was going through.*

Alcohol is a sin for me is because it comes before God. *Gotta have it.* My relationship with Dave became a source of sin for me because it too came before God. I was in endless pursuit of Dave's answer to *What am I not?* rather than pursuing *Who am I in God's eyes?*

Secrets Make You Sick

Since Dave died, I have taught my children that secrets make you sick. We don't keep secrets. I share the truth of what happened to their father in appropriate detail for their ages. I try to be honest about my own struggles with addiction and what it has cost me. We talk about the pain and struggles they encounter in school and in life. I truly believe it is safer and healthier in the long run than denial.

Finding Joy

Back in 2004, while we were still living in Louisiana, I found myself feeling overwhelmed by sadness, suspicion, and fear about my marriage. I hadn't smoked since I first got pregnant, but I started to again, sneaking outside late at night.

I remember one night in particular. It was cool for a summer night. I was sitting on the dewy grass, staring at the clear, starry sky; all I could picture was Jesus on the cross.

You are the only one who can help me through this.

That was it. That was my prayer. Looking back on it now, I think He has been faithful to me in that, whether I always recognized it or not.

Right now, I am working on finding joy. God gave me five kids for a reason; I had never seen it that way. Now I know he has a purpose.

I've enjoyed raising my kids, every part of it. I've enjoyed the demands, the cooking, the cleaning. I've enjoyed living in the places we did and being active in their schools. When we first moved to Michigan following Dave's death, I took care of them first and foremost. But then it got old. And I got tired.

Now, with my older two gone, it's hard in a different way. I find myself with idle time. Sometimes I connect with God or work my steps in the Alcoholics Anonymous 12-Step program. I realize that, for the first time in a long time, I can do things for me. I'm trying to refocus; I'm forcing myself to find joy in the little things. It's still hard sometimes.

The other day, my son Stephen lost his cell phone while ski-ing. Because I was there, he was able to take my phone to the top of the hill and find his, which was buried in the snow. He was so happy to get it back. That brought me joy.

Caleb and his friend cooked dinner for everyone the other night. Each of the kids invited a friend, and afterward we all went to the movies. That brought me a lot of joy.

My youngest called me last week to say she would be back from her field trip by eight thirty. "Will you be on time to pick me up?" she asked. I was. As I drove her friend home, I heard all about their day. There was a point in time when I didn't give a care about such things; now I know it is precious and fleeting.

Power to Persevere

If I could say anything to women or men in my situation or David's, it would be to persevere. Survive.

It is now eight years since Dave died, and I'm just beginning to see light at the end of the long, dark tunnel I've been living in. Looking back, I am still not sure what I could have done differently. He and I were each unhealthy in our own ways; together we became toxic. But out of our mess God created five amazing lives, a beautiful testament to his power to redeem and restore our brokenness.

Trust in him. Invite him into your mess.

Acknowledge in your heart that he is the only one who can get you through this.

> "See, I am doing a new thing! Now it springs up;
> do you not perceive it? I am making a way in the
> wilderness and streams in the wasteland."
>
> — Isaiah 43:19

Resources

Here are some resources to help survivors and their loved ones begin the process of pursuing hope and healing.

Books

- *The Wounded Heart: Hope for Adult Victims of Childhood Sexual Abuse*, by Dan Allender
- *Out of the Shadows: Understanding Sexual Addiction*, by Patrick J Carnes, Ph.D
- *When a Man You Love Was Abused: A Woman's Guide to Helping Him Overcome Childhood Sexual Molestation*, by Cecil Murphy
- *Leaping Upon the Mountains: Men Proclaiming Victory over Sexual Child Abuse*, by Mike Lew
- *Victims No Longer: The Classic Guide for Men Recovering from Sexual Child Abuse*, by Mike Lew
- *The Courage to Heal: A Guide for Women Survivors of Child Sexual Abuse*, by Ellen Bass and Laura Davis

Counseling

- **Christian Family University**, Rob Jackson, MS, LPC, offers counseling, free weekly teleclasses, and other resources to support sexual integrity and recovery from sexual addictions and abuse: 888-891-HOPE (4673), ChristianFamilyUniversity.com

- **Focus on the Family** provides free online consultation and referral to qualified, local, Christian counselors: 877-233-4455, FocusontheFamily.org
- **American Association of Christian Counselors** offers a free national referral network of state-licensed, certified, and/or properly credentialed Christian counselors offering care that is distinctively Christian and clinically excellent, www.aacc.net

Advocacy

- Brave Step, bravestep.org, strengthens men and women impacted by sexual abuse through inspiration, education, and personalized care
- Darkness to Light, d2l.org, empowers people to prevent child sexual abuse
- Help for Guys, help4guys.org, a complete resource guide for male victims and survivors of abuse
- Prodigals International, prodigalsinternational.org, promoting freedom from the bonds of sexual addiction
- RAINN, rainn.org, the nation's largest anti-sexual violence organization
- SARA (Sexual Abuse Resource Agency), saracville.org, eliminating sexual violence in our community
- SNAP (Survivors Network of those Abused by Priests), snapnetwork.org, peer support organization

CONNECT WITH THE AUTHOR

Connect with Nanette Kirsch:
Visit denialbook.com
On Twitter @denialbook
On Facebook @denialbook2017
Email: nanette@denialbook.com

END NOTES

Preface

1. The Reverend Timothy Keller, "Series: 1 Corinthians: Leader Talks, 2004–2005: Scripture 1 Corinthians 6–7" (Timothy Keller Sermons, Gospel in Life, Redeemer Presbyterian Church), February 7, 2005.

2. Nice Cumming-Bruce, "Vatican Tells of 848 Priests Ousted in Decade," May 6, 2014, http://www.nytimes.com/2014/05/07/world/europe/vatican-tells-of-848-priests-ousted-in-last-decade.html.

3. "Yellow Dyno Statistics: Child Molesters," accessed September 9, 2014, http://yellodyno.com/Statistics/statistics_child_molester.html.

4. "Priests Commit No More Abuse than Other Males," Pat Wingert, Newsweek, April 7, 2010, http://www.newsweek.com/priests-commit-no-more-abuse-other-males-70625.

5. Ibid.

6. "Prevalence: 1 in 10: Estimating a Child Sexual Abuse Prevalence Rate for Practitioners: A Review of Child Sexual Abuse Prevalence Studies," Catherine Townsend and Alyssa A. Rheingold, PhD, August 2013.

7. "Statistics: Child Sexual Abuse: Who are the victims?," Parents for Megan's Law, accessed September 9, 2014, https://www.parentsformeganslaw.org/public/statistics_childSexualAbuse.html.

Chapter 8

1. Patrick J. Carnes, *Out of the Shadows: Understanding Sexual Addiction* (Simon & Schuster, 1983), 1.

2. Carnes, *Out of the Shadows*, 4.

3. Clarence Page, "Another Alpha Male Caught Behaving Badly: Why Do They Do It?" *Baltimore Sun*, March 18, 2008.